ALL OF MY
FRIENDS
ARE RICH

MICHAEL SARAIS

ALL OF MY FRIENDS ARE RICH

MICHAEL SARAIS

A CIP catalogue record for this book is available from the
British Library

ISBN: 978-1-8380160-0-5 (Hard Cover)
ISBN: 978-1-8380160-1-2 (Paperback)
ISBN: 978-1-8380160-2-9 (E-book)

Cover Artwork by Fedor Barkhatov (fedos.art)
Internal Formatting by Evenstar Books
Edited by Paul Ryan and Susan Keillor

michaelsarais.com

CLOUDY DAY
PUBLISHING

To my mother Helga and my best friend Sara.
The most fearless women in my life.

CHAPTER 1

-£960.57

'A/C 4480 30Sep. Your remaining balance overnight was £39.43. As this is near your limit, please ensure you have enough money available to cover any payments.'

FUCK. I SCREAMED INTERNALLY. There might've been a possibility that I screamed externally, too. I couldn't hear myself over the agonising existential cry for help that nearing the limit of my overdraft was sending my soul into. Payday was still ten days away, and all I had in my fridge was a half tub of Flora spread and three cloves of garlic. I did have some unopened quinoa in the cupboard, so that was a titillating and nutritionally complete meal waiting to happen.

I was early for my appointment. About twenty minutes early. I have somehow always managed to be punctual for everything. Not too sure why, as no one would ever be punctual. Teachers, trains, friends one sees during a premature midlife crisis, and doctors most certainly weren't.

The extra time would give me a solid chance to reassess my life budget for the following few days and hopefully manage the impending anxiety of either not eating for over a week, or making Sara feel sorry for me and guilt-trip her into paying for the entire bill when we'd meet up for a meal out.

It was probably going to be the latter option.

I was alone in the waiting room. A dry, beige, boring waiting room. There were three magazines on the coffee table—the March issue of *Good Housekeeping,* an *Elle* from May and some car magazine. I didn't even try to look at that one. The chairs were incredibly uncomfortable and slightly unstable. They made a squeaking noise every time I breathed. My jeans were so tight, it hurt to cross my legs. I also had a crotch hole from where my thighs would rub onto each other. A small price to pay to look vaguely decent in a jockstrap. I didn't fear a leg day, but I did fear my whole arse would suddenly make an appearance after a miscalculated move that could potentially rip my jeans apart. Also, thanks to my bank alerts, I was now fully aware I couldn't replace them. Not even a pair of Primark jeans. The £9 kind.

My shoes were muddy, desperately asking to be washed, but it was just one of those things I'd forget to do until a friend would point out how disgusting they looked. To be fair, I didn't mind looking somewhat scruffy when seeing Dr Grey, a name I found incredibly hilarious as a long-time viewer of the best medical show in existence.

A more run-down me would better project the constant dread of living I was actually feeling for the majority of my waking time and compel her into feeling sorrier for me. An emotion I needed her to have in order to keep prescribing me happy little pills that would bring me happy little joy, especially when swallowed with a glass of Malbec. Or two.

'I will be with you in five minutes!' she said. Her head popped out of the door of her office.

Her hair was messier than usual. A busy day, for certain. There were plenty of depressed millennials in London. Or people that desperately needed validation from a professional.

I was one of them. Officially diagnosed as bipolar. And also, actually desperate. Soon unable to pay for rent and/or Netflix.

I deleted the text from the bank so I wouldn't see it again for another few days and put my phone on silent. I was mentally prepared to tell the juicy tales of my past week with a dramatic spin.

'Leo Cotton, please come in!' she said.

I lit up. My new prescription was only a few cries and a slight panic attack away. My foot was tapping on the floor incessantly; my palms were sweaty. I pulled my hair back and finally stood up.

I walked inside and she was on a phone call. I sat down next to her, whilst she brought up my patient chart.

'Well, you can tell Paul Dommett I have other patients!' she said, in an unusually assertive way. 'Yes, I get it's a delicate—'

I felt like I shouldn't have been there hearing that private conversation.

'I'll be there as soon as I'm free. Goodbye,' she said, hanging up the phone. 'Sorry, Leo.'

'Paul Dommett? The talk show host?' I asked with a cheeky smile.

'It's been a rough morning, I apologise. How are you feeling?' she asked, with her more usual peppy tone.

'Alright?' I said with caution. Wouldn't want her to think I was *actually* alright.

I could never get used to the fact that the office of a psychiatrist isn't actually as glamorous or inviting as it appears on American TV. In fact, this one wasn't much different from the room you may be diagnosed with chlamydia in. Unless you're a Dean Street Express kind of gay. In which case this office would be by far more colourful, like a Leicester Square cocktail bar for straights, although with fewer guys covered in shame to stare at.

There was definitely shame here, but it was mostly coming from me. The guy who would check their ex-husband's social media on the daily and their gross shiny new boyfriend's stories on Instagram, while spilling wine all over himself and ugly crying.

I was that guy.

'Did you get a chance to look into the material I suggested during our last session?' she asked with the tone of a defeated schoolteacher and her slow student.

The material was stupid. The pamphlet—written entirely in Comic Sans—asked for me to change my behaviour, just like that. It was essentially a *Marie Kondo* guide for the aggressive bipolar to rid oneself of negative influences that may affect the precarious balance between the severely depressed and the homicidal maniac that lived within me for most of my twenties.

I actually did have a look at it. It was positive thinking crap, and I wanted no part in it.

'I gave it a bit of a glimpse, but I find it really hard to concentrate. I can't say these meds are working all that well. I know you said they would take time to kick in, but I can't keep living in this bubble where even reading the *Evening Standard* becomes a hurdle. I'd like to write again someday,' I said, while my voice was starting to shake.

Get it together, Leo.

'That's okay,' she started writing on her pad. 'Do you have anything planned for this evening?' she asked with an optimistic smile.

I actually did. I had to go meet up with my ex-husband Jake to look after our dog while he'd go take his trash boyfriend to an outdoor cinema and watch some god-awful play.

Jake and I decided to adopt a dog a year after we got together, a beautiful grey and white Siberian husky named Squall Leonhart, after *Final Fantasy 8's* main character. I loved Squall more than anything in the world, so it truly felt like a double break-up when I had to leave him with Jake. I'd get to see him and spend time with him when the happy pair would go on dates or holidays together.

I went from being Squall's daddy to his unstable dog sitter; an unpaid one at that.

'I am going to my old flat to look after Squall for a few hours,' I said with my teeth nearly grinding to dust.

'Oh,' she said, struggling to stay awake.

'It's fine. I am actually looking forward to it. I haven't seen the fluff ball in a while and my friend Sara is coming over with some wine, so that's a much better evening than the one I had planned in my head.'

'Which was what?'

'To bathe with my toaster,' I said with a smile.

She didn't like that one.

'Leo, you know we take suicide "jokes" *very* seriously here,' she said with a death stare.

'I am sorry. I don't actually intend to kill myself. The pills really prevent me from doing that,' I said. 'I am much better, I promise.'

'Just make sure you keep taking them every day.'

Why wouldn't I?

———•——————●——————•———

Forty minutes of "*this is the crisis number. Please call them before you think about jumping in front of a train*" later I was well on my way to my old flat. My hair was starting to succumb to the humidity and my face probably looked like a tired, dehydrated, puffy mess, but I was so excited to get some dog love.

Obviously after snooping into every single drawer in the house.

Unhealthy? Yes, but I never said therapy was working.

My old flat was just off a residential road in Putney. Ground floor small flat with a garden and a neighbour who'd call you at all times of the day to question random noises coming from the apartment. Martha used to hear Squall barking even when he wasn't home for days. She didn't get out much.

It had just started to rain, so I proceeded to walk a bit

faster. Didn't want to look more of a mess in case Marc was already there.

Bleurgh. Marc. Marc Rhodes was the piece of trash my ex-husband decided to stick his wiener in on a regular basis. He was the kind of guy I promised myself I'd never date or ever give blood to. I'd tick the option to never donate my organs if they were going to such a little bitch. He was constantly out partying, first in line to do a tour of every gay Pride in the country, consistently wearing mesh t-shirts, crop tops and denim shorts. Someone who'd caption their Instagram posts with, *"When your friends buy you a drink and you're doing Stoptober. Oops."* Or, *"On Fridays we wear black."*

The guy was three years younger than me and earning a six-figure salary.

Fucker.

Meanwhile, I was nearing my thirtieth birthday, and I'd plan my shopping trips based on when *Tesco* would sell nearly expired hummus for 25p and sad cucumbers for under 15p.

I couldn't say he felt particularly threatened by my charm or success, but I did like to think I was the one with the brains. The brain that got away, even. When not on antipsychotics or drunk on £4 Aldi wine, of course. Then I'd be just as dumb as Marc.

The gate door was in front of me. It had recently been painted a shade of dark grey.

Jake loved doing housework, while I'd mostly pick what to watch on Netflix. That was our dynamic.

I opened the gate which surprisingly did not make a loud noise anymore, and got to the front door.

Smelling my old life was nostalgic. I knocked, even though I had a secret copy of the key. Like a mad psychopath.

'Oh, there you are,' said my already displeased 6'4" ex-husband.

Squall, on the other hand, ran towards me and put his paws on my chest. He was excited to see me. In a world where bleeding to death seemed like the single most perfect evening, this was the kind of pickup my fragile ego had needed.

'He's so happy to see you,' came out of Jake's mouth.

I couldn't focus on anything else he was saying, as there was a freshly inked giant tattoo sleeve sported on his left arm.

'What the hell is that?' I asked, while probably looking like I had just sucked on a mouldy lemon. Drenched in bleach.

'Oh, this? I just felt like it,' said my almost forty-year-old ex-husband.

This was Marc's doing. Marc was the kind of person to have stupid hippy tattoos all over his body.

'How very *eat, pray, love,*' I said. 'So where are you heading tonight?'

Like I didn't know already from Instagram.

'It's an outdoor screening of *Madame Butterfly* in Regent's Park.'

I cackled as I saw the rain outside.

'Fun! I hope you don't mind; Sara will be coming over to keep me company later, just so that I can be having some fun too. Not play-under-the-rain kind of fun, but... you know.'

He grabbed his keys and pretty much ignored any of my sarcastic attempts at mockery.

'I should make my way as I'm already late. You doing okay otherwise? Therapy going alright?'

'It's an absolute blast, thank you for asking,' I said while having a quick flashback of me pounding down a tub of vegan Ben & Jerry ice cream just two nights before.

'You sure? You seem a bit on the high side.'

'That's not how it works, Jake.'

'Okay, as long as you're taking your meds—'

'I can function enough to remember to take a pill every day,' I interrupted him. 'I am not your responsibility.'

'True,' he snapped. 'Well, I will see you later.'

'Enjoy your evening!' I said with a fake smile while closing the door behind him.

It was wine time.

———•————————●————————•———

An hour and a little over half a bottle of *Casillero Del Diablo* later, I opened the door to my gorgeous should-really-be-a-model friend, Sara Langaard.

'Hey, woman,' I said, with cartoon hearts in my eyes.

'Have you started without me?' she asked, sounding somewhat surprised.

Sara was a 5'9" skinny twenty-eight-year-old with long, straight light brown hair, huge green eyes, perfect teeth and a relatively large toned arse that looked incredible in skinny jeans.

She was also a heavy smoker and a near alcoholic with a slight hint of disordered eating, but I liked to focus on the positives. Like most chatty, beautiful and stylish women in London, Sara worked in public relations and events management.

'This fucking journey took forever,' she barked while entering the house with a bottle of wine in each hand. 'I didn't like it when you lived here, and I certainly do not like it now.'

'Like you ever came before.'

'Jake gone already?' she asked while looking around.

'It's just you and me. And the husky, my love. I am surprised you have managed to come here so quickly. You're not working until midnight today?' I teased.

'I am sure you know my boss had somewhere to be, so we all got to sneak out earlier.'

Marc was Sara's boss. God damn Marc. Same guy my husband decided to fuck all those times I stayed at home watching reruns of *This is Us*, munching on soy nuggets and trying to remove dog hair out of my beard.

'Your boss is an annoying cunt,' I exclaimed while pouring a hefty chalice of red.

'Oh, that he absolutely is,' she said while taking her shoes off.

She sat on the sofa, grabbed her glass and put her phone on the coffee table.

'The flat looks different,' she noted.

She wasn't wrong. Gone were the framed movie posters and PlayStation games stacked on the shelf to make room for Indian printed emerald green cushions and paintings of random women wearing a burqa. The place indeed felt different. I did not exist in this reality. There were no more photos of Jake and Leo on the chest of drawers, no more

Buffy the Vampire Slayer memorabilia in the study and no more me. Anywhere. 'Me' was never to be found again in this place. That was my old life.

There was something extremely self-harming about having to spend one day a week in what used to be my own home, but it was my only chance to cuddle with the dog, and I would take that as often as I could. Even if that meant having to sit in the ground zero of my previous life while my ex-husband was taking his new boy to all the restaurants I used to be taken to.

He could always choke on something, I hoped.

'What's been going on with you? How was your day?' she asked, while sipping loudly.

'Oh, you know. Usual stuff. Bared my feelings and got a new prescription for *Quetiapine*. The best day. How was your work?'

'Forget about work. I have something to tell you,' she said, with an ominous smile.

I looked at her suspiciously. Like she was about to tell me that Marc was pregnant. Or that she was about to die. One of those.

'Alfie...' she muttered, with a dramatic pause.

Her tone made me think she had caught her boyfriend cheating or found out something bad about him and I was extremely nervous to hear that as I wasn't mentally ready, drunk or medicated enough to be there and console her.

'Yes?' I prompted.

She chugged the entire glass I had just given to her.

'Do you notice anything different?'

'I don't notice anything. Ever,' I said. 'You should have learnt that after that time I let you speak to Ian McKellen with coriander between your teeth.'

'I fucking hate coriander too.'

'Tell me!'

'He kind of asked me to marry him...' she whispered.

'He did what?'

My jaw dropped. Hard.

'He proposed.'

She blushed. Sara would never blush. Sara had turned into girly mush. I took a humongous gulp of wine, tried to tone down my psycho eyes and held her hands.

'That's...great? It's great, right?' I wasn't sure.

'Yes! I am so happy! And I couldn't wait to tell you.'

She girl-screamed. Worrisome.

'I am so excited for you! Oh my god!' I gushed.

She was the first one of my friends to become engaged. I was the first one a few years before. First one to get married too. And first one to get separated.

There was a truly small, stupid, negligible part of myself that was incredibly sad at the prospect of losing my girl to a straight man I'd barely trust with a kettle, but I didn't think I had ever seen her so excited about something that wasn't a Cartier watch or a box of sixteen Domino's chicken wings. This was a big deal. This was life changing.

My life, that is.

'How did it happen?' I asked.

'Oh. That's not important,' she said in a dismissive tone.

'Did he put the ring on his penis? Can he fit the ring on his penis?'

'Of course not, you douche. We came back from a night out, and he just did it there and then. In our flat. Before

12

vomiting profusely on our bedspread. It still counts.'

She was hiding something, but I couldn't quite put my finger on it.

'Are you sure it was a real proposal?' I asked, sceptical.

'Yes. Of course, it was. I think he nearly shat himself from the fear.'

'Alfie shits himself every other day!'

She put her hand on my thigh.

'I got engaged, Leo.'

'Yikes, this *is* serious,' I said while slowly absorbing the notion. 'You're getting married!'

'Yes,' she calmly responded.

'Wow. You.'

'Don't use that tone now,' she inhaled. 'It's not that unrealistic for someone to want to marry me.'

'I'm just processing...'

'Good news, though. I'd like for you to be my best man.'

'Of course!' I gave her a hug. 'So...you had roughly twenty-four hours to absorb the notion. You thought about the when? The how? The where?'

'I'm thinking somewhere fun, a nice sunny day. I'm thinking a badass hen do with all my friends at a luxury villa, or something.'

Fuck.

I internally screamed. I possibly externally screamed. I couldn't hear myself over the inner struggle of being left to rot without my best friend and the slight excitement of being there for her. Abroad.

'Of course, I am going to be your best man! So, where's this sunny location you had in mind?'

'Greece, I reckon,' she said. 'Alfie's parents live there and it's gorgeous. They also have a garden that may as well be a national park.'

£39.43 in my overdraft.

Shit.

CHAPTER 2

-£260.57

I was sitting in the manager's office by myself in front of a trade report I had written six words for. Sara was getting married. My forever single girl was getting married to the guy I thought she was dating as a joke.

Sara spent most of her twenties sleeping with muscly black guys that played football. Professionally. The playing-football-thing, not the sleeping around. The girl that would openly flirt with other guys while being on a date with another was now about to walk down the aisle with a 5'10" beardless *One Direction*-looking fella. I didn't quite know how to process that. On one hand I had to be happy for her. I never once took her relationship seriously, but it was then clear that she actually really loved the guy. They had moved in together a few months earlier and I thought that would have been the end of it.

'Leo can you please check your staff on the shop floor?'

A squeaky voice could be heard through the door. My bitch boss Katherine was on patrol. I was trying to hide from people. Like most days.

I was an assistant manager at a luxury department store. I had to work under Katherine, someone I used to manage before I took a leave of absence for my bipolar meltdown and absolutely hated. Lazy and entitled, she somehow scored a double promotion while I was gone.

'Don't worry, all sorted!' a much more pleasant voice ensued. 'Hey girl!' said a bald and bearded individual entering the office.

Dominic, the only person I'd save from the fire I wanted to set in that store.

'Hi, sweetie,' I muttered.

'Bitch face Katherine is leaving in a few minutes, so we can drink a few cans of gin & tonic without anyone yapping at us,' he gushed.

A man who knew the way to my heart.

'You okay?' he asked, while sitting on a chair. His *Bleu de Chanel* aftershave was engulfing the air inside the office.

'My friend Sara got engaged and asked me to be her best man,' I said hastily.

'Ew,' he quickly exclaimed.

'No, I am very excited for her! But it's Sara, of course. Which means everything will be over the top and expensive as fuck. She's doing the wedding in Greece. Mother fucking Greece. I can't even afford to get to zone four in London.'

'Shit, babes. Is that why you didn't come with me to the party in Brighton last week?' he asked. As if I ever had any intention of travelling for over an hour to go to a house party with creative assholes and drag queens with beards.

Dominic came from a good family and liked to dive his face into a pot of cocaine every weekend, and for some reason he somewhat liked the retail job. Something my poor, frustrated, broke arse did not understand.

'I have a few months to save some money, which is something I have never done before. Also, my life is as frugal as it can get. Do I really want to give up my one night a week where I have a couple of bottles of wine at a bar?'

'We both know it isn't just one night a week,' he interrupted. 'Or have you forgotten that time I had to send an Uber to pick you up from Canary Wharf because you went home with that tall asshole with the moustache from *The Glory*?' He put a hand on my shoulder.

'Dating is vile, sweetie,' I sighed. 'I should probably stop trying to find myself a rich man that can maintain the lifestyle of all my very privileged friends,' I smirked.

'Your favourite co-worker will always give you a hand.' He reached out to my neck.

'I know you will. And it's not just about the money. When did my garbage humans that I call friends start being decent enough to get married to other people? For love, even.'

'Ha!' he crossed his arms. 'You were the first one.'

'And look at how it ended. Are all my friends going to start nesting now?' I wondered out loud.

'I doubt it, but hey, I am here if you want to satisfy your "husband" fantasies.' He winked.

'I already had a husband. Heck, I am currently technically still married. I can assure you there aren't any husband fantasies that don't involve some sort of murder-suicide. Thanks for the offer, though.'

'Anytime, my dear. Anytime,' he said while grabbing two cans of *Marks & Spencer* gin and tonic from his backpack. 'Just knock a few of these down until you're happy for your friend.' He winked while pouring the cans into a paper coffee cup.

I was happy. Sara was my everything. My ultimate life companion. Was I maybe being jealous of having to share her with the whitest of guys in London? Was I jealous of her being happy? Did I have a weird fetish where I enjoyed seeing my friends being as miserable as me?

Nah, that couldn't be it. I was just overwhelmed by the information. I was happy for her. I was happy to be there for her.

This is growth, Leo.

Then I proceeded to sip my cocktail-in-a-can bang in the middle of my work shift.

I dropped my keys on the floor while trying to open my front door.

Clumsy bitch.

I wasn't too sure whether Andrew would be home, but I wasn't particularly keen on having flatmate bonding time.

Andrew was a truly pretty guy. There was nothing rugged about him. He had big, poofy, dark blond hair usually styled in a quiff. Hard enough to get a small bird trapped in there.

He was very slim and would wear *Polo Ralph Lauren*

jumpers, beige chinos and brogues most of the time. He was the kind of person you'd say "good boy" to and pet his head dearly. If you were into that.

He was the responsible adult. He managed to buy his first flat at thirty-two. I was a few months away from my thirtieth and I was so far away from the property ladder, I may as well have been a five-year-old homeless kid. Andrew had a spare bedroom and, honestly, was feeling pretty lonely. He focused so much on renovating the flat that he barely had the chance to realise he was now living alone in Streatham.

Streatham.

He very kindly sublet his second bedroom and allowed me and buckets of dog hair which, after a year, he was still finding around the house.

How I missed my Squall.

'Hey doodle,' I announced while entering the flat.

Music was playing. Like weird, royalty-free elevator music.

Something was up. I entered the living room and... horror.

'Hi!' he said, awkwardly.

He had company. There were at least ten people in the flat. Andrew was having dinner, and I had completely fucking forgot.

'Hello everyone,' I mumbled.

All I could see were white people dressed in pastels having a jolly good prosecco and probably talking about the best resorts in Marrakech that wouldn't serve spicy vegetables.

'You have made it!' he gushed. Genuinely happy to see

me.

Was he pretending? Was I invited? Did I forget? Was I a bit too drunk from the work cans? Damn, I looked bad.

'Leo, you know most of the people here, I think?'

I looked around and recognised a few faces. I guess my speech wasn't the only slurred phenomenon happening in my body.

'Yes, of course. How are you guys?'

Literally no idea.

Most of them continued their conversation. Not a fun one to remark, but most of them did nod at my presence.

'Sit down for a drink,' said good little Andrew while pouring.

Alcoholic me was saying yes, but antisocial me wanted to slap everyone and then hide in his room. Under the duvet.

But, alas, I consented. I loved me some free booze. And all my friends kept providing me with it that day. You can't be ungrateful when you're so damn close to the poverty line.

'How was work?' Andrew asked while handing me the glass.

Ugh.

Dreadful question. At least in public, because it would normally prompt people to ask shit such as:

'Oh, what do you do?' enquired a curly-haired, hooked nosed and incredibly bright toothy little homosexual sitting on the chair across from me.

Name? I wanted to say Craig or Tom, but I had never been sober when we were introduced the first few times. Not to mention, each time Andrew talked about his friends, they all kind of sounded the same. Now that I was sitting with so many of them, they kind of looked the same too.

'I work in retail,' I unenthusiastically said with a sour expression.

'He's a manager,' Andrew quickly interrupted.

Like that sounded any better. He was so very attentive at trying to pick me up any chance he could. He was a good guy.

'Yes. I manage a group of horny, incapable kids to attempt to sell expensive clothes to the rich Arabs that come to Knightsbridge, so we can hopefully not succumb to the inevitable doom that is glooming over most of the British high street,' I said, smiling nervously.

Tom/Craig seemed a little grossed out.

I was wearing a tracksuit and a t-shirt with *Crash Bandicoot* on it, to be fair.

'Yes, isn't it terrible what's happening to all our stores?' They all somewhat agreed in a weird collective murmur.

I was so gutted to be stuck in that conversation with such boring people.

I had this whole grand idea to just warm up some spaghetti in the microwave, have a shot of something and go on *Grindr* for some sex validation from other gross men.

I was planning not to brush my teeth and have a glorious wank.

Now I had to entertain for the absolute bare minimum that wouldn't be considered rude, which I had calculated would be at least fifteen minutes. Ten if I faked a migraine.

'They're a terrible bunch there anyway,' said Andrew, coming to the rescue. 'They are extremely disorganised and are in desperate need of good press. They still haven't banned fur or exotic skins. It's pretty gross in this day and age,' he blurted in his polished Oxford accent.

'Oh, I do love a bit of fur. Is that bad?' *Tom/Craig* spewed through his big, stupidly whitened teeth. My face, no longer friendly, managed to crack half of an angry smile.

I chugged the entire glass of prosecco in one alcoholic gulp.

'Sorry guys, I actually have a really early morning tomorrow,' I said, blatantly lying through my far less white teeth. 'I think I am actually going to head to bed. I am knackered.'

Andrew understood I wasn't a fan of that little shit sitting in front of me.

'Of course. Have some rest. Goodnight, Leo.'

Haha!

I was horny and ready to send my nudes to half the grid of gays in my area.

It was 10 p.m. and I was desperately seeking anyone to be doing some complimenting-my-junk before bed. Or I wouldn't be able to sleep that night. Or forgive myself.

My bedroom looked like the last episode of any season of *American Horror Story*. A dreadful incongruous mess. The insane amount of underwear I owned prevented me from doing laundry often. It would also ensure that for over one week, once the underwear drawer would start emptying, I would get to wear some of the skankiest jockstraps, thongs and weird lacy numbers as regular undergarments. It would make my getting-changed-at-the-gym situation very exciting for everyone looking.

The gym was a sacred place where I'd fuck the most. Something about men lifting 20kg dumbbells gets everyone horny once inside the locker room.

That evening was not laundry day. It was a long working day that needed to end with virtual sex with someone. A little exchange of nudes and then *bam*! Spunk on the tea towel I kept in my nightstand.

I took my trousers off and sat on my bed. I opened Instagram as a warm-up, and there it was. "*Ugh, I guess,*" was Sara's caption. Sara managed to make her engagement announcement cool.

Most basic tramps would write, *"I said yes,"* but all those people deserved a beating.

Sara told the world by telling Instagram.

She had just about one photo of Alfie posted in the three years they had been together. She wasn't one to overshare, but she shared this. Proudly.

I had to make a plan. What would I wear? Who would I go with? How would I get to Greece? How the fuck could I even pay for any of that? This was going to be lavish. Her parents were loaded. They bought Sara and her sister a flat each without batting an eye.

I sometimes wondered what my life would have been like if I were born into that family. I wouldn't have had a heroin-addict father who left used needles around the house while my mother worked three jobs to provide for me, for one.

Perhaps I wouldn't have needed to watch my mother

wilt at every session of chemotherapy. Maybe I wouldn't have needed to bury her as my adult life was about to start.

How nice it would have been not to be an orphan at twenty-two.

I looked at the side of my bed and there was a dirty glass with wine stains from the night before and, drum roll, at least a glass and a half worth of wine left in a bottle.

Score.

I poured it down while carefully blowing the dust on the glass away. Took a sip and fired up Grindr. A quick load and there they were. The gays, the indecisive and the weirdos in my area. Like a cock buffet of repressed assholes with mother issues united in the pursuit of a face to direct their cum into. Life couldn't be better.

'*Hey.*' '*Hey!*' '*What's up?*' '*Fun?*' were all sent by different faceless profiles. I didn't need that. I wasn't actually sure what I was into that evening. I probably should have just opened *Pornhub* and looked for a seriously depraved scenario I could beat my—vegan—meat over. Think *"hillbilly orgy"*, or *"bleeding twink chokes to near death,"* or any category I'd be desperate to remove off my browser history in case of a police raid.

That evening I craved contact. I craved attention. I wanted someone to tell me I looked hot. I wanted someone to lust over my cock and tell me how big and veiny it was.

I had plenty of father issues, in my defence.

'*Hey,*' one of those profiles wrote.

I ignored. Realistically you wouldn't respond to a stranger saying 'hey' twice to you in the streets. It's weird.

Shit, Tom/Craig was showing near me. His name was actually Dean.

Who knew? Did I ever know? Although the most shocking news was that he was just thirty-one years old. And he wasn't afraid to show pictures of him travelling to all the places. That's the exact kind of twink that needed choking. Not by me, though.

Picture received.

I was intrigued. I loved a photo. A Grindr photo could tell you a lot about the kind of gay this person was going to be. Were they a closeted 'straight' husband sharing the bare minimum for them to get pounded behind a bush in Streatham Cemetery? Were they a hairy bumhole under an orange light and a loose-fitting Andrew Christian jockstrap?

The possibilities were endless. I was curious, so I opened it. It was the double 'hey, hey' person. They had a bit of a stubble, a bit of a belly and possibly a bit of a lazy eye. I wasn't attracted, but I wasn't a monster. I was going to at least acknowledge the effort.

'Hey', I responded. Feeling cool. Mysterious. Feeling I was way hotter than he was. Out of his league, but still nice about it. Like the Lady Diana of British penises.

'What are you up too?'

Misspeller. Lovely.

I was dealing with the average Londoner. Poorly educated, but brave as hell.

'Not much.'

I was trying to keep my cool so that I could prompt him to give me a compliment shower.

'You're chest looks hot.'

It hurt. I had the compliment I was waiting for and it came complemented by one of the grossest grammatical miscarriages I would have normally broken up engagements for in the past. There was just no excuse for it, but at the same time he was actively endorsing all my efforts I made at the gym.

I was flattered. I was drunk, really. Not enough to misspell basic English, but definitely down that alleyway. He asked me if I wanted fun. I ignored. I did want fun, but there was really nothing fun about me trying to change my underwear and sneak out of the flat. Trying to avoid that angel of a flatmate and those horrible bitching friends of his, including that moron Dean and that photo he took in South Africa fondling a poor penguin.

No, ma'am. I was also kind of hungry and in desperate need to tackle that tub of *Pringles* I hid to avoid the calories.

I proceeded to dive into my shorts drawer and grabbed the tub. The crisps were paprika flavoured. Exotic, yellow and definitely already opened from another drunken meltdown. Still crunchy-ish. I was fairly content. I was shoving two at a time into my mouth when he demanded the inevitable: a cock pic.

As partially horrified as I was by such a forward question, I was actually not in the mood to have a wank anymore, but I was in a mood to fuck with this probably proud owner of several cat paintings, so I did. I sent my most glorious dick pic. The one. Taken from the angle that makes it look like one of those things you put under the door to stop drafts from coming through. My tool never looked bigger. I wanted him to feel thirsty, but at the same time go to bed annoyed that he wasn't going to get any. Mainly because my mouth had orange powder on it and I had zero intention of brushing my teeth, but also because I had already put a pair of velour joggers on. And no one was going to get those off me without a good reason.

'I'd love to suck that off,' he sent without hesitation.

My work was done. I was a *Pirelli* calendar model. I got a socially inept man to have a full raging boner in front of a screen and it was all thanks to me. I was a charity, really. I ignored that message, and I was just getting ready for bed. My ego was fulfilled. And then he typed again. This time making things far more interesting for the both of us.

'£?'

That had not happened before. Sure, I had seen some hairless Brazilian torsos offering massages near Paddington station, but this had not directly happened to me yet.

And in Streatham? I didn't buy it. Someone had just been stabbed a few nights before over some chicken nuggets. I wasn't going to be the dumb skanky gay that gets murdered because of a drunken desperate desire to make extra money to join their best friend in the quest to have the badass unrestrained wedding experience she had always envisioned.

Or was I?

'What do you want?'

I typed, feeling like the sluttiest Vivian Ward cosplay.

Silence. I waited for a good three minutes.

'£50 for a blow job.'

I wasn't a fan of blow jobs. I had a horrible gag reflex, and frankly, I wasn't too fond of the misogyny of it all. I didn't like getting my head shoved into someone's pubes and I was definitely not an admirer of the taste.

For £50, though, I could probably literally suck it up.

He wasn't done with the specifics.

'Cash on the table. You come in, put your pants down, cum and go.'

This changed everything. I was getting paid to receive a blow job. This sounded great. Easiest £50 of my life. I could cum on demand. He may have wanted the long-ass experience, but realistically I could make it all end in five minutes and have his mouth full of my potential children *and* my wallet filled with cash. Something I had not seen in quite some time. It was tempting.

Although a small part of me still had a slight fear of having my throat slit by some rando in their flat full of knitted cushions and cat toys scattered across a carpeted staircase, my fingers took charge and typed themselves.

'What's your address?'

CHAPTER 3

-£210.57

HAD DONE IT. I WAS A MAN. I had reached peak gay whore in London. Seven minutes of weird, fake, boss dominator bullshit and a whole lot of grabbing a head with a very receding hairline and shoving my cock inside its very, very whiny mouth later, I had ka-chinged fifty whole quid into my bank account. That's right, Halifax. Not only was it payday, but I had also added a second income onto my sad, overworked current account. And it wasn't that sad. Heck, it was far better than many other drunken, horny encounters I had after a long day of being bitched around by Katherine, the botched lipped bitch who couldn't tell you Ireland was an island if her dumb life depended on it.

I had someone cry on me. I had someone burp into my mouth. I had had it with just about any weirdo with my extensive experience with London hook-ups. This was vanilla. This was the lemon sorbets of hook-ups. Yes, he did have a weird tattoo on his back with *Madonna*'s autograph. And I did imagine this nearly middle-aged man going to Madge herself with a Sharpie, asking her for an autograph and then quickly walking to the first Hep-C wielding tattoo artist in the area and begging them to ink him as quickly as possible. But I ignored it. I had a sloppy mouth down my crotch, I hadn't showered yet, and I could swear there was a 'Yes sir' thrown in there. I couldn't tell because I was grunting and pretending to be Liam Neeson. But there were definitely tears. Deepthroat tears.

Little Gary. He even introduced himself. Afterwards, saying 'cheers.' He even put on a manly voice like he wasn't the one screaming like an opera singer when I had his nipples squished between my fingernails. Gary was willing. And I was willing to raise some funds. If I had to use my penis to get there, then so be it.

I didn't get any other messages after '*Thanks, it was great. Let's do it again at some point,*' but I was confident I'd see little Gary very soon. He'd be waiting impatiently for my broke self on those lonely nights to get his balls emptied. Onto his own hands. Because I wasn't touching that. Not with that measly fee.

So even though my whore CV had only one entry in it, my accountant brain was already calculating how many times I could penetrate that poor pot-bellied man's willing mouth for wine money. Or the wedding pot, as now I had to think about something else that wasn't my liver.

'*Man, call in sick! We are lunching out!*'

I was happy to. Even though I told myself I'd refrain from frivolous lunches for a few months, I would always make an exception for Sara.

We were going to meet at *Dean Street Townhouse*, an outright robbing bastard of a restaurant that would charge me twenty quid for some vegetables in sauce and two potatoes.

Still elated from her engagement, she was going to splurge. She would get a steak, and she would most definitely not barf it afterwards.

Dean Street Townhouse was just across the road from the *Dean Street Sex Clinic* and *Burger & Lobster*. Both very valid places for you to catch crabs in. I imagined my father going in, arms full of holes, getting his AIDS diagnosis. He would then crawl around looking for people to share needles with.

I'd never go in there.

However, we would sit outside the restaurant and scope the queues to spot anyone I may have slept with in the past.

It was our little game. Now I was worried it was all going to turn into discussions about types of dresses, flowers and whether her sister would turn into a psycho wedding planner. I hoped not. Sara was a badass. She wouldn't just turn to mush for this.

It was a beautiful day in October. When done right, autumn was my favourite season of the year. I liked crisp, cold, but sunny days. I was walking through the small roads of Soho, which looked entirely different in the mornings. I was wearing a pair of Chelsea boots that were actively killing my feet, so I'd walk faster in order to sit down as soon as possible. Sara was certainly not going to be there yet. She was always late, and I was always early.

I was nervous to experience our new dynamic. Would

she just monopolise all conversations and make them wedding-related?

I approached Dean Street and surprise, surprise, Sara was already sitting at a table. Outside, so she could smoke. Bottle of red wine already placed in the middle of the table. I couldn't believe my own hungover eyes. My main mission was to avoid telling her about the whole sex-for-money thing. She was creeped out enough by sex apps on a regular day, let alone going into a middle-aged man's house to earn a few pounds.

'Hello gorgeous,' she said, while putting her hand over her eyes to avoid the intense sunlight behind me.

'How nice is this?' I said, while sitting down and genuinely appreciating the nice weather.

'Great day to call in sick, aye?' she winked.

She knew the way around calling in sick at my workplace. After all she had also worked there in the past. Only she, however, would get to a so-called dream job.

'Why did you get the day off?' I asked, curious.

'Meh, just felt like I needed one,' she said, trying to light a cigarette. 'I have been doing late evenings every single day, while Marc is getting to fuck off across the globe for meetings with clients.'

I wasn't particularly in love with the idea of my best friend being in the same workspace as my ex-husband's child lover, but I did enjoy hearing the gossip and how rank his personality was. It would add fuel to my hate fire.

'I am so sick of his little mood swings and his bitch fits,' she puffed. 'I think I might slap him one of these days. And will dedicate it to you, if you wish.'

'Oh, yes. Merry Christmas to me!' I smiled and grabbed

a menu. 'What are we feeling?' I asked, scouting the menu for a dish that didn't contain dead animals.

'Oh, I have already decided,' she smiled with her obvious I-am-about-to-murder-a-steak face.

'What's Alfie been up to, by the way?' I questioned.

'He's been very keen to announce our engagement on social media,' she laughed. 'I swear he's the future bride. I have had so many friends of his congratulating us. I can't help but think he's been going around town with one of those pink and black sashes and a veil.'

I did have to go through some sort of slideshow of their relationship and five very excited stories on Instagram of him being extremely ecstatic over asking this incredibly complex woman to be his wife. For however many years before the inevitable divorce.

'I'll have this weird butternut squash number,' I said.

The cheapest thing on the menu.

'You sure that's going to fill you up?'

It had to do. I would always prefer to drink my lunch-out money. Drinking while on anti-psychotics was actually a great way to buy less alcohol, as I'd feel smashed after one or two bottles.

'Yeah. Had a big breakfast anyway.'

I was starving.

'So where in Greece are we doing this thing?' I asked, so I could already look at cheap flights to buy with cock money.

'Santorini.' She didn't hesitate.

Sara would go there often and get spoiled rotten with all kinds of trips and presents from Alfie's retired parents.

Why did I have to be so poor?

'I am thinking April.'

A sensible option, as any later I'd roast under a suit.

It was only a few months away. How many limp, wrinkly, grey-haired dicks would I have to suck in order to get to the island without having to kayak the Mediterranean?

I was freaking the hell out. Inside, of course. Amongst all the other life freak-outs I'd carefully shove deep down below.

I was doing just great.

'I think it's going to be so much fun,' she started pitching. 'For my hen do, I have this whole idea of having all my friends together, rent a villa, maybe with a pool, or a Jacuzzi, maybe a chef to make good food...'

My bank account was screaming.

'I will have to invite him, though,' she cautiously whispered.

Of course, she had to. I was so mad at the fact that for god knows how long, I would have to deal with bloody Marc dipping his deformed little toes in my life. A quick glimpse at his social media and he had already managed to make Sara's engagement news about him. He posted something along the lines of "*My little work angel is getting married,*" along with a photo of them together. I shook my head in disgust.

Not only had he taken my husband and was slowly attempting to buy my dog's affection, but now he was putting his tentacles all around my best friend's neck.

I could, of course, take the high road and pretend not to care, but unfortunately, I was just that petty, jealous and bitter.

And then I realised he'd probably bring Jake as a plus one. Sara was going to re-create *Ex on the Beach* and I was just going to sit there and watch them have a pre-honeymoon right in front of my disgusted eyes.

'We need to find a way to not make it awkward,' she said in a decisive tone. 'I want you to have fun, and I don't want anything to get in the way of that.'

Nice words, but I couldn't find a way around it, other than sending a call to harvest his organs and sell them in the black market.

'I'll be fine. It's all about you.'

She was the most important person in my life. I wasn't going to let this drag queen in the making ruin Sara's special day.

Nope.

She finished her cigarette and put the butt in the ashtray. Really squashed it.

'I have to tell you something, and I am not entirely sure it's my place to tell you.'

I looked at her with a hint of worry. What other ground-breaking news did she have? Why so serious?

'...but we always tell each other the truth, so I think it's better if you're prepared.'

'Shit, what's going on?' I asked, impatiently.

'I think, and I am not fully, fully sure, that Marc is moving in with Jake soon.'

My mouth suddenly dried up.

Fuck. Fuck Jake. Fuck these cretins for making me feel miserable on a daily basis.

I was forgotten, replaced and soon, this guy I spent so much time hating, was going to live in my flat, with my husband and my dog. He was going to live the life I thought I'd live for far longer than I actually got to. Marc was going to walk my dog and feed him. Marc was going to sleep night after night in the bed I owned half of.

'Wow,' I muttered.

My eyes were glossy, and I was ready to cry. I was so ready to cry.

Damn. I started crying.

'Hey. Hey!' Damage control was in full motion. 'I am sorry,' she said. 'We knew this was going to be a possibility. We were prepared. I wanted to tell you before Jake will, because I don't want you to be ambushed by the news. I know you like to prepare arguments in your head beforehand.'

She smiled. I smiled a little in response. She was right. Every time I'd get into an argument with anybody, I'd get completely overwhelmed, and most of the time I wouldn't be able to mumble a word. Jake was shit. We'd been separated for nearly a year by then, and it took me many, many months, to truly come to grasp with how much of a selfish shitty little person he had become.

Not that he hadn't been while we were together. Nobody prepares you for the amount of gaslighting you receive when you're diagnosed with a mental issue. Nobody prepares you for how much you'll be abused on the matter. All of a sudden, you're a liability, and your emotions are just symptoms to be discounted.

'*That's why you get fired from every job you have.*' Or, '*You have no idea how many guys I had to say "no" to because I was too respectful to you.*' He would throw those at me quite often.

As most people, I wasn't aware of my condition. I knew something was wrong, but I thought it was due to circumstances. London could have been partially responsible to cause that. You're surrounded by an illusion of perfection. Your friends are leading perfect lives, strangers are leading perfect lives, and then there's you. You haven't quite figured out how to exist in such a reality. You haven't wrapped your head around how to coexist with your condition. You haven't quite understood what you're good at, what your calling is.

Jake was a fucking arsehole.

'Hey, you need to get over this,' she insisted. 'You need to start living your life. I know it's not the life you had imagined, but you have to start somewhere. You don't need to wait for Jake, because he's moved on a long time ago. I am sorry.'

My tears kept on coming. I couldn't pace myself. I couldn't even say anything. I had come undone. Once again.

'You're worth so much more than this,' she said while reaching for my hands that were covering my eyes. I shook it off.

'Am I?' I managed to hiss. 'What is my worth? Nobody gives a flying fuck.'

'I do,' she declared. 'I am sick of you selling yourself short because you feel like you're missing out. He essentially psychologically abused you for years. He made you feel like you, your opinions, your actions didn't matter. He treated you like you were inferior and worst of all, crazy. You're so much better off without him. Trust me.'

If only I were better, though.

'Look, we will get over this as well, but you should really start talking divorce and move the fuck on,' she said.

I took a breath.

'...and I am not the only person who really gives a fuck about you. I don't think I have to remind you my dad very much sees you as the son he's never had,' she said, caressing my hand.

'Okay, you are right. I'll have a serious think. Can we order something, please?' I said, tired.

'...But this isn't done, okay? I love you,' she said.

I was so done, though.

———•————————●————————•———

Four bottles of wine later and my payday had already suffered a severe beating. I had another month to go through and I had spent pretty much a quarter of my living money. The emotional conversations were happening more and more often. I had been crying so frequently, I was expecting an intervention on my dehydration. I suspected my meds were not working well enough. It was awful to think, but alcohol was the only thing that would quiet the voices in my head. The only thing that would eventually numb me enough not to feel shit.

I was well anesthetised at that point of the evening, though. Enough to feel a hint of horny in me.

Was I in the right state of mind to see a random guy? Or was I going to make the sensible choice and actually go home to sleep?

I turned Grindr on just to see what was going on. I

hadn't been on it since the night before. I was greeted by a '*Fancy coming again tonight?*' text from Gary. The time stamp was a few hours before, but maybe he hadn't finished without me yet? His house was just on my way home.

Eh. Screw it. Why not?

'*Still keen?*'

It didn't look like he had been online, but surprise. There he was.

'*Yes, please. Same £?*'

Now I was feeling pathetic.

'*Yeah.*'

And then he asked me to come over soon. Easy enough. I probably should have taken a shower, but I would rather be taking one afterwards. To cleanse.

The house was just down the road, in a leafy cul-de-sac. There was for sure someone else living with him. He gave me the impression it was a man, but I was pretty sure it was an eighty-year-old lady. No self-respecting man would be caught dead in a house with floral tapestry in every room, way too many cat toys without any visible cats and a chair so covered in dust, I assumed it was just someone's ashes scattered on it.

His room was upstairs. I needed to take my shoes off and then take them with me. He'd whisper when he'd see me. I understood. Although those stairs were noisy.

He was in front of me, making way for his bedroom. Curtains were drawn. Khaki green with a pattern. DVDs everywhere. Stacked messily. A *Star Wars* poster and two Madonna ones. The more I'd look around, the more Madonna stuff would pop out.

He closed the door behind me. He was nervous again. You could tell he hadn't been doing this often. Not that I was, but I was the kind of person to feed off other people's insecurities. Because I was so insecure all the time. I also felt like I was playing a character. This incredibly butch, sporty, aggressive sexual being. I was gracing Gary with my presence. My busy schedule. Everyone wanted to suck my cock, and it needed to feel like a privilege for him.

I scouted for the money, and it was ready on top of the dresser. Perfect.

He was breathing heavy. I took my jeans off. I then took my top off, but kept my cap on, backwards.

I stood in just my pants and sports socks, semi-hard, showing off my bulge like a tease. He couldn't wait. He put his face on it. Licked it through the fabric. Sniffed my pants and rubbed his face on them. He put one hand in his pants and placed his lips on my now hard dick. I took control. I quickly pulled my pants down, the elastic band just below my balls, then grabbed his hair from behind and shoved his mouth onto my pulsing cock.

He closed his eyes, made some noises. I did the same.

I was trying to enjoy this. I was playing my character, I was guiding his sucking, I was in control of his breathing.

I grabbed his hair and stopped the blow job. He looked at me while kneeling, his mouth still open and wet. I leaned and spat into it.

He gobbled.

He had liked it, but I asked if he was enjoying himself anyway.

'Yes, more,' he whispered submissively.

I obliged. Spat again into his mouth. Got some around

his face as well.

Good.

'Get on the bed,' I ordered.

He wanted to be spanked. That's what he asked for last time, and he was just begging for it to be done again.

He quickly took his sweatpants and underwear off, then swiftly jumped onto the bed with his face down and arse up.

He was presenting it to me. I moved over and grabbed his bum cheeks with both of my hands. I squeezed them hard and then spanked one.

Fairly hard, quick.

He made some noise. I ran my finger down his crack.

He was dry; I wanted to tease his hole.

I wanted him to want me to fuck him. I was sure I could ask more for fucking.

Fucking would take much more effort.

He was moaning. I put my finger into his mouth to get it wet. I shoved it down.

I wanted him to gag. I rubbed my now wet finger down his crack again. Put the tip of my index inside his tight hole, just the tip. Then spanked his other cheek.

I flipped him around, so he'd be lying on his back and I sat on his face.

I got my arse hole just on his mouth and then put my hand on his neck and choked him.

His tongue touched me; I rubbed myself on his face.

His moaning was so loud, I was fully into it.

I moved away slightly and then shoved my entire dick into his mouth, while my hands were on his forehead. I'd get deeper and deeper and he'd be touching his dick.

Then I took mine out. He gasped for air.

'Cum in my mouth,' he gushed.

This was a quick visit, so I was happy to put an end to it.

I grabbed my cock. I made him put his hand on my chest and quickly proceeded to wank over his face. I could come quickly, and he was ready for it.

'I am going to cum,' I said.

'Yes, please sir,' he responded.

That got me excited. I shot my load into his mouth, then on his cheek and one last shot on his stubble.

He came on his belly, a big load.

I sighed. I was a bit sweaty, but not excessively. It didn't feel like I had done a lot; frankly, with the whole thing lasting no longer than six minutes, I wouldn't pay as much as he was about to.

'Cheers,' he said in a breathy tone.

I got up, grabbed the towel conveniently placed by the bed and cleaned up my hand and my dick, then threw it at him. There was a lot that he needed to get off.

I dressed myself quickly.

'Plans for tonight?' I asked awkwardly, to fill the silence while I was tying my shoes.

'Just TV and chill.' He had a bit of an Essex twang.

Bit sleazy.

I took the money from the dresser and quickly glanced at it without necessarily counting it in front of him. It felt about right.

'Thanks,' I said while making my way out.

I also realised I probably should have waited until the

end of the staircase to put my shoes on, but it was too late at that point.

I quickly went down and left, closing the door delicately behind me.

It was drizzling out, a little chilly. I was tired. I needed to get home.

Shower. I needed one badly.

CHAPTER 4

-£237.41

'TWAS A CLOUDY SUNDAY. I was sitting at a restaurant, by myself. I had gotten there early, as usual. I was waiting for John, my most attractive male friend. I couldn't see John much as he'd be travelling all the time, and he was generally the shittiest at texting back. I'd ask him out and receive a reply a few weeks later, months in this case.

John was a bit taller than me. He had small blue eyes, a dark auburn stubble, short bleached hair and his arms and hands were covered in tattoos. He wore unbelievably expensive and weird-looking designer clothes for all occasions and he'd smoke a truckload of weed every evening. He had a deep voice and a huge smile. I had just spotted that smile entering the restaurant. My eyes lit up.

'Hey noodle,' he exclaimed while raising his hands in the air to give me a big hug. He smelled delicious. Tom Ford, for sure.

'Sorry I'm late. Tube was shite,' he said.

He was wearing an oversized hooded jacket. It felt like it was made of teddy bear. It made him look huge and fluffy, but then he took it off and reminded me of how much skinnier than me he was. He sat down with me and I couldn't stop staring at his t-shirt with a big Pikachu on it.

He owned some bizarre stuff. He squeezed my hand on top of the table like an old grandma.

'I have missed you,' he said, as if he wasn't the only reason why it took so long for us to meet again.

'I missed you! Where the hell have you been these last few weeks?'

I liked to nag.

'Ugh,' he muttered. 'I just have been super busy with work and have been anywhere but home.'

John was an esteemed fashion buyer. He had been to Tokyo at least three times that year. Tokyo was my dream. I had never been to Asia, but I had promised myself I would go to Tokyo to celebrate my thirtieth birthday, while Jake would celebrate his fortieth. My thirtieth birthday was five months away, and of course there was no Japan trip planned for me.

I hated that.

The waitress came over with two glasses of prosecco.

'Oh, that's the stuff,' he said, while grabbing the glass like a caveman and gulping half of it in one go. 'I am really fucking sick of all the travelling.'

Quite triggering, but I let it slide.

'I just turned thirty not even a month ago, and I want to have a chance to just sit down at my flat and fuck around on Tinder for a few hours, you know what I mean?'

That's *all* I would do.

'No, I get it,' I assured him. 'Is it a boyfriend you want, John?'

John had a bit of an odd relationship with guys. He was the type of person to attract all kinds of oddly attractive guys with all kinds of attachment issues. Daddy issues, drug issues, anger issues, anything, really. He'd go for the most immature, needy ones and would constantly get himself into trouble.

'It's been ages,' he said. 'I have been single for so long, and I see people settling down and having children literally all around me. It's a fucking nursery every day at the office. They're just popping them out one after the other.'

I giggled. I remembered working in an office environment. Women would indeed be popping every few months. In retail, not so much. I was surrounded by people that had barely left university or people over fifty that had been with the company since World War One, granting them a ridiculously high salary and almost infinite holiday. They were so close to the finish line and lived so cushily that they wouldn't dare try finding a new job. And damn rightfully so.

Me? I was the severely underpaid assistant manager who'd end up doing all the things my staff were slacking at. Such as speaking to customers for one. I had this whole plan I'd go back to retail to be able to save enough money so that I'd be able to afford a studio flat with a garden and have Squall living with me again.

I couldn't forgive Jake for getting it all. He got the dog, he got rid of me, and now he was going to get a shinier new flatmate he could have sex with. It just wasn't fair.

'And speaking of settling...' he continued. 'Mother fucking Sara Langaard.'

All this while I was either filling the till points with paper bags or staying at home eating instant noodles or, since recently, putting my dick into someone's mouth for £50 a pop.

'Yeah, isn't it the slap on the face we all needed?' I said, kind of joking. Kind of. 'I never would have gambled on her to be the next in line.'

'Her boyfriend is so, so damn hot though.' He squinted. 'He looks young.'

I laughed a little.

'Isn't that your type anyway?'

'Yeah, pretty much. I recently got into trouble exactly because of that.'

His dating horror stories were always entertaining to me. I enjoyed hearing other people's struggles. Made a difference from my usual mental ramblings.

'I see this hot guy on *Grindr*, yeah. Perfect, mixed race, tall, skinny and he sends me the filthiest shit. Asks me to come fuck him, and I head there straight away.'

I was staring at him while sipping the rest of my prosecco.

'I go inside his house, and he just jumps on me. He takes me to his bedroom, and we fuck. Raw. Hot. And then when I am finished, I looked around and thought this guy looked somewhat familiar.'

'And you couldn't tell until after you jizzed onto each other?' I poked.

'Yeah, I was too horny. And you know I can't really see anything. He could have been anyone. I'm so fucking blind,' he giggled. 'Then I go *fuck, this is my boss's son.*'

I spat my prosecco.

'And I swear I think he's seventeen,' he added.

'Jesus fucking Christ, John.'

My best friend was a child molester.

'I got dressed in seconds and *ran* out the bloody door,' he said while grabbing the menu. 'I'll be soo fucking *fucked* if I get found out.'

I wasn't even fully surprised as this would be so typical of his conquests. He always attracted this kind of drama.

'You seeing anyone?' he asked casually. 'I swear it's been a while now. Or are you back with the hubby?'

Hell no.

I didn't want to date; I wasn't even interested. I was so angry at the world, it was hard.

'Nah, not really. I can't be arsed. People suck.'

I didn't think I was quite ready to tell him about my little side hobby, but I decided I needed some outside input.

'Right, I'm going to run something through you, and you are going to tell me if I'm being an idiot. I have been doing something...' I teased mysteriously.

'Drugs?'

'No!' I scrunched up my face. 'Someone has been paying me to suck me off. A neighbour.'

He smiled.

'That's hot. How did you get around that?'

'Just someone on *Grindr*,' I said dismissively.

'Oh. Because I heard there is an app where you can basically just do that. *Seeking Arrangement* or something?'

'What the heck is that?' I asked, blatantly curious.

'I think it's some sort of dating app, but it's about finding a sugar daddy and such. Someone told me about it at work. I'm not into it because old men are disgusting.'

'Yeah, I don't think I'd be into it.'

I was into it.

Hi, daddies.

———•————————●————————•———

Leaving John was always a bit weird. We'd exchange a way too long of a hug. I'd never know if we were supposed to kiss at some point, but it would never quite happen.

Except this time, I wouldn't spend time dwelling on it. I was too curious to open up the app store. If there was an app out there that would make the process of scouting willing-to-pay idiots a lot easier, who was I to deny myself such a helping hand? It was also very sleekly designed, so that made it very pleasing to look at. Had to create a username. I believed in branding, so I kept my name and uploaded my best shirtless photo.

It was a good enough photo for me not to be ashamed in case I ever became famous and it surfaced from the dark depths of the internet.

It was one of those rare photographs to treasure dearly because of how well light, filters and shadows seemed to have cooperated that one time.

The profile was being set. I wrote mostly truths on the 'about me' section. Avid reader, semi-regular gym-goer, animal lover, likes travelling and all the bullshit people want to hear.

In reality, people want to hear how quickly you

crumble emotionally when shit goes down and how much of an annoyance you'll be to them. Or whether you'd still put their sweaty balls in your mouth when you're having a depressive episode. That'd be real stuff.

I wasn't too far from home. I was planning to activate my spanking new Seeking Arrangement account and hopefully come back to a few requests.

I really wanted to be able to get something for Sara after all. I was so sick of being the friend that never gets anyone a present because of, well, poverty.

I had a little chilled evening planned with my flatmate Andrew.

We'd try to spend some time together in front of Netflix and just enjoy each other's company. I really missed that intimacy with someone, to just sit next to each other and not necessarily say anything. Also, it would make for an extremely cheap dinner as Andrew would buy absolutely everything, wine included. He was very attentive at how shit my finances were, and he was happy to help. He could have charged a lot more to a stranger for my bedroom, but he was my saviour in my time of need, and I was very grateful to him. And my other friends. Regardless of how inadequate their lifestyles would make me feel.

I was just about to get my keys out and there it was. A text from Jake.

'When are you free for a chat this week?'

My heart was pounding. I didn't appreciate confrontation. Some people feed off it, but I was an only child. Didn't have to fight for much. I may have been born with only a few resources, but they were usually all directed to me.

Fights with Jake were tough. I had such a hard time expressing myself that I usually wouldn't be able to say anything.

I wished there was a way to re-do arguments. With more preparation and research, I could have been the king of debates.

Unfortunately, that's not how life works. People like me just hear the accusations.

I was being dumped one more time, this time for good. I was shaking with anger but couldn't do anything.

'Sorry, I am late,' said a panting voice from behind.

I could hear the clinking sound of multiple glass bottles in a grocery bag. Andrew was running towards me with goodies.

'Hello gorgeous,' I said, putting my arm around him.

He was wearing grey sweatpants and flip flops.

'Are you wearing one of my caps?' I asked, entertained.

'Yeah, I'm incognito. My hair is a mess. I fell asleep watching shit on Netflix and only just woke up. Was meant to be well into the dinner preparation process, but hey, better late than never.'

I proceeded to open our front door.

'You okay?' he asked, noticing my absentness.

'I am very good. Your look makes me deeply happy.' I smiled. I hated seeing him worry.

'Oh, fuck off. Is curry alright? There wasn't much at the store. Forgot we had nothing at home and the big shop is closed.'

We walked upstairs.

We lived on the first floor. We shared the building with another three flats, but I'd rarely see any other people.

Such a contrast from my previous life, where neighbours would actually put Christmas cards and biscuits in your post box.

I wondered for a second if they were still addressing them to 'Jake, Leo and Squall.'

I wonder if they had noticed Marc coming and going from the flat yet.

'Oi. Why are you being so quiet? I want none of this sad shit tonight. It's my evening and I want to vent,' he said, juggling all his grocery bags.

'Nothing. I am just preparing all the jokes for when you take my cap off and I get to see whatever the hell is going on with your stupid hair.' I smiled. 'It's just excitement coming from me. By the way, do you need help with those bags?'

'Too late, Leo.' He shrugged and smiled.

I opened our front door. The house was spotless, even though he had probably been napping for three hours.

'Has the cleaner been?' I wondered.

'Nah, I was bored. Was on the phone with my sister and she wouldn't shut up about her husband, so I put some headphones on and vacuumed. She didn't even notice the noise,' he said, putting the bags on the table. 'Right, I'm going to start chopping all this crap. Can you pour the wine, pick some music and keep me company in the kitchen?'

Good trade.

I put my phone on a dock with the first 'chill playlist' available on Spotify and I launched myself onto the first bottle. It had a cork.

'Are we celebrating something?' I asked.

'No, you know I hate shit wine. And I swear it only takes you two extra seconds to use a corkscrew.'

'I could get hammered within those two extra seconds. Speaking of which, did you go out last night?'

'Oh. Ha! I have been on a shit date.' He rolled his eyes.

'Tell me more,' I said while pouring two hefty glasses.

Andrew was just as unlucky as John when it came to dating. It was like all the weirdos were conspiring to make both of their lives semi-miserable.

I'd introduce them, but I had a slight crush on John—mainly platonic, but he was just that hot friend you kind of always want to bang. The idea of him having sex with another of my friends was terrifying.

'Oh, he was just really odd and off-putting. He cussed quite a lot.'

My face contorted in confusion.

'I swear constantly,' I said.

'I don't know. Maybe I am just too used to you. But also, he was a bit too "masc" for my liking?'

If there was ever such a thing.

'Really? Since when are you bothered by that?'

Andrew was a terrible kisser and a very passive bottom. You'd think an alpha guy would be right up his alley. Or his bumhole.

'Yeah, but I don't watch sports or play them. Also, I looked like a gremlin next to him. I should really go to the gym or something.'

'We tried that,' I interrupted him. 'You nearly threw up.'

He also took a sip of wine.

'I did throw up. But I do want a hot body. Why does it

have to be so hard?'

He loved a good whine.

'I don't know if I want to see him again. What if I have to get naked in front of him?' he asked.

'You look good naked!'

I wasn't lying.

He somehow had a very attractive bubble-butt and virtually zero visible body hair.

'What have *you* been up to these days?' asked the master of subject change.

I was on the verge. I wasn't happy to talk again about Jake and Marc.

It wasn't the healthy option for me to bottle off my anger towards them, but it was better than annoying my friends once again.

Also, Andrew would be horrified if he found out I was going to strangers' homes—well, *one* stranger's home, to exchange sex for money. Beyond horrified.

'Nothing, just been seeing friends for drinks and bitching about work.'

I finished my glass.

'Speaking of which...have you been applying for any writing jobs?'

Ugh, no.

I was lazy, and I did not like rejection all that much. In general.

I wished there was a job that would just pay me to play video games or guzzle an entire bottle of red in five minutes.

'I don't know, doodle,' I sighed. 'I don't want to start something new, be the newcomer, learn things. I am tired.

I am too old for this crap.'

He gave me the eye.

'You're four years younger than me. And, without you getting too cocky about it, you're one of the most intelligent people I know.'

I smiled.

I liked to think that, but life experience proved me wrong again and again.

'You need to get out of this,' he continued. 'You're just going through the motions because you're hurt, but everything could be so much better.'

Cute. Cheesy, but cute.

'I don't know what my dream is anymore. There is a part of me that wants to do something meaningful, with impact, maybe write my memoir,' I said. 'I could bore other people with my mental struggles, with my money issues, with my raging jealousy.'

'Maybe it's too deep of a conversation for a Sunday,' he said, pouring more wine into my glass. 'I just want you to feel normal again. Yourself.'

I wanted that too.

'I'll think about it. For real.'

But not really.

I looked down at my phone and I had an unbelievable amount of notifications, all coming from *Seeking Arrangement*.

My profile had gone live.

'What's that?' Andrew tried to take a peek.

I put my phone down.

'Phones off. It's *our* date night,' I winked.

'Look at you speaking like an adult. Well, good. There

is something that has been going on at work, which I'd love to hear your opinions on,' he said.

I wasn't listening. I kept trying to glance at my phone screen.

It took a little over an hour after food, wine and a bit of a Netflix documentary for Andrew to pass out on our sofa. He wasn't much of a drinker and he'd get cosy fast. I put a little blanket over him as he was always cold, and I quickly moved into my room.

I took my phone out and things were interesting, to say the least.

The "sugar daddies" in the app *knew* what they were doing, straight to the point.

None of that 'hey' nonsense, just plain transactional.

I was impressed.

None of them had display photos, but I wasn't too surprised.

Martin was presenting a very interesting proposal.

Age range was 60–75.

I couldn't even imagine living that long, let alone having sex with someone that age.

I had done old, but never past fifty-five. What were five or twenty years more than that going to do?

Martin was essentially looking for someone to be his, *ehm*, companion for a business trip in Sofia, Bulgaria.

Odd fucking country. I had never been. Kind of a random place to have business in.

I couldn't do that, could I? That would have been

incredibly irresponsible!

What if this old man turned into a psycho and harvested my organs while I was tied up to a bed with leather gear?

Also, would I be able to take the time off work?

Could I lie to all of my friends about my whereabouts?

I knew that even John would have slapped some sense into me and called me stupid.

However, this was a free trip, with fancy hotel stay and, best thing, a whopping five hundred pounds in cash.

I could so definitely do with an extra five hundred pounds.

Was sticking my dick into a wrinkly old man a few times worth it?

Damn right it was.

'*I'm interested.*' And...send.

CHAPTER 5

-£431.98

I WAS SITTING AT A TABLE IN A RESTAURANT at Gatwick airport. A steakhouse, of all places. Waiting for my seventy-year-old date to arrive. There's a sentence I never expected to say.

I was doing a very stupid and irresponsible thing and I was slowly regretting it the more I sat there waiting.

I felt like no one in the world was ever on time for things. Let alone early, like me. I didn't want to order a drink because I didn't want him to think I was just ordering things to add to his bill. Even though that was exactly how things were going to go down, I wanted to at least give the illusion of the *boyfriend experience*.

I had my back towards the entrance of the restaurant. I didn't want to sit and stare at every single man who'd enter the premises and either get my hopes up or be horrified by them.

I was starting to worry about my appearance. What if he was so used to collecting gay hoes online that he would just come to the table and laugh at my face? It was unlikely, but definitely a possibility. I wasn't one to be excessively self-conscious about my looks. Not because I thought I looked particularly good, but mainly because I'd always pick people that I knew would find me attractive. I'd look for someone *fairly* good-looking, but not necessarily an Adonis. I needed to feel like *the* more attractive one.

Twisted, but I never claimed to be particularly healthy.

This was going to be a cakewalk. What I was fearing was my potential lack of enthusiasm in the bedroom department. I knew there had to be sex stuff. When you're a gay man, you have the luxury of knowing that no matter what you look like, what awful things you're into or however unbathed you are, there will be someone out there willing to have sex with you. Even someone who looked like a model. You just had to cast your net and hope for dad issues.

My shoulder was touched.

Pet peeve.

'Good evening,' he said.

I smiled. A fake smile, like the one you'd give a priest. One you wouldn't want to fuck.

'Hey!' I said enthusiastically.

I didn't know what to do. Get up? Yeah, that seemed about right, but then? Hug? Handshake? No. Mister randy goes straight for a peck on my lips.

Fucking weird. I wouldn't do that to *anyone* I'd be meeting for the first time, but the old-ass man felt completely at ease kissing someone over forty years younger in the middle of a restaurant.

I was starting to feel a bit iffy about the bedroom stuff. I kept my eyes open during the smooch, and I couldn't help but notice the unbelievably long hair coming from the tip of his nose. Not inside a nostril, but on top of the nose. Weird, long white hair.

I was the kind of person who would never tell people if they had something in their teeth, let alone a monstrous strand of silver hair being birthed by the greasy skin of their nose. Also, very big nose. A large, vast terrain for that sequoia of a hair.

He was smiley. He seemed pleased to see me.

Had nice-ish teeth. Couldn't be sure if it was his natural teeth, but I wasn't dying to find out.

He was bald, but that wasn't a deal-breaker. He was wearing a light blue polo, some beige khakis and some brown deck shoes. Outfit-wise, it wasn't much different from the kind of stuff Andrew would wear. Perhaps less tight.

'You're really gorgeous,' he said.

This was the beauty of going on a date with someone who was fully awake when the moon landing happened, or when World War Two ended. They just had a way with words.

'I'm a mess,' I rebutted.

'I am glad you said yes to the trip,' he said, opening the menu. 'Not many people would trust a stranger to spend time abroad.'

Who says that?!

I was shitting myself. He was obviously foreshadowing my demise through organ harvesting, and I still sat there like an idiot, waiting to order an alcoholic drink.

'Would you like some wine?' he asked, innocently.

'Yes!' I nearly shouted. 'You get the honour to pick for us.'

And to pay for it, you stupid.

'Sure thing,' he responded.

He put his glasses on. I was then sure that the hair wasn't just there for decoration, but it was also a necessity, in case the spectacles slid down his enormous greasy nose.

'Are you bringing any sexy underwear in your luggage, young man?' he smirked, staring into my soul.

I did bring some underwear, but the thought of putting this man into the same context as *sexy* was doing nothing to put me in the mood. I wondered how much I needed to drink to actually perform well sexually. I had the sex conversation with him before, via text. He claimed to be a bottom, because he had trouble keeping his erection going, which wasn't the most promising of statements. Maybe he was going to turn out as one of those old gay men who always have a drug stash. Maybe I could actually go through with sex if I had one or five lines of cocaine. Doubtful.

'Can we have a bottle of the *Cotes du Rhone*, please?' he asked the waiter.

Decent choice.

'Is that alright with you?' He smiled at me.

I smiled back. After all, that was my job.

'So how was work today?' he asked, while laying a napkin on his lap.

I couldn't help but think I would have to sit on that lap not too long after.

'It was okay. It's not a particularly exciting job. I get to be around pretty clothes all day, though.' I snacked on a breadstick, as I was starving.

'I can see that,' he said, his eyes scanning my outfit.

I was wearing a very tight t-shirt. I wanted my baby muscles to show.

'...and what do you do, Martin?'

From what I understood, he was one of those British pensioners who just loved buying properties abroad for cheap and renting them out. He said we were going to visit a property and that he was going to the bank to have some meetings.

'You're more than welcome to either come with me, or perhaps have the day to yourself to visit the city or use the hotel facilities. Like a massage, maybe?' he winked.

Gross.

But I loved a massage. That was a good option. Thought I'd be stuck with bad grandpa the whole time. At least I could add Bulgaria to the countries I had visited.

The waiter finally came to pour our wine.

I was about to relax, at last.

———·—————●—————·———

Martin wasn't much of a drinker, so he only allowed himself two glasses, while I chugged most of two bottles. It seemed like I could handle it better, though. He was touching my cock through my jeans while in a lift, on our way to our hotel room at the airport.

I appreciated that better than him trying to kiss me. I didn't want that at all. The man had a steak for dinner.

Dead cow breath on my tongue was not what I was craving.

We entered the room. Pretty standard, albeit quite spacious.

'I really need a shower,' I announced, straight away.

'Absolutely,' he said while putting my hand luggage down. 'I'll see if there's anything to watch and maybe order us some more drinks?'

The man knew what he was doing. But so did I, hence I immediately ordered a bourbon.

I was planning to take the longest shower, so he would fall asleep and not be expecting anything frisky.

Silly me.

I took a shower worth the entire yearly supply of water for a small island, but unfortunately my companion wasn't as tired as his face looked.

My eyes were not ready. Martin was lying on the bed, wearing *a jockstrap.*

'*Christ*,' I thought. I probably owned a very similar pair myself. Same kind I'd wear when all of my everyday undies were dirty in the laundry basket.

Suddenly it all dawned on me, what I was doing.

This man was renting me. He was renting my body to do whatever he pleased with it. It was my job for the night. I would have to get my towel off, drink my bourbon, and then advance onto the bed and fuck this man's brains out.

He decided to lie on his stomach, so his whole crumpled arse was on display.

Suddenly the idea weirdly made me hard. Barging my way through, make this man hurt a bit, making him moan, or even scream. I kept thinking about all those times

Jake told me he had to work late while he was staring at someone else's anus, ready to fuck them behind my back.

I shook that image off and found myself aroused enough to give this man what he had paid for.

'Looking good,' I said in a flirty way.

'Your drink is on the table, stud,' he said without looking at me, face on the pillow, just waiting for me to do my thing.

No one had *ever* called me stud. Didn't care for it much.

I gulped the bourbon, and it went straight to my head.

I was ready.

I uncovered myself, threw the towel on the floor and made my way to him. I didn't want to kiss him or use my tongue on any surface at all.

I was the alpha, so he had to do as I said, even if he wanted me to do other stuff.

I squeezed his buttocks. They were soft, flimsy. No hair. A perfectly smooth pair of cheeks I was about to lather in lube.

I gave him a bit of a back rub to help with our "chemistry."

I touched him all over. He was in ecstasy. I rubbed my cock down his arse crack; his breathing was getting heavier and heavier. His lungs were probably collapsing, but I just took it as a sign that he wanted me to fuck him.

I put another dollop of lube on the tip of my fingers and slowly entered his hole. It was loose, easy to access. I could tell this would be an easy task for my dick. I grabbed a condom and tried to open it with my teeth. I had trouble for about ten seconds, but I eventually managed to open it with my hands.

The condom was tight, but very well lubricated.

I was ready to go.

I grabbed his hips and pulled them towards me. He was still presenting his arse to me, up in the air, while his face was on the pillow—an ideal position as I didn't want to see his face.

'Gentle, please,' he begged.

The tip of my cock entered him quickly; he was loving every inch of it. I slowly made my way in until my whole cock was buried in him.

He *howled*, from pleasure.

I then started vigorously thrusting, giving him the fuck of a lifetime, no mercy.

I was slapping my balls against his taint so loudly I had forgotten for a second that I was having sweaty sex with the very same pathetic man I was earlier having dinner with.

He was a very giving bottom and had a major tolerance for pain.

He was pushing his arse onto me so I could fuck him harder and harder.

It was really going far better than I thought until my penis slipped out.

No biggie.

I grabbed my cock and tried to stick it back in, but something felt wrong.

It was a lot stickier this time around. I thought we needed more lube, but the smell wasn't leaving much doubt.

I looked down at my hand and saw the worst.

A handful of *shit* and a trail all over my cock.

His arse was all smeared too, because of how hard I was fucking.

The stench was impossible to ignore at that point and I had drunk way too much to pretend it wasn't there.

I was about to heave, but I managed to say *just one second*, and quickly made my way to the toilet.

I removed the dirty condom straight away and threw it into the bowl.

I washed my hands with boiling water and soap. I could still smell the shit.

It was like it had made its way into my nose and was there to stay.

I looked at myself in the mirror. I felt like Carrie, just drowning in shit. My pupils were dilated from mixing my meds with copious amounts of alcohol, my hair was messy, and my face was flushed. I was in a hotel room with a man over twice my age, fucking him for money and dinner, to then be taken to a foreign country without telling any of my friends or family.

Shit.

Literally.

CHAPTER 6

-£344.58

'C AN WE PLEASE SEE EACH OTHER SOON?'

I hadn't seen Sara in a few days, and I wished I could share the tale of this trip with her. One day, just not anytime soon. I replied to her with a '*yes, please*' from the taxi that would take us to the hotel. Martin hadn't booked one in advance, which was pretty fucking dumb. So far, Sofia hadn't really managed to make a good impression. The airport was small, and as soon as we came out, we were bombarded by drivers trying to get us to go with them. No Uber there yet. I was surprised to see *my man* pick a random driver in the crowd and just follow them blindly. That was not how I'd usually roll. The driver was speeding like a maniac and all I could think was how embarrassing it would be for me to explain this situation to other people if I got into a car accident in Bulgaria with my sugar grandpa.

He seemed fairly chirpy and alert. He was still quite smiley, even though when I came back to bed after *shitmageddon*, I was not in the mood to fuck him anymore.

The room kept stinking. I couldn't escape it. I think he was mortified by it, but at least he sucked me off in a spectacular way. There was something very alluring about grabbing this head of flesh, with no hair on and then shove my cock all the way in it, until I sprayed my warm cum directly into his throat like a feeding tube. He swallowed it all, a true pro.

I couldn't imagine going into so many details with Sara, but I thought it was worth telling her one day. In case one of these repressed old faggies decided to slit my throat at some point. Obviously I wouldn't tell her that her wedding news and plans were the key to me finding this new business venture.

'It's quite the pretty day,' he said while looking out the window. I was melting. It was nearly thirty degrees outside and there was no air conditioning in the car. I was wearing thick jeans, so I could only imagine what sort of cheesy situation was going on in my balls department. Or, worse, Martin's.

'The hotel we're going to is very nice,' he explained. 'Hope you brought your bathing suit, as the pool is magnificent. There's a hot tub too.'

I was looking forward to that. Hopefully I'd get to experience all the amenities by myself and not being followed by my creepy grandpa, trying to cop a feel any chance he could. We had only known each other for less than twelve hours, and I was already quite sick of having his veiny hand on my inner thigh. He'd look at me while doing it, and smile.

Yikes.

The car was ready to park. The hotel was huge. I didn't think we were close to the city centre, but according to my Google Maps, we weren't too far. I was curious to see what that would look like, because until then, the city hadn't really delivered in the beauty department. The environment was plagued by massive high-rise buildings, all grey and dated. Billboards everywhere, discoloured and tacky, displaying businesses that didn't deserve billboards. It wasn't the usual London designer ones, just local stores selling bathroom sinks and taps. The city centre was hopefully going to look more effervescent.

I was also curious to see what kind of gay guys lived here. I had never met a Bulgarian before, not even in London.

We got past reception, and the hotel was indeed amazing. Marble everything. Black, white with copper accents. Giant pots of fresh flowers everywhere with almost no people around.

I didn't get to see many fancy hotels while growing up. Mum would often mention how much she dreamed of staying at a luxury resort and be pampered all day.

When I become a famous writer.

'Wow,' I gasped.

'Do you like it?' he asked me while riding the lift. There were two other men in it, so this time he didn't dare to put his face onto mine.

I couldn't have managed another close encounter with the big hair on his nose. I wondered if I'd ever find the courage to tell him at some point during the trip.

God, I hated confrontation.

The lift doors opened onto our floor, all carpeted and spotless. Again, almost no one around.

He opened the door to our room, a junior suite. We were quite high, seventeen floors above the world. I was categorically terrified of heights, so I wasn't keen on staying too close to the windows. Sofia didn't exactly click as the capital of health and safety, so I proceeded to the bedroom where we were greeted with fresh fruit, champagne and chocolates, along with various *extra special* toiletries, such as face creams, body lotions and eye masks.

The man had clearly spent some money at that hotel before.

I was knackered. The flight at 6 a.m. wasn't exactly an adrenaline booster.

'Why don't you rest a little?' he suggested.

'Are you going somewhere?' I asked as I was already crawling inside the bed.

'I have a few meetings scattered, so I won't be back until evening. Take your time and relax. I'll see you at dinner.'

He gave me a wet kiss, a bit gross.

I could make peace with it as that was *it* for a few hours. If I played my cards right, I'd only have to have sex with him once that day and I could live with that, especially if he took extra care and tried not to shit on my cock.

Sweet dreams, Leo.

───•────────●────────•───

I woke up around three hours later, confused about my

surroundings. For a second I had forgotten where I was.

I wasn't sure what to do with my free time, so I decided to do what every sane gay guy would do: I opened *Grindr* and put '*show me around*?' as a screen name. I was fishing for some really cute guy to take me around town, so I wouldn't get lost or kidnapped.

I couldn't say the choice of men was overwhelming. It was almost like homosexuality wasn't really a thing in Sofia. Most guys were far away, but the few that were within walking distance were surprisingly friendly.

Incredible looking guys, I may add. All were complimenting my body or my hair. It was almost too good to be true.

Was I *gorgeous* in Bulgaria?

One, in particular, took my breath away. He was muscular, with dark grey wavy hair, stubble and a banging chest.

He said his name was Petar. I was horny.

I had missed having sex with someone I actually wanted to have sex with. I wondered if it would be okay for me to go out and about and get pounded by a complete stranger, while on a trip with another stranger who actually paid to own my body for a few days.

My penis made the executive decision for me, so I instantaneously asked for a location. I couldn't risk asking him to come to the hotel as I had no idea when Martin could come back.

I jumped into the shower and into a pair of denim shorts as quickly as I could.

I figured I was going to bottom on this occasion. Those muscles were made to beat me into batter. I chugged a few sips of bourbon from the bottle in the minibar, chewed some gum, and I was out of the hotel.

The area was *interesting*. It was all very grey and run down. I went down a hill to find multiple stalls selling fruit and vegetables. All seemed very affordable, and people were surprisingly enthusiastic. Then at some point there was a voice coming out of speakers all across town. I couldn't understand a word, but I shat myself, nonetheless. I thought it was some sort of warning we were getting attacked, or that a missile was coming our way. No one moved. Not a single soul seemed to care about the voice. It was like a call to prayer ignored by everyone. So, I acted cool and ran to my guy's house. Flat buildings seemed to all have an open front door, so I went in straight away.

'Leo?' he shouted from the top of the staircase.

'Yes,' I responded promptly, excited to see this guy's face in the flesh.

He was wearing a tight white vest. His chest was incredibly defined, and his arms could lift me and throw me into traffic. The man was very, *very* good looking.

We kissed as soon as we were close enough to each other. He closed the door with his leg and lifted me to take me to the bedroom.

I was very much involved with what was going on between us, but I couldn't ignore the house décor. Everything was somewhat flowery, with tables covered in lace. Crystal glasses behind glass-doored cabinets. Bit of good ol' Jesus scattered around, but I stopped giving a crap once Petar proceeded to kiss my neck and push his bulge onto mine. It was intense.

We got naked very quickly, and I loved everything that

was in front of me.

I turned us around so I could be on top of him, and I immediately went down on him. Not circumcised, not freakishly long, but optimum girth.

I wasn't a fan of giving blow jobs, but that one went into my mouth as fast as an anvil free falling down my slutty throat. He was a gentleman; he didn't hold my head to take over with the skull fucking. He was lying there, enjoying what was happening and caressing my hair.

I wished he lived in London. I'd climb him as my full-time job.

He managed to grab a condom and put it on his cock with just one hand, something I had never successfully achieved in my sexual career. He gently lubricated his fingers and rubbed my hole, and then he slowly made his way inside me.

That's when he took control.

He flipped me, so he would be on top of me, with one of my legs over his shoulder while he kissed me passionately.

I had turned all my thoughts off; I was just enjoying the moment and how great his cock was making me feel. It went on for about fifteen minutes and every single one of them felt pretty fucking great.

Bulgaria was doing me good.

'I'm close,' he said in that *very* endearing accent. I wish I knew sex talk in different languages. I was so horned up that I put my face in front of his cock to let him know I was ready for him to shoot his load on it.

Not something I'd normally do, just on special occasions. Because semen is rank.

He didn't look like he was expecting me to ask for it so

bluntly, so he smiled a little. I was gently licking his balls, and that's when I could feel him quivering.

He shot a thick load on my lips. It was so hot. I was licking every drop of it, but that's when he surprised me again. He managed to cum once more, on my chest. And then again all over my cock. I didn't even know that was possible. A triple orgasm? I thought it was just a female myth. Or something pigs did.

I was covered in Petar's man butter and I didn't mind. I'd keep this mental image on file every time I'd want to get hard. It was that hot.

'Did you come?' he asked, while catching his breath.

'Not yet,' I responded, with semen still dripping off my lips.

That's when he decided to suck it out of me. Never had I come that quickly into someone's warm mouth. He smiled again, like I had just delivered agave into his throat.

He gave me a towel to clean myself off and then laid himself next to me, fully naked with his hand on my hip. It was intimate, and sexy as hell.

'Hello,' he said, cracking another smile.

'Hey there, Pete.' I moved slightly to grab my clothes, and he stopped me.

'Wait,' he said. 'Don't you want to stay for a bit? Tell me about you?' His giant hazel eyes were mesmerising.

Uhm, where could I start?

Dear Petar, I am a frustrated retail worker nearing his thirties who is currently abusing the very last of their attractiveness to exploit old men and receive money in exchange for sex so that I can afford to pay for fun activities for my rich best friend's wedding?'

I couldn't. Even if I'd never see this beautiful guy again.

'I can stay for a second.' I relaxed. 'What would you like to know?'

I touched one of his nipples gently.

'How's London? I've never been.'

I liked talking about London. London was my longest-lasting relationship.

'London is a lot,' I said, for lack of better words. 'There's everything you could possibly want. There's a very good chance that if you want fresh pancakes at 3 a.m., you'll probably find somewhere in London that makes them for you, or if you want to adopt a Filipino baby at 5 a.m.'

He ran his hand through my hair.

'You are very handsome.'

I wasn't used to that kind of treatment. Not from people that didn't want something from me. Martin called me handsome just the day before, but it was only to get into my pants. This guy had already gotten into my pants, and I was ready to go, yet he took the time to say it.

It was refreshing.

'What do you do, by the way?' I probed.

'I'm a photographer,' he said, proudly.

Of course, he was a photographer. I looked around and there were dozens of photographs hanging. Mainly black and white. Very impressive ones.

'So, you'd like to photograph London?'

'I'd like to photograph you.' He kissed me gently.

'Me? I should be photographing you! You're the one with the embedded eight-pack.'

'Yes, you,' he said, while getting up to grab a DSLR and starting to fiddle with it.

Who knew having incredible sex, an engaging conversation and about an hour of posing nude in front of a camera for a stranger would be my best memory from Sofia?

———•———————•———————•———

I was still daydreaming about my sexy afternoon, when Martin asked for my attention at dinner, later that evening.

'Sorry, I think I am still a bit tired. Perhaps I've had a bit too much relaxation today.'

I Wasn't lying.

'You look good for it, though,' he said.

I couldn't help but notice the giant hair wasn't there anymore. I wonder if some random Bulgarian businessman told him, maybe stopped him in the street. Gutsy.

One time I didn't tell Sara she had something stuck in her teeth for about an hour and I thought she'd disown me. Now she'd ask me constantly and question my integrity.

I missed her, and all my friends. I felt incredibly far from everything.

I'd get to go home the day after, though.

'So, have you done this before, Leo?' he asked, quite abruptly.

I wasn't sure what he meant, so I entertained him.

'This?'

'Yes, you doing what you do. With men like me,' he said cautiously. 'You seem like a very smart guy. I really enjoy talking to you. I was just wondering *why* you do this. You could do anything.'

Damn right, Martin.

I was flattered, but also a little insulted. I didn't think I was a part of the sex worker community, but assuming they were all unintelligent struck a nerve. Smart people have sex too, Martin.

'I am sure there are other people out there doing this who can also read books, Martin.' I smiled, cheekily.

'No, of course. You just really seem to be confident and I very much like that.'

I grabbed my glass of wine and gulped a sip.

'Is this something *you* do often?' I put down the glass.

'When you get to a certain age, it can become very lonely,' he said. 'Growing up, we didn't have apps or all these clubs where you can be yourself. It took me over fifty years to come to terms with my homosexuality. I have been married to a woman and I have children. I've missed out on being with beautiful young men when I could, and not many want to do that now.'

'That's right, I don't often think about it,' I said. 'I was born into an era that celebrated homosexuality, or gender fluidity, or the general message that it's okay to be yourself and love whomever you please. You had to go through a great part of your life ignoring your true instincts and doing what society wanted you to do.'

Suddenly this ordeal wasn't as slimy as when I first participated. He wanted someone to go back to. He didn't want to be in a hotel room by himself. I wasn't just there for sex. My company, my conversations, my observations and general presence were the reasons why he was paying me to be there with him. I was sure he wouldn't have batted an eye if I had told him I had spent the afternoon with a Bulgarian hunk taking tasteful nudes and having circus sex. He didn't buy me; he was just renting me.

'I couldn't imagine that kind of world. I think sexuality is the last of our problems, nowadays. We are very privileged in that aspect.'

I took a bite of my vegetable tartlet.

'But my generation isn't happy, either,' I added. 'Suddenly we have gotten what *your* generation has fought for, but we are still riddled with mental health issues that keep being stigmatised by a majority of the population.'

All references were casual, of course.

'I think the bar for happiness has gone a bit too high these days. I have days where I am completely content just sitting outside my porch, in Bournemouth, reading a book and sipping a nice glass of wine,' he said while cutting through a steak. 'Sometimes I feel lonely. Such is life.' Grandpa was becoming more interesting throughout the dinner, but I just couldn't shake off how creeped out I was by his general behaviour around me. I wondered if he had any other older gay friends who he could share this tale with, and if he'd tell them how I was in bed, how long my cock was, or how unaware I was of national politics. Maybe they'd all be laughing in a circle, thinking how cool they were for being able to own a toned, young gay guy for a few days.

'As promised,' he announced, while passing a white envelope over the table. 'Thank you so much for keeping me company. There's a little extra, as you've been so good to me.'

Fuck.

Now I *definitely* had to fuck him that evening.

Oh, how I wished I was drunk enough to mentally replace his face with Petar's.

I wondered what he was doing that evening.

Suddenly I felt a bit of melancholia at the idea of not seeing him again, probably ever.

CHAPTER 7

£376.22

'*LOOKING FORWARD TO TONIGHT!*'

One of Sara's closest friends, Abigail, was in charge of arranging the fun for her birthday bash. Abigail was also my friend, an absolute badass. She was a chatty, loud, witty as heck all-around fabulous woman and we'd have a great time together.

Also, it meant that she would have to get in contact with Marc, something I absolutely wanted no part in.

'Do you think Jake is invited?' Dominic asked me while we were finger spacing clothes on a rail.

I hadn't thought about it. 'I have no idea,' I responded, bluntly.

'Did you want to come with, by the way? I'm taking John, but you're more than welcome to join.'

Dominic and Sara had met a few times. I knew Dominic wouldn't want to come, but I was learning to be more polite with the people around me.

'Nah, I have a big rave tonight,' he said, proudly. 'Thanks, though! Will you be alright in terms of money? I heard *Hakkasan* is expensive.'

He wasn't exaggerating. I had a quick look at the menu while I was supposed to be working and realised I could just about afford the bread. I was hoping we'd have dinner quickly and then move somewhere else for drinks. Or I'd be *mega* fucked. Yes, I had some extra money from the blow jobs and my little Bulgarian field trip, but that was all going to my "*best man fund.*"

'I think I'll be alright. I'll just sit next to Sara and will probably eat next to nothing.'

Sara's eating ventures were notorious. Some days she'd binge all kinds of foods, some days she'd just drink wine and some days she'd plain forget to eat. I was hoping for the latter that evening.

'Also, I've eaten a couple of meal deal sandwiches, so I'll be stuffed way before I get there.'

I realised even then how sad that sounded.

'If you need any money...' he started.

'Oh, god no,' I immediately interrupted him.

'Well, you know, you just went away, surely that must have cost money?'

If only he knew.

I hadn't heard from Martin since we separated at the airport. The moment we landed I was done with that arrangement, and I think he knew. I didn't think there was going to be another trip with him anytime soon. I wasn't even sure if he thought the money was worth it. I wished there was some sort of rating system within the app.

Come up with a god damn excuse, Leo.

'I got a *Ryanair* flight for five quid,' I stuttered, nervously. 'Haven't exactly dabbed into my non-existing savings.'

'*Ryanair*? Gross, sweetie!' he frowned.

'I think we are done with this for tonight?' I asked, impatient to leave that damn store.

'Yeah, fine by me. We have been here for way too long anyway,' he said while removing his long-sleeved top and revealing a mesh vest underneath.

'You don't waste time!' I said while giggling at his hairy chest coming through.

'The quicker I get out of these clothes, the quicker I'll be on the dance floor fucked on MDMA.'

Solid plan.

All I had was a bunch of pills that would make me sleepy and fail at stabilising any sort of mood I had.

'You coming tonight?'

Jake decided to text me for the first time since his '*we need to talk*' announcement. Was he going to Sara's party? To tell me about his plans with Marc, perhaps?

God damn, I didn't want to face that.

Not on my wifey's birthday.

———•————●————•———

I had managed to chug a couple of gin cans in my Uber, on my way to the restaurant. Three of them, to be exact, and I was merry. I could see Sara smoking outside the venue, and I immediately asked the driver to drop me there. She was by herself. Odd.

'Hello, woman.'

I went for a hug and a kiss on the cheek. 'Happy Birthday.'

Her whole face lit up. 'Thank you.'

'You okay?' I asked, concerned.

'I had a fight with Alfie this morning and he still hasn't fucking showed up.'

'Fight over what?'

'It's fine. Nothing particularly serious,' she scoffed. 'I am just so tired of dealing with his shit.'

'Hey, hey. You guys just got engaged. You shouldn't be tired of anything.' I tried to perk her up.

'Oh, I don't know. One day he acts like a normal human being, but there's all these times he acts like a child.' She rolled her eyes. 'Am I supposed to feel like this all the time?'

'You don't feel like this all the time,' I put my arm around her waist. 'I can call him and see where he's at, if you want.'

She looked at me, stepped on her cigarette and smiled a little.

'No. We are going inside, and we are going to have some serious drinks.'

Troublesome.

'Please don't do anything stupid,' I said.

'Such as…?'

'Don't get all flirty with other guys just to prove a point.' I gave her a stern look.

'I don't do that,' she said, while opening the door to the restaurant.

Like hell you don't.

We entered the restaurant, and it was all rented out for Sara. Abigail had to have pulled some serious strings for it. I wasn't sure what kind of money would be able to achieve that. Everything was very pretty. Flowers at every table, some black balloons here and there, and a very enticing open bar.

'Where's John?' she asked me.

'Oh, he's late; he will probably come in an hour or so.'

I was trying to get the bartender's attention in the meantime.

'Don't get too frisky, you two. Don't want the added drama of dealing with my gays hooking-up with each other.' She winked. 'I know the way you look at one another. Don't think I haven't noticed.' She had also managed to get some attention. 'Two glasses of champagne, please. And leave the bottle.'

She meant business. 'So, what have you been up to this last week? I have barely seen you or heard from you.'

She'd just worry if I told her the truth.

'Nothing much, just working loads. We are a bit understaffed, so I have to do the dirty work with Dominic.'

She was looking around to scout people.

'Oh, he should have come. I like him.'

Didn't think she did.

'That's alright. You'll just have my full undivided attention.'

She handed me one of the glasses. 'Cheers.'

'Happy birthday, my baby girl.'

That was when I had noticed Jake in the background, by himself.

'Has Jake come here by himself?' I asked, perplexed.

Sara turned around to have a look at where he was. 'Uhm, no. He came with Marc, but he's probably talking to some other people from work. Or doing cocaine in the bathroom.' She tapped her nose.

'Ah, lovely.' I couldn't believe this was still going on between them. Jake used to hate drugs, and while I may have had a slight little problem with alcohol and depression, that was always a deal-breaker. Maybe Marc gave a hell of a blow job. I decided to go to Jake and talk. It was the perfect occasion, plus I didn't want to spend the entirety of the party trying to avoid the inevitable conversation.

'I'm just going to go speak to him really quick,' I reassured Sara.

'Alright, but don't ruin this for yourself. I'm planning a long celebration, and I can't have you all angry and mopey in a corner, okay?' She gave me a kiss on the cheek. 'I love you.'

I smiled and walked towards Jake.

He was on his phone, as he was for most of our relationship.

'Hiya,' I said courageously while tapping on his forehead.

'Oh, hey. You're here,' he replied, with no sense of surprise or faint glee.

'I am. How long have you been here?'

Small talk. Small talk was painful.

'Maybe twenty minutes? Not too long, anyway. Did you want to talk? Maybe we could go outside.'

I accepted the offer and led the way outside. I tried to find a corner where we wouldn't be surrounded by pissed people trying to smoke.

'What is it, then?' I asked, quite bluntly.

His voice was breaking, out of nervousness; I wondered if anything unusual had happened. 'It's about the flat. I wanted you to know that Marc will be there temporarily for a few weeks.'

A few weeks? That's not what I was expecting. Was he just lying to me? My face showed clear confusion.

'He is renovating parts of his flat, and he needed a place to stay. I know what we discussed in the past...'

I was pissed off. 'You said no one but us would be Squall's owners, and now you have your guy live with him?'

His face turned red, his voice struggling to find the right words. 'No, it's not like that. He just needed a place to stay for a bit...'

I wasn't buying it. 'Marc is loaded. He could probably afford to pay for this whole party. Why wouldn't he go to a hotel or rent a flat?'

'Because I asked him to. He is my boyfriend...' I interrupted him.

'We are still married, Jake,' I said, like it meant anything.

'Look, I don't want to push anything you aren't ready for, but it's been a year now. And I have been looking after your dog for the entire time.'

'*My* dog. It is always *my* dog when you get pissed off. You seem more than happy to whore him around to meet your shitty friends and score cool points, though,' I quickly blurted, without much thinking.

'Oh, whatever.'

'You know what, do whatever you want. It's not like you have my best interests at heart. Just follow your dick, like you always have.'

I was planning to get back in, when he stopped me. 'Don't do this. You know it's not fair. I am just being honest on what is happening, so that you have time to prepare and you don't have another mental meltdown.'

I couldn't say anything back. I just nodded and went back inside.

Bad choice, as my best friend was now having a good ol' chat with my nemesis and a few others. I was about to head there and bite the bullet, when a pair of hands squeezed my chest from behind.

'Hello, arsehole.' John had arrived and gave me a hug. 'Sorry I'm shit.'

I was happy to see a friendly face. Also happy to see someone I'd gladly get drunk with while I waited for Sara to be free from the devil.

'So, where have you been? Did you do anything with what we talked about last time?' He pinched my cheek.

'Of course not.' I half-smiled.

'Ah, boring. What did you have to do? Did you get a hot daddy at least?' He sat on a stool by the bar with his elbows on the counter.

I knew he was about to start his whisky-on-ice spree.

'Get me one too,' I said, parched.

'Sure.' He asked for two doubles.

My man.

'Will you really not tell me? I told you about my underage conquest, which, *by the way,* not so underage, I luckily found out. But I still feel like you owe me one now.'

We both laughed. He looked relaxed; he had probably smoked something before getting there, although I couldn't tell. His aftershave was overpowering.

'There you go, my noodle.'

I couldn't get to the drink soon enough. That's when Abigail made her way to us, by the bar. Her loud voice could be heard by the entire room.

'Hey, you two!' Her long, burgundy hair was wrapped in a messy ponytail. She had dressed up for the evening: jumpsuit and chunky heels. She looked much more polished than usual. We three-way hugged.

'Has anyone seen Alfie yet?' she asked, not exactly whispering.

'I think he'll be a little late,' I naively replied.

'Oh, he's probably fucked up with Sara and being a dick,' she quickly slurred. 'This is a really good time to talk about the hen do for Sara, assuming they're actually going to get married.'

My heart started racing. Any sort of situation that would involve money I didn't have made my palms sweat.

'Oh yeah, are we going anywhere fun?' John asked, while tapping his oversized rings onto the side of his glass.

'I think we should fly somewhere, rent a villa and get absolutely hammered by the pool,' she enthusiastically illustrated. 'I'm thinking Ibiza or somewhere else in Spain, where gin & tonics are as big as a fucking aquarium.'

The idea was thrilling, but in my head I was trying to calculate just how many limp dicks I'd have to suck or sit on to be able to afford the hen do trip *and* the trip to actually attend the wedding. I was the only twenty-nine-year-old in that room not to have a savings account, or my own home, or a decent job that that allowed me to 'work from home.'

'I was just talking to Marc.'

Ugh. I already hated what was about to come.

'...and he said he's done events like these before and we are looking at about a grand each for the whole thing. That should ensure constant drinks and potentially a cook too, which I think would be perfect,' she said.

I had accidentally swallowed too big of a gulp. 'A grand?' I asked, hoping I had an aneurysm while she was explaining.

'That's alright, I guess?' John interrupted. 'Leo, I can pay for both of our deposits if you need more time?'

'No, no, of course not.'

Huh, the lies I'd tell. 'I mean we don't need to pay straight away, right?'

It was October, after all.

'I don't think so.' Abigail seemed to understand my economic situation without actually addressing it out loud. 'I think we should just think about how many of us there will be and go from there. Mister best man, we could probably discuss activities, decorations, etc. together. I don't think there will be many others who know Sara like we do,' she teased, while messing up my hair.

I smiled, looked at my phone, and immediately started scouting for some paid jobs on my apps. I was in Mayfair, so the odds of a gross businessman paying for sex would be quite high. It had become somewhat easier to spot the paying "clients" on *Grindr*. Yes, there were a lot of men just looking for regular, quick sex; however, I had narrowed the age range between forty and seventy-five years, with user names or descriptions that would imply "*generous*" or "*rewarding*" and with a photo that looked professionally taken, wearing a suit and leaning against a plain background. The better the photo, the higher the chance of this man being a "*no-nonsense, straight to the point*" kind of douchebag. I wondered whether *Carlos* would be up for some Leo time.

'*Hey, mister,*' I sent, along with a shirtless photo of myself. '*Doing anything this evening?*'

I was in a rush to get the ball rolling. Or his balls rolling. On my face.

———————•———————————•———————————•———————

I was terrified of the bill coming. I had sat at a table with all my very successful friends and had an unbelievably expensive tasting menu drenched with a continuous stream of alcohol. All the various black American Express cards were lying in the middle of the table. No one seemed fussed; no one was sweating profusely waiting for their turn to put their pin. It was £190 each. I was shitting myself, worried that I wouldn't have enough in my account. I would *never* check my account, as I didn't want to face that anxiety every day. I could always use my sex savings, but I didn't want to tap into the wedding celebration pot.

While I was waiting for the card machine to get to me, I kept keeping Mister Carlos intrigued. I was wasted, and it was probably a very bad idea, but I asked £120 for sex. And he had accepted to send an Uber to pick me up. He also just wanted to top me, which would make it a very easy pay check. I didn't have to perform or do anything difficult. I had to lie there and just take it up my arse. He didn't seem too big from the photos, so I was confident I could get the whole thing within me and finish in just a few minutes.

'Whose card is this?' the waiter questioned.

It was the only Halifax Basic Account on the plate. I could see Sara making eye contact from across the table. She was waving her card. I could read *'I'll pay'* through her lips.

'Don't worry,' I mouthed, stupidly proud.

I tapped my pin code into the machine, and magic. It went through.

Relief. I immediately put my card back into my wallet and got off my chair to speak to Sara.

'I feel like I haven't seen you!' she said, drunk off her tits. 'I've missed you.'

She gave me a big sloppy kiss on the cheek.

'I am going to have to go now, hun,' I said in a whiny child tone.

'But we are all going dancing now!'

'I know, but I am very drunk, and I do have to go to work early tomorrow. I'm sorry.'

I didn't.

'Alright, but let's do lunch together soon. Just me and you.' She hugged me.

'Sounds good, baby girl. Happy birthday.' I gave her a kiss and walked outside to wait for my Uber. Jake was also outside, solo. Was he going home by himself? I couldn't believe he'd refuse a night out dancing.

One of the reasons he had broken up with me was that I wasn't social enough. Now he was about to move in with

Mister Socialite himself and he was bailing?

He saw me and walked towards me.

'Hey, you going home now?' he asked, oddly friendly. Tipsy, perhaps.

'Yeah, it's time to go for me.'

I decided not to ask about Marc's absence. I was hoping they had a big fight.

'Do you want to grab a quick drink together before going home?'

My eyes were wide open. I was taken aback. I believe I wanted to; I wanted to have a moment with Jake together. Unfortunately, as soon as I was about to utter a word, my Uber stopped right next to me.

'Maybe some other time, then,' he said, then waved.

I got into the car not saying anything. Why I still loved such a man who hurt me so much, I couldn't understand. But there I was, leaving a potential reconciliation to head to a man who was about to channel all of his sexual frustrations onto me.

The Uber stopped just a few roads past Hammersmith station. I got out of the car and banged my head on the roof, hard. I wasn't sure whether going to a random sex date that drunk was a good idea, but alas, I was already there, and I had chewed on gum for the whole car trip, so my breath situation was hopefully under control. Carlos gave me quite a lot of instructions to get to his flat, which would require at least an *alert* level of drunk, which I wasn't too sure I possessed. I was on a mission to make the whole ordeal as quick as possible, so I could go to bed, where it wouldn't be an issue if my head was spinning constantly. I rang the buzzer which automatically opened the gate. It was one of those complexes made of multiple buildings, and I had no clue where to go. Flat 78 seemed far, and the numbers didn't seem to make sense in the dark. I walked straight, or as straight as I could, so that I could at least get to the higher numbers. It was around midnight, and I could only hear my own steps. No one was around. I started walking faster, as I wanted to minimise the time I'd be spending by myself outside. Sometimes London at night can be scary. Finally, I heard a voice coming from above me.

'Leo?'

I looked up and a short man with only a few tufts of hair around the sides of his head was standing at the top of a flight of stairs.

'Hey!' I shouted.

I was walking up the stairs and I couldn't help but analyse his looks. Big round glasses, a silk robe and a pair of leather slippers.

'Come in, quickly,' he said in a Spanish accent.

At least we seemed to agree on the 'quickly' part. I got inside the house. It was a quaint little flat. The door opened onto a living room, with a big paisley red and beige sofa. A lot of artwork was hanging on the walls, with the common element of red. The house was filled with little objects, an inconceivable amount of stuff, probably gathered throughout the years as souvenirs. Cabinets upon cabinets of what seemed like Spanish War memorabilia.

'Would you like to drink something?' he asked politely,

while removing my jacket and hanging it.

'No, thanks,' I said.

Yes, I said no.

The more I scouted for clues about this man's life, the less I wanted to get naked with him. 'Have a seat,' he said, while pointing me to the sofa.

I was nervous this was going to turn into him illustrating a set of rules with a PowerPoint presentation. I sat down and noticed from accolades and photos in the room that Carlos was a teacher, or must have been a teacher in the past, judging by his age. He walked towards the sofa, and I was expecting him to sit down next to me, but I wasn't so lucky. He quickly unzipped his trousers and pulled out a fairly short dick surrounded by grey pubes. Not fully erect, but right next to my face. No one had been so direct before, but I guess I was bound to find different personalities. I was just about to open my mouth, when he grabbed the back of my hair and shoved his dick into my mouth as quickly as he could.

It tasted unwashed but didn't smell like it. Or maybe that's just what old cocks tasted like. He was thrusting and trying to push it as far as he could, something that would usually bother me, as I had always had a terrible gag reflex, but this was a very innocuous penis, so there wasn't much struggle there. He then took his robe off and removed his trousers completely. He slapped me on a cheek a few times to open my mouth and said '*good boy*' more than I cared to hear.

On second thought, I *wasn't* drunk enough for it. I kept on sucking until he slapped me again to get up and then he guided me to the bedroom. I only had a few seconds to notice my surroundings. This man was very fond of religious figures. The bedspread was rough, like it was made of thick wool. I'd usually sleep with the window open and a fan in front of my face. I doubt I could ever sleep in wool. He pushed me on the bed, abruptly. He turned me around so I could lie on my stomach and then pulled my arse towards him. I wasn't sure what was happening. I had a bit to drink, sure, but I wouldn't allow this old man to fuck me bare. But that was not what was about to happen. He wanted to spank me, hard. I was glad he couldn't see my face, baffled, weirded out.

'Yeah, mother fucker!' he shouted between spankings.

It hurt. A lot. And he'd spank the same bit, over and over. I tried to make sex sounds each time, but it was getting more and more painful, and he seemed to enjoy it a little too much.

He didn't disclose that he wanted me to be a submissive bottom during our chat. I would have asked for more money, or not showed up. Fuck this guy and his issues. I decided to take matters into my own hands and speed up the pace of this bullshit encounter.

'Fuck me, please,' I whispered.

I knew that limp sausage wasn't going to hurt anywhere near as much as his hands were.

He was ecstatic. It was clear from his stupid smiley face that he thought he was some sort of Hispanic sex god. He quickly jumped onto the bed, back on the frame. I proceeded to remove his t-shirt for some reason. Not sure why that'd be better, but at least I could bite his nipples hard if he got trigger-happy with the spankings again. He pulled my head and put his balls in my mouth. Big, hairy balls.

I couldn't wait to brush my teeth once I got home.

Meanwhile, he grabbed a condom from a drawer in his nightstand and attempted to put it on his little noodle. There was way more latex than flesh to work with.

Good.

I immediately abandoned my position between Ballsville and Musty Buttholeland and jumped on his waist, with my hands on his man tits. I had to take charge. I wasn't going to be this man's little bitch, regardless of what our economy dynamic actually was. I lubed up my hole and sat on his little dickie, ready to ride it as quickly as possible, until it would prematurely release itself. That's exactly what I did.

'Slow down,' he muttered, but I wasn't listening.

I went faster and faster and not even three minutes later his lament graced my ears. Carlos was done. His decrepit little swimmers were now in an oversized condom and I could finally fuck off home.

'Sorry,' he said.

For the spankings? For being such a weirdo? Or for coming too soon? The last one was a blessing.

'So hot,' I said, to make him feel better. I was getting worried as I hadn't seen the cash yet. 'Time to go,' I announced.

He put his robe back on and grabbed his wallet. 'I'll call you an Uber.'

I didn't expect that, but I couldn't say no. It would have been a bitch to get home at that time of the night on public transport.

'Thanks, Carlos.' I smiled at him.

'There you go. Thank you. You're beautiful.'

I was a sucker for a compliment.

Thanks, dad.

I grabbed the money and quickly shoved it in my pocket without counting it. It felt thick enough, unlike what I had to put in me that evening.

'I'm just going to head out for the car. I'll see you soon,' I whispered while still tying my shoes. He wished me goodnight and closed the door behind me.

It was drizzling out, chilly. I walked quickly toward the main gate, my arse cheeks still hurting. That night didn't feel right. It didn't feel like I was in control. I had managed to soften the blow of Sara's birthday bill, but I had to pay a price.

CHAPTER 8

£334.44

DOMINIC AND I HAD THE SAME DAY OFF WORK. It just sucked that it was on a dreary, dark, rainy evening. He came over to watch Netflix and play with the pup. Both Marc and Jake had to work late, so it was the perfect chance to snoop around.

The flat had been invaded by Marc's presence.

'Christ, there are photos of them hanging on the walls now!' I shouted.

One was at the Ritz, with the two of them wearing suits and looking dashing. I had the same photo with Jake. It was our first anniversary.

'You know they actually got to stay at the Ritz?' I asked, bitterly.

'That shit is expensive,' Dominic said. 'Wonder whose cock he had to suck to get that deal.'

Like Dominic couldn't afford it too.

Everyone but me seemed to be able to do those things, while I could barely splash on a £6 bottle of red wine, instead of the usual £4.50.

'Have you found anything else?' an inebriated Dominic asked from the living room.

He was wearing jersey shorts, even if it was cold outside. He wore the same outfit for most of the year, all black and comfy, oversized hoodies with slutty vests underneath.

'Nothing juicy,' I responded, while putting down a couple of business cards with Marc's stupid name on them.

I loved Dominic's company. He made me feel good and appreciated. He also bought me vegan pizza and wine every time I'd be upset or too weak to leave my bed. He was also one of the only people who wasn't too tired of hearing me rant about Jake.

I sat on the sofa, grabbed my chalice and put my legs over Dominic's. He liked that; he liked massaging my feet—something I found very erotic.

'How was Sara's birthday? Did you have fun?' he asked.

All I could remember was the salty bill and my post-party activities.

'It was good, but her fiancé wasn't there. I still have to catch up with her on the matter, because I feel like they haven't spent much time getting along since the engagement.'

Dominic removed my socks and kept massaging my feet. It felt good.

'How are you feeling about all this?' I wasn't sure what he meant. 'This is your first friend getting married, isn't it?'

It was. I got married at twenty-six to a tiny number of friends and my mother's ashes. Sara helped with most of the celebration expenses. She took me away to France for my stag do, and we partied, hard.

'I'm okay,' I responded after a long pause. I didn't want it to be a case of being emotionally drunk. It happened way too many times.

'Remember, you can always talk to me. I will listen to whatever, regardless of how pathetic it may feel sometimes.'

I felt soothed. Truth was, I actually had my doubts on Sara's relationship, but I never had the courage to tell her. Alfie was erratic, immature, and at times just an awkward person to be around. Sara was the sun, an incredible force who sometimes had to dim herself in his presence.

'I am mainly worried about how much this is going to cost me, and we are not exactly hitting department budget at work, so the idea of receiving a bonus seems quite feeble.' I sneered.

'Well, remember we have a private event coming up soon in the store. That might perk up the sales. And we'll be there together, so we'll make it fun.' He moved my legs to get up and reached for my head. He gave me a little pat and then gave me a big kiss on the lips. 'I'm going to grab more wine, okay?'

He took the house keys and left the flat. Meanwhile, my phone was buzzing with messages from a guy named Jimmy, from the *Seeking Arrangement* app. He seemed normal enough, although he wasn't based in the UK. He was an Englishman living in Germany, employed by the government. Unlike the majority of people I'd spoken to through the app, he wasn't a thousand years old. He was thirty-seven and didn't look like a wild animal. We were having some nice interchanges, and he was really keen to meet.

'*Cologne is tremendously boring, so I try to get away every chance I get.*'

It sounded like this was another man who liked to go away with his 'sugar babies.' I preferred that as well, as I didn't want any acquaintances seeing me having dinner with all these different, much older than me, individuals. Having dinner with Martin in Gatwick, or even in Sofia, was an odd experience. I could see people at other tables looking at us, thinking we were father and son, and then being completely horrified when he would kiss me on the lips multiple times in public. Jimmy seemed different.

'*I'd quite like to get away too,*' I replied.

I drank the last few drops of wine and lay down on the sofa while petting little Squall, who was sleeping peacefully on the cold wooden floor. I had also been thinking about Dominic kissing me. I knew he had a mild crush on me, but it seemed like he was trying to get closer and closer to get physical with me.

Then my phone buzzed again. And again. I picked it up and held it far from my face as my eyesight was getting a bit blurry.

'*Paris, then?*' Jimmy was keen. '*All paid, plus reward, of course.*'

Ooh, la la.

I got back home quite late. The house was dark, except for a tiny lamp Andrew would always keep on for me, so I wouldn't trip and break shit. I put my keys down and looked at the mail pile. One stood out as being thicker, with an embossed design all over it.

It came so soon. Sara and Alfie's save the date. That bitch had decided on a date and didn't tell me.

'*Sara and Alfie are getting married. First of April. Santorini. Invitation to follow.*'

I only had a few months left to come up with the money. I had to step up with my extra-curricular activities. I was waiting for confirmation from Jimmy, but if all went well, I was going to go to Paris for a weekend and get £700 for it. Not too shabby.

I took a tablet of Quetiapine and went to bed immediately, too tired to brush my teeth or remove my contact lenses. A long day at work would await me in the morning.

The shop floor was decked for the event. There was a bar, a DJ, canapes, goodie bags, z-list celebrities. Sara didn't organise this one, but she was going to come anyway to make sure everything was going right. I'd have to ensure my staff would behave like normal human beings, and not the usual bunch of running geese I had to deal with on a daily basis. Dominic and I had to dress up as well. Full black, with name tags on display, something I hadn't worn since my first week on the job. We looked exactly like waiters. The music was loud, ideal to barely hear other people. Katherine was kissing every invitee's arse.

She was loud, and insufferable. You could tell people had no interest speaking to such a crass, annoying human. She was watching me like a hawk. It was going to be next to impossible for me to grab a flute of champagne without her noticing.

I was standing up still, just looking around. My staff were actually doing their job, speaking to people and putting clothes through the till. Perhaps I'd truly see a bonus in November.

Sara was talking to the bar staff. It was utterly fascinating to watch her in work mode. She was assertive with a smile that wouldn't crack, but not afraid to come across as a bitch in order to get things done. She was wearing a short navy dress, with her long legs bare and suede ankle boots which would make noise, even with the loud music. Her hair was up; she probably got too hot running around. I decided to bother her for a bit. I was way too exposed where I was, and I didn't want to risk being stuck talking to some orange-looking girl who'd tell me the tales of how exciting it is to tan in Marbella.

I was making my way to her, when I heard a familiar voice. 'Excuse me?'

I turned around. *Fuck.*

Fucking Marc.

'Leo, could you help me?' he urged.

I didn't think I'd ever hear my name coming out of his mouth.

'Yes?' I stammered. Blood ran straight to my head. Regardless of how shit I thought he was, I found him a bit intimidating. His confidence would throw me off; we were such different people.

'I saw a shirt a few days ago that I must have, and I figured you'd know which one since you're in contact with the clothes almost every day.'

Arsehole.

I hated vague descriptions of things. It would elongate the experience and I'd have to do the guessing game for a far more extended period of time.

'What kind of shirt?' I enquired, expecting see-through black, like most of his wardrobe.

He smiled. Big white teeth. Bits of grey hairs scattered on his beard, even though he was a few years younger than me. Hair slicked back, as if monkeys had jizzed on it. Multiple long necklaces around his neck and a very unbuttoned patterned shirt. Everything about him irritated me. His voice was deep, yet oddly feminine at the same time.

'I think it was silk? With flowers against a dark navy background.'

I knew exactly which one. It was a £900 shirt. I loved that one.

'I think I know what you mean. I don't believe we have your size left, though. We sold one this morning,' I jabbed, with a little smile.

'Awe, that's a shame. Could you double check in the back, please?' he insisted.

Fucker.

'It's not super urgent...' he continued. '...but it would be perfect for Japan.'

Of course, he'd get to go to the one destination I always wanted to go to.

'Oh, I love Japan,' I said, thinking this was going to be our one topic of conversation.

That's when I had a chill running down my spine. It couldn't be. He *wouldn't*.

'Yeah, we are going to celebrate Jake's fortieth birthday,' he exclaimed.

My face felt hot, and I glowered. What a piece of shit. I couldn't believe Jake would do that to me. The trip I had arranged for years, he was going to share it with Marc.

Tokyo was *our* thing. I was livid. I was furious I had to find out from such a little cunt. My back felt like flames were coming out of it.

'I'll go check,' was all I could say back. I wanted to say so much more and call him out for the atrocious piece of trash he was, but all I did was go to the stock room, close the door and scream. Loudly.

I was hurt. I had had enough. I was done with Jake and his bullshit. Fuck it all.

CHAPTER 9

£1094.65 (Payday!)

THE EUROSTAR HAD JUST ARRIVED at *Gare Du Nord*. The bright sunlight was warming my face. I had to wear sunglasses. I had a very comfortable ride— Jimmy bought a first-class ticket. I also didn't have anyone sitting next to me, so it was easy for me to get up and go to the bathroom over twenty times. I drank two cans of Monster Energy way before we got to the Channel, so my bladder was in constant movement.

I had been avoiding talking to most of my friends, as I couldn't shake the anger off from finding out about Jake and Marc going on the trip I so desperately wanted to go on.

'Oi, man! When do I see you?' Sara texted. I wondered if she knew about it.

I'd ask her when I'd get back.

The station was frolicking with people, even though it

was barely nine in the morning.

'I am here. Looking forward to seeing you!' Jimmy texted.

He had flown the evening before and already unpacked. We would stay at his friend's house, which had plenty of spare rooms. I hated meeting new people, but when doing encounters with strangers from the internet, I much preferred being around people, no matter how irritating it might be to be nice to them. I was sure one of these men would turn out to be some ear-collecting murderer and I was going to be found with my intestines hanging out of my body while lying on a Hilton bed.

The station itself was windy. My hair kept going everywhere. I had pulled it all back, as lately it was unmanageable, but I'd still let it grow a bit, for the time being. I was sure one of my friends would stage an intervention when it got to Jesus length.

I could see Jimmy waving in the distance. He looked short, although he was only a bit smaller than me, maybe one inch. He was wearing a beige trench coat, a pair of straight cut blue jeans and white trainers.

'Bonjour,' he said. 'Welcome to Paris.'

His voice was soft, with a bit of a South London accent. Probably partially lost having to speak English in Germany.

'Hello there.' I moved my weekender bag to my other shoulder.

He reached for it. 'Want me to carry that for you?' he offered.

Nice. I appreciated that.

'Oh, no, don't worry,' I said.

He gave me a little brush on my back. I was glad we didn't do the kiss-as-soon-as-we-meet thing Martin seemed so fond of. Also, no weird hairs growing out of Jimmy's face, although I could detect a balding spot at the back of his head, not too noticeable. He just seemed to have quite thin, light brown hair. Very clean, probably one of those people who washed their hair every day.

Crazy ones.

'Taxi or metro?' he asked.

I had only been to Paris once, with Jake. I didn't mind the metro, and it would probably take less time.

'Up to you,' I responded.

You're the one paying.

'Let's do a taxi, then.' He waved for a car to stop, just outside the station.

We were going to head for Le Marais, the Jewish/Gay quarter. Also, my favourite spot for delicious falafel. We sat down at the back, with his thigh rubbing against mine. He seemed shy, not very talkative, but he'd stare at me for a prolonged period of time, with a half-smile.

'Are you okay?' I asked, embarrassed.

'Yes, yes, of course, sorry,' he apologised while scratching his nose. 'You're just very handsome.'

I still wasn't used to hearing compliments.

Jake frequently did that at the beginning of our relationship. Then we both gained some weight, got resentful, and even during our last phase of the relationship, when I had lost weight and put on some muscle, he still wouldn't see me.

'Oh, thanks. Means a lot at nine in the morning.' I giggled. In a manly way, of course.

The taxi stopped at a very narrow, one-way street. Jimmy paid in cash; he seemed to have quite a lot of euros in his wallet.

As a Londoner I'd often forget cash existed. I grabbed my bag and got out of the car.

'This is the door,' Jimmy said while pointing at a big black gate.

Seemed promising. We walked through it, to then open another door, a brown one which led to some of the tiniest and steepest steps I had ever seen, even by Parisian standards.

'Nicolas lives on the top floor, so it's quite a walk.' He laughed, slightly out of breath.

'I haven't done cardio in weeks. You're honestly doing me a favour,' I blurted, while also being out of breath. He was walking in front of me, with his arse right on my face. I was impressed. He was clearly someone who rode a bike. Or younger guys, as it would turn out. He had keys to the flat, so we quickly got in. No one was home.

'Nicolas handles a couple of properties used for Airbnb,' he explained. 'He will be home later, but our room is over there,' he said while pointing at the nearest door.

The flat was spacious. There were a lot of newspaper articles hanging on the walls. It was Nicolas' boyfriend's work. He was a journalist. Every surface had a fair share of memorabilia, especially Roman little statues. Not too atypical for a gay home. The ceiling was made of large dark brown wooden panels. It looked nothing like it did on the outside. Cosy place, much better than any hotel room.

Unless these guys turned out to be annoying as fuck.

I walked into the room and put my bag on the bed. He came into the room as well and closed the door behind him.

'Do you need help with unpacking?' he asked.

I looked down at my tiny bag with barely two changes of clothes and a few pairs of underwear and refused.

'Are we going to go out and explore?' I asked, excited to have some food.

'Yeah, absolutely,' he said enthusiastically. 'Can I kiss you?'

That came out of nowhere.

'Sure,' I conceded.

He came close to me and gave me a soft, light kiss with some tongue. Bad kisser. He went for it again, this time with a bit more energy. Still bad, but not horrendous. I could feel his hands grabbing my crotch; he wasn't just after a kiss. I wasn't sure what he wanted to do, but as soon as he knelt to get my zipper down, I knew he wanted to blow me.

'Can I?' He looked up, with puppy eyes.

I was sitting on a train for three hours, so I wasn't fully sure what I was brewing in the smell department, but alas, I let him do his thing. My cock was hard, and he latched on it straight away with his small mouth. It felt good; he knew what he was doing. He may have been a god-awful kisser, but he certainly knew his way around a man's member. He was sucking hard and fast; he wanted me to come quickly. I hadn't masturbated in a few days, so I was ready almost instantly. I warned him, as that seemed like the polite thing to do, but he seemed like he couldn't get enough.

I grabbed the back of his head and shot my load straight down his throat. He moaned. I shot two or three loads and released my grip on his head.

'Nice,' he said while wiping his lips.

If that was going to be the theme of the weekend, I was in for a fine time.

'Want me to...?' I asked, without much intention of doing anything.

'No,' he interrupted. 'Later this evening,' and left the room.

I zipped myself back up, my cock still semi-hard for the impromptu suckatron. I was flustered. And starving.

———•————————●————————•———

Paris looked whimsical, far better than it did when I visited with Jake. It rained all day then, and I had brought a cold from London. There was no sexiness in the so-called most romantic city in the world. This time, though, the sun was warm and blinding. I was wearing a striped t-shirt to keep up the French theme. Jimmy looked smitten as he walked next to me.

'I used to walk down this road all the time, when I lived here,' he declared with pride.

'What made you leave?' I asked, confused by the bizarre choice of leaving Paris for a minor city in Germany.

'Purely work,' he groaned. 'They offered a lot more money for me to move out there, so I just took it. I lived in Tunisia for a few months too, same reason.'

I was surprised. This guy had been around.

'How was that?'

He gave out a little chuckle. 'It was interesting. Being gay there was a bit of a hassle, but it's always surprising to see how many there are.'

I thought it was an interesting way to describe a country.

'So, the sexual aspect is the make or break feature of your favourite place to live?' I teased.

'Ha, not necessarily,' he confessed. 'After all, I can always get a fit guy like you delivered to me.' He winked.

I got the joke, but *yikes*.

'I'm joking, by the way,' he reassured, while putting his hand behind my neck.

I laughed too, as I didn't want him to think I had zero sense of humour. I probably would have made a similar joke myself. If I were a freak.

'Where the heck are you?' popped on my phone screen.

I hadn't texted Sara in a few days, and that was unusual for us. I didn't like lying to her, so for some reason I'd find not talking to her a better option. Also, she knew I couldn't afford to go out of town, so she'd ask for specifics.

I needed to say something.

'Hey, baby girl. Just been busy this week. Catch up next week?'

Easy enough. Sara would worry too much about my state of mind.

'So, what do you do, apart from working at a department store that you hate? What do you like doing?' Jimmy asked.

What *did* I like doing? 'I wish I was the kind of person who'd answer something like 'going out,' or 'playing sports,' but I mainly like playing video games, drinking wine and eating. Oh, and I try to go to the gym. I don't enjoy it. I just feel like I have to do it. Gay code.'

He smiled. His eyes closed when he smiled. It was endearing.

'No hobbies?' he asked.

'I used to write quite a lot when I was younger, but I don't have much inspiration lately...'

'That's interesting. Write what?'

'Oh, I'd take inspiration from real-life events and I would turn them into allegories. I have never finished anything, though.'

'You should give it one more shot. It would be silly not to.'

I sighed.

'What about you? Apart from giving *spectacular* blow jobs?' I smirked.

His eyes were shining. 'I enjoy travelling very much. I get lonely a lot and going to places and meeting new people is what I love the most,' he said.

'So, what do we have planned for tonight?' I asked while running my hand through my hair. Guys seemed to like my thick, dark brown hair. Something many of the men I was meeting didn't possess.

'We'll go for dinner with my friend, if that's okay with you.'

I was curious to meet his friend, so I was game.

'Maybe we'll have a drink at a gay bar or something,'

Good stuff. It was already shaping up as a much better weekend than my little Bulgarian trip.

That is without counting the incredible circus sex I had with mister photographer in what was clearly his mother's house.

Can't have it all, Leo. Can't have it all.

———

I felt comfortable. I'd usually be nervous as hell and hardly ever eat on those kinds of dates, but Jimmy, Nicolas and his unnamed 'very French' boyfriend put me at ease. We went to a sushi bar, and Jimmy ordered the entire menu. I was the only person going for the vegetable pieces, and I was scarfing them one by one.

Le boyfriend was a tad irritating, but I blamed that on the Parisianness of it all.

'How could you like Marie Antoinette? I wish she was here! I'd cut her head!' he shouted at some point in the thickest French accent.

There was a lot of hand moving and voice raising from his part. He had obviously encountered the argument before. One dynamic I couldn't quite wrap my head around though, was Nicolas. He kept touching my leg every time he spoke to me. And even casually having his leg very close to mine. It was a small restaurant, so I gave him the benefit of the doubt. Or not. French people are slags. So, no surprises there.

We walked away from the restaurant after Jimmy paid for the entire bill. Something like £600 for the four of us. The man had cash to spend. He put his arm around me and gave me a little peck on the cheek.

'You good to go?' he whispered, tenderly.

'Yeah, absolutely. Thanks for dinner.'

He seemed to be enjoying himself.

'How's that one down there?' Nicolas suggested, while pointing at a very loud, dark bar with a queue of very attractive gay men trying to get in. Just like the restaurants and a majority of apartments in Paris, the bar was tiny and jam packed.

With sausage.

Nicolas went to speak to the bouncer. His little tight jeans made his bum appear disproportionately big compared to the rest of his body. While Jimmy looked like he was an everyday cycler, his friend plain looked like he had some serious injections. He seemed the type anyway. His upper lip was plump, and he looked like he'd do a sunbed on the daily, for sure. Not my type, but I could see why others may have taken a liking in him. He was very outgoing and loud.

He explained he had grown up in South America, so that would probably line up with his behaviour.

Only a few seconds later, and we were in.

Sara would have been proud. This was her specialty too.

The boyfriend left us to work at home, like a bore. No one would miss him, though. As soon as I walked in, I felt arms trying to hug me from behind. It was Nicolas.

'So, what would you like to drink?' he asked, very close to my ear.

No doubt he was flirting with me. I indulged it. It wasn't often I'd see so many guys trying so hard to get into my pants.

'Gin & Tonic?' I said.

'Right away,' he conceded.

Jimmy didn't seem to mind, but I didn't want to push

it. After all, I didn't want to be thrown onto the streets for being a hoe on our arrangement.

I got my drink, and it was huge. I forgot how much more generous the rest of Europe could be when serving drinks. The music was cool, very camp. The dance floor was hot. People were dancing on each other. It was sweaty, but in a good way. I wasn't much of a club dancer, but as soon as the alcohol hit, I would get down and dirty, to then regret it the day after.

Nicolas? That was his element. The guy could dance, and he did that with just about anybody. Jimmy was shyer, but he was still game. He was more focused on me having fun, which I thought was nice. And he made sure I never had an empty glass in my hand, which was even nicer.

***———•———————●———————•———

We got home at around 2 a.m. Per Nicolas' idea we'd chill at home with more music and drinks. I was already seeing double, but I could potentially drink a bit more. We sat on the sofa and got comfortable. Nicolas was only wearing boxer shorts, and Jimmy removed his socks and his jacket. I got hot very easily, so I also decided to strip to my pants.

'Nice bulge, mister,' Nicolas emphasised.

I was flattered.

'So, what's your opinion on French men, Leo?' he slurred.

Jimmy had his arm around my neck.

'They're very direct, *monsieur*,' I admitted. 'But many of them are handsome devils. You sure we're not bothering the boyfriend, by the way?'

I didn't want him to have a heart attack seeing us all lying on each other.

'*Non*, he's upstairs, sleeping like a log,' he chortled. 'I'm more nocturnal,' he said while sipping his drink and putting his legs on the sofa.

I had a vague idea of where it was all going, but I wasn't sure if it had been planned in advance. I felt equal parts cornered and intrigued. Jimmy didn't seem to have much of a reaction.

'So, have you guys fucked in Paris, yet?'

That was Nicolas' way to get to know Jimmy's new friend, apparently.

'We have not,' Jimmy expressed. 'I suppose we are waiting for you to go sleep.'

I turned to Jimmy almost surprised he'd been so straightforward.

'Ah, you don't have to worry about me,' Nicolas replied, while lighting a joint. 'You guys want one too?' He offered, while reaching for a box full of them.

'I'll take one.' Jimmy took one and lit it himself. 'We can share one if you want.'

I wasn't one for drugs; none of them had ever appealed to me. Also, as embarrassing as it was, I couldn't physically smoke. I just couldn't do it properly since I had only tried once, when I was maybe thirteen. The so-called 'weed scent' was hard to ignore on my clothing, especially for such a detective like my mother. She didn't react very well, likely due to my father's weakness for recreational drugs.

I declined and put my legs on the sofa, slightly touching Nicolas feet and I laid my head on Jimmy's chest.

'Shall we play a game or something?' Nicolas asked while puffing away. Relaxed as ever.

'I think I'm a little too drunk for games,' I cautioned. 'I'd lose straight away.'

Jimmy laughed, lightly.

'Oh, that's no fun,' Nicolas groaned. 'Maybe I should just go to sleep,'

'No, please stay,' said Jimmy. 'Or at least give your guest a goodnight kiss!'

I turned around to Jimmy; he knew what he was doing.

'Well, if you insist.' Nicolas put the joint down and crawled towards me, going over my distended legs and being effectively on top of me.

'Goodnight?' he said, with his face one inch away from mine. He grabbed the back of my head and put his tongue in my mouth, softly, but deep. Meanwhile, Jimmy was putting his hands under my pants. I was getting hard. Nicolas then moved onto Jimmy and kissed him as well. I was getting hot. They took my t-shirt off together, while I removed Nicolas' soon after. His body was chiselled, waxed chest, tanned. Jimmy was kissing my neck from behind and playing with my cock, now fully hard. I was worried about this activity being done in the open, in the living room, but neither one seemed concerned. Maybe this was an occasion that happened relatively often.

My pants came off, and Nicolas immediately reached for my cock to shove it in his mouth. I wasn't sure who was the better sucker between the two, but they both made me feel really good. Jimmy got up to grab the joint from the table and re-lit it. He was standing up watching Nicolas slobbering all over my dick and touching himself.

Two puffs later and he handed me the doobie. I had no choice but to try and smoke it. Seemed easy enough. I put my head down, and Jimmy joined to suck my cock along with Nicolas. Not sure if the weed was having its effect but having two warm mouths fighting over pleasuring me and making out together was an exciting feeling.

Jimmy started biting my nipples, while Nicolas moved lower, using his tongue all over my scrotum. I was relaxed, and I had to do nothing but lay there. I wasn't sure what was happening anymore. I knew I was enjoying every second of it. I noticed Jimmy grabbing a bottle from the table. It was the first time I had noticed the lube. Had it been there all along? How early in the evening was this planned? Or was it just always sitting there, complimentary for guests? He grabbed a dollop and lubricated his arsehole, still wearing his grey t-shirt. Nicolas moved away to kiss me on the lips again, while Jimmy proceeded to slowly sit on my hard dong, bare. I really wanted him to use a condom, but I was feeling so damn good, I couldn't slow down the action. Also, right before I could even say anything, Nicolas had lowered his pants to give me a taste of his member, thick, uncut, completely shaven. Jimmy was riding me, and Nicolas had my head between his thighs. My breathing was heavy. I found the situation extremely erotic. I didn't have that much experience with having sex with two people at the same time, but this felt organic and natural, adjectives I never thought of when thinking of sex.

Nicolas sat on my face, with his perfectly waxed hole right on my mouth, his arse cheeks hovering my whole head. A great position for him to make out with Jimmy, not that I could see much from there. That's when I decided I wanted to fuck Nicolas, hard. It would be easy, with my saliva still dripping from his hole. I moved Jimmy away from my cock and immediately turned Nicolas around. My cock slid right in. All the way in. Nicolas moaned loudly. I grabbed his waist and fucked him hard, while Jimmy was sucking him off. He was so conveniently tight; I could only hold off for a few minutes.

My hair and my face were soaked with sweat. My whole body was shiny. Nicolas reached for my arse to push myself even further into him, faster, harder. He was begging for more and more. That's when Jimmy begged us both to come all over his face. We were nearing the end of it all. I pulled myself out of Nicolas, with my dick perfectly clean, luckily. We started making out while both having a wank directed at Jimmy's face, with his mouth wide open. When Nicolas grabbed my hair, I knew he was close to finish, so I grabbed my cock and jacked off as fast as I could. We both came a few seconds later to a very willing mouth. The synchronised '*aaaaah*' could have woken up the whole Marais, but it was way too late for me to care.

'Fuck,' Jimmy whispered, with his mouth covered by our loads.

My legs ached. Everyone seemed exhausted.

'That was hot,' Nicolas panted, while using a tissue to clean himself up. I went straight for the bathroom to both clean up and brush my teeth. I looked at myself in the mirror and saw my flushed face, my eyes bloodshot. I was exhausted, ready for bed, and that's when it hit me. I didn't pack my pills for the trip.

Shit.

For the first time in over a year I would be going to bed without them. Would two pill-free days have a weird effect on me? I hoped not. Dr Grey warned me not to miss taking the pills as it would increase the possibility of having a hypomanic episode.

That wouldn't be good.

I brushed it off for the time being. All I wanted was to get in bed, maybe fuck Jimmy again. Just the two of us. Burn some extra adrenaline so I could fall asleep easily.

Yeah, that sounded like a good idea.

CHAPTER 10

£1785.09

Going back to London after sunny, indulgent, sex-crazed Paris was an adjustment. I had sex with Jimmy a whopping fourteen times. A couple of those included Nicolas, which made it that much more interesting. What truly sucked was going to work straight after the Eurostar ride and working a late shift in addition to that. I was knackered. However, I had some duties to attend. I hadn't seen Sara since the douche-y party we had at work, and we could barely talk to each other then.

'Come to Angel for drinks!' she texted.

We had some wedding matters to discuss and after such a long weekend dedicated to myself, I was ready to spend time with my true soul mate. It was almost ten o'clock and my shoes were splashing onto the wet pavement. My hair needed washing; Paris cigarette smell still stuck onto it. I nervously pushed it back, scratching my scalp slightly.

My whole body was feeling itchy. Perhaps the missed Quetiapine was starting to have an effect on my body. I needed to take it as soon as possible that evening.

I was aiming for an early night, eleven at most. Three drinks, maybe.

A few crossroads later and I arrived at my destination. I could see Sara from outside. She was wearing a thick knitted dress and big, chunky boots. My girl was feeling the winter. I was expecting her to be with Abigail, but she was speaking to a guy instead.

'Hello, princess!' I announced with a wide, dorky wave.

'Hi, hun!' she rejoiced, with a tight, drunken hug.

'How much have you drank in my absence?' I enquired, clearly jealous, as I was busy as hell dealing with my rascals at work and Dominic's day off. Bad combo.

'Not a lot, actually. We finished work late. Shit day,' she said, while looking through her small handbag.

'Oh, almost forgot. This is Duncan!' she added, while pointing at the guy with huge, deep blue anime eyes sitting next to her.

'I'm Leo,' I stuttered, while tending my hand to shake his.

'Hi there,' he said, with a Scottish accent and a big bright, slightly crooked smile. Sara was already surrounded by gays, through work, life and everywhere she went, but this one looked different. He wasn't a fashion gay. He was quite slim, wearing a light blue denim jacket and a white t-shirt. His hair was messy, wavy, with no product in it. His stubble was light brown, with a ginger hue.

'He is my assistant,' Sara interrupted. 'I'm going to smoke a cigarette and I'll be right there with you.' She grabbed her debit card and handed it to me. 'Get yourself a drink, please,' and she went outside, cigarette in one hand, phone in the other.

I ordered a large glass of house red wine and it was quickly poured in front of me. I hated meeting new people and making small talk. That was work for me. Now I had to babysit the little Scottish assistant.

'I gather you're the best friend,' he said, smiling through his eyes.

'Yeah, a toxic one at that,' I responded, sarcastically.

'Oh, she only had nice words for you,' he replied. 'She sold you short, though,'

'Short?'

The bitch.

'Tell me more!' I urged.

'Oh, she said you were a bit of a mess.'

I smiled back. 'She was being nice. I'm a *huge* mess.'

He grabbed his pint of Guinness and took a sip. 'Eh, don't think so,' he expressed, while looking at me. 'How long have you guys known each other?'

How long? I couldn't even recall a time without her.

'God, I think ten or so years now. Babies, basically,' I lamented, with just a hint of nostalgia for the times that had gone. 'Have you worked with her long?'

Duncan leaned back on his seat. 'No, this is actually my first week! She probably thought I looked really pathetic and asked me to go for drinks.' He raised his glass. 'Here I am. Several drinks later.'

It's hard to forget your first night out with the woman. Or to remember it.

'It wouldn't be a Sara initiation unless you go home

and throw up your guts at the end of the evening,' I teased.

'Oh that's 100 percent in the cards,' he said while laughing loudly.

'Sexy.'

'Oh, I wish. Just very gross, explosive vomit.'

His accent made every word much more endearing than their meaning. I lifted my glass, and we clinked.

'So, how's being an assistant?' I asked.

'I'm not a *personal* assistant,' he pointed out. 'It's just *one* position below her.'

'Oh, don't tell her *that*,' I said.

I was enjoying the back and forth. Sara's colleagues would usually be vile queens with a Birkin and a full make-up bag.

'Ha ha, I know. No, it's nice. It's very different from what I did before. I worked in accountancy.'

My eyes were doubtful. 'You had a previous job? You're like twelve,' I said, while scouting him up and down.

'I'm thirty-two years old!'

'What? Lies!'

He genuinely looked twenty at most.

'I'd show you my driver's licence, but it's super-duper embarrassing.' He giggled. 'Just trust me on this, please.' He quickly brushed my hand with his.

'I was gone two minutes and you two are holding hands already?' said a very inebriated Sara. She sat down next to Duncan and in front of me. 'Isn't he adorable?' She pinched his cheek.

'Be right back, just need the loo,' he announced, while getting up and escaping Sara's hand.

'He is indeed adorable!' I confirmed. 'Very unlike the

rest of your queens at work.'

'Don't be mean,' she said, while putting her finger on my nose. 'So, let's get to the important stuff. Where the fuck have you been these last couple of days?'

'Nowhere. Just had a few dates,' I said, without much conviction.

'Of course, that's what you'd be doing,' she said, with a hint of disappointment. Almost as if it wasn't an exciting enough excuse.

'Why, what's up?' I gulped a big sip of my very pungent pub wine.

'Well, I was hoping you'd tell me when you're free. I want to go wedding dress shopping.'

'Oh. Is it like the movies? A montage of you trying hideous crap while your bridesmaids and I get pissed on prosecco?' I was very excited at the idea.

'It better fucking be.'

I hadn't heard mention of him yet, so I felt like I needed to ask. 'Are you and Alfie okay? I feel like I haven't spoken to you properly since he didn't show up to your birthday.'

She squinted. 'He did. You were just too drunk and gone to see him. He came late. He apologised. All good. For now.'

She rolled her eyes up.

'You sure?' I wasn't too convinced.

'Yes, he's not beating me up, Leo,' she scoffed.

'I was worried about the other way around, really.'

'Ha, fuck off,' she said, while throwing a piece of napkin at me. 'You look a bit ill. Are *you* okay?'

'Yeah, I'm just tired from work, that's all. Usual shit day.' I brushed it off.

'Have you been applying for other jobs?' she nagged.

'No, I have been too lazy.'

Meanwhile, Duncan had made his way back to the table, drying his hands on his skinny jeans.

'These toilets are rank. Were you guys shit-talking behind my back?' he questioned, looking at both of us.

'Absolutely.'

'No, just about to kick Leo in the arse for staying in such a shit job, when he could be doing so much better.'

'Oh, what do you do?'

'Shop girl,' I responded, while doing jazz hands.

'He is a manager of a luxury department store.'

'Oh cool!' he exclaimed while smiling at me.

'Assistant,' I pointed out, without much enthusiasm.

'He hates it, but he won't do anything about it.'

'Oh, what would you like to do?' he asked.

'He is a really good writer,' she responded, before I could even mutter an answer.

'Don't you love when you get to that stage and your friend just holds the conversation for you?' I said, while throwing a napkin ball at her.

'Writer? What kind of writer?'

'The one who doesn't write,' I retaliated, snappily. 'I don't think anyone would even want to read my crap.'

'Oh, my god! Just sit down and do it!' Sara rolled her eyes and looked at Duncan. 'Do you know how many excuses I have had to hear for the last decade?'

'Pleeease, let's talk about wedding dresses. Show me your mood board,' I said, attempting a subject change.

'Mood board? Who did you take me for?' she said with a corrugated expression, as if I had asked her to shave her head bald.

'Oh, god. Wedding dress! How cool!' Duncan exclaimed.

'You are more than welcome to join,' she said, oddly. Then looked at me, cheekily. She was up to something. She was always up to something.

We ended up all teasing each other and drinking until two in the morning, when I finally passed out in an Uber that would hopefully take me home. Not the healthiest start of the week.

———•———————•———————•———

I woke up to a phone bursting with notifications and a pillow drenched in sweat. I fell asleep wearing my clothes and with my contact lenses stuck to my eyes. My mouth felt like a station toilet and all I wanted to do was to throw up everything I had ingested in the previous ten hours. Unfortunately, I wasn't a fan of vomiting. I'd endure the sense of nausea and go onto my far more nauseating day at work. I needed coffee, desperately.

I was pleased to see Duncan had followed me on Instagram a few hours before. I got onto his profile and he looked exactly like in real life—always smiling, always with a Guinness in hand. A few trips here and there, but no photo that indicated a boyfriend.

Grindr was also bursting with messages by random people, one of which was Gary, who I hadn't seen in some time. Since my other men were paying so much more, it became redundant to see him, but I guess I always needed wine money. Also, the amount of effort required was a lot less.

Later this eve? I texted him. I wondered if I could fit a date with someone else straight after. I knew it was overkill, but I really wanted not to worry about money for the engagement party.

I took off my dirty clothes from the night before and jumped straight into the shower.

I sat in the tub, while the hot water fell on my head. The last few weeks had been intense. There was a part of me that was still downplaying the fact that Sara was actually making real plans for the wedding. An engagement party? Dress shopping? I couldn't quite wrap my head around it. And Alfie? Was I really that thrilled for my best friend to get hitched with someone so unreliable? What was 'reliable' anyway? I followed stranger men from the internet all the way to other countries for money. No one knew what I was doing. If I got murdered, no one would know. I loved morning thoughts.

I also didn't forget that Jake and Marc had planned the trip to Japan that Jake and I had discussed doing together since the very beginning of our relationship. I couldn't believe that Jake would be capable of hurting me so much. I needed to tell him. I needed for him to hear me out. That's what I'd do that evening. I'd let myself be blown by Gary, take the cash, buy a bottle of wine and take it to Jake, hoping the little shit wouldn't be there.

I had underestimated how tired I'd be after work. I was surprised I could get hard at all with Gary. He wasn't the sexiest person in the world, with his stupid face and mouth constantly hanging open. Even when he didn't have a dick in his mouth. Somehow, I had managed to make him happy and come on his arse like he so wanted.

I was on my way to Jake's flat to discuss our shit. Luckily, Marc was away for some crappy event, so I wouldn't have to worry about seeing him in what used to be my home. My hands felt freezing cold, while my head felt warm and damp. I was probably catching a cold. Unfortunate, since I had taken so much time off work to be a whore across Europe, so I couldn't really afford sick days anymore. I was just in front of the main door, with two bottles of Shiraz.

Jake opened the door, with Squall quickly coming out to greet me. His light blue eyes made my heart melt and his white fur went all over my black jeans. Coming home to this every day was perhaps the main thing missing from my life.

'Hey,' Jake said, with a smile. Had he been drinking already? I hadn't seen him smile for so long. I wondered if he was plotting something. 'Sorry about the mess.'

'Oh, please. You know me.'

'Well, you know,' he justified, while closing the door behind me. 'Wine? I already had two glasses.'

'Sounds great,' I responded, while taking my jacket off and heading for the sofa which had been replaced recently by a much smaller, designer-looking, dark grey piece.

'You got a new sofa?' I asked, knowing damn well where it could possibly come from.

'Yeah, you know I have always hated the old one. It was time to get something different,' he explained, while handing me a huge glass of red and sitting next to me.

'I'll miss the old one. I spilled so much wine on it and it never showed. That brown fabric was magic!'

He looked like he had a haircut that day. His hair always looked blonder when cut. His beard, slightly darker, was groomed as well. Much shorter than usual.

'I am surprised you wanted to meet up. Usually we barely speak, outside of Squall's arrangements,' he said.

'Well, I did want to discuss a certain matter.' I quickly gulped half of the wine in the glass, then looked at him. This had the potential to be a pleasant evening, and I didn't necessarily want to ruin it by arguing again. 'Actually, forget about it. Let me unwind. Work has been a nightmare.'

'Okay,' he conceded. He quickly grabbed his phone and started scrolling. This used to be a major pet peeve of mine. Jake would constantly be on his phone, obsessively. During the last months of our relationship that's all he would do. I knew he was probably talking about my bipolar diagnosis to his friends, or worse, mocking it with Marc and just flat-out not caring about it. All this while I'd be sitting at home, thinking of suicide.

The one glass turned into two bottles, and at that point we were joking around and watching sitcoms on TV. A great time to address the elephant in my head.

'So, are you planning any more holidays?' I asked, like a naïve Red Riding Hood.

'I'm not sure yet.'

'Really? No major holiday next year?'

'Nothing concrete yet, but where is this coming from?' His face contorted.

'Do you want to maybe just tell the truth? Or am I to find out when you ask me to look after our dog in your absence?'

'Leo, I promise that—'

'—you promise you're not thinking of going to Japan with your boyfriend?' I interrupted.

'How do you even...?'

'Your boyfriend has a big mouth. And he knew what he was doing when he told me. I'm surprised he hasn't boasted about it with you once he got home. Maybe with an evil laugh at the end of the tale.' Our merriness had officially ended.

'Leo, it only came up in conversation maybe once. I made no plans whatsoever.'

'He is buying clothes for it. I should know, as I had to put them through the till myself! You know how fucking humiliating it is for me to just be ordered around by him? Can you fucking empathise for once? I would never do something that shitty to you. *Never.*'

'Okay, that was not cool, but it's not like I can't go to Japan because you want to go, and you can't afford it.'

'Jesus fuck. Do you have to go the exact fucking time we had planned to go? *Happy fucking birthday, Leo. Please look after the dog while I fuck around in Tokyo with my idiot boyfriend?*'

'You're out of line.'

I got up from the sofa. My blood was boiling, my hands clenching. I pulled my hair back and took a deep breath. I had so many feelings bottled up; they were all dying to come out.

'I'm out of line? Did you ever try to even think about

how you'd feel if I did all of this to you? If I abandoned you as soon as things got a little tough and then went on with life like I never existed?'

'Leo, you know full well things weren't good. It's not up to me to sort your mental issues out.'

'Fucking hell.' My eyes became glossy.

'I'm sorry.' He got up to touch my shoulder. 'I know I have been an awful person. But when you had your bipolar meltdown, I was also going through stuff. My dad was dying; I had no energy to support you as well.'

'I was there. I was there to support you even at my weakest state. Even during the time I was prescribed all sorts of medication that I could barely leave the bed. But you didn't give a fuck, because you were having sex with a younger, cooler, bouncier version of me. Marc doesn't have all this baggage. Marc is great, isn't he?'

'Are you off your meds now?'

My jaw dropped. 'Oh, my fucking god. I am leaving.'

'Hey, hey, I'm sorry.' He stopped me. 'I just want to be sure you aren't doing anything silly.' He looked straight into my eyes.

I looked back at his. That green hue, looking genuinely worried. I wasn't sure if the wine had taken over, but I had forgotten what I needed to say.

'Breathe,' he whispered.

I wasn't crazy. This wasn't a symptom. I was fucking angry, sad, fed up. My emotions had taken over, and I was craving to be seen. I kissed Jake, and he didn't try to stop me. I was tip toeing to make myself taller, grabbing the back of his neck.

For a second, it felt like the first time we kissed.

He put his arm around my waist and kissed me back. I knew it was a bad idea. I knew I'd regret it, but I couldn't let go.

He took my shirt off and threw it on the floor. It was clear this was going to go further. He picked me up and took me to the bedroom, almost launching me on the bed. He took his trousers off and helped me out of mine. His massive cock pulsed out of his underwear, stroking mine. He kissed me on the neck, while I looked up at the ceiling, then I closed my eyes, while he gently kissed my nipples. I grabbed his back, while he was pushing his dick still wrapped inside his underwear onto my arse. I wanted him inside me. I needed to connect. I took my underwear off and he immediately turned me around. My head was on the pillow and I was waiting for him to enter me. I hadn't had sex with Jake since we were last together. I was nervous, but at the same time it felt so right. I was angry at him, but only because I still loved him, deep down. It only took him a few seconds to spit into my hole and then push his knob into me. It was rough. He was so big I'd often bleed because of it. He spat some more, and then managed to enter me, all the way in. He was lying on top of me, kissing me, and slightly biting my ear. It was painful, but manageable. The alcohol helped. I felt secure under him. He wanted me too. I could feel it. I didn't want it to end. He was thrusting faster and faster. My dick was dripping with precum.

'I am going to cum soon,' he breathed. I was too. I was covered in sweat, but I couldn't get enough of him. I wanted more.

And then he did. He shot his load inside me. I could

feel it drip out of my hole.

He was exhausted and threw himself on the bed next to me, panting heavily.

Then everything got quiet, like he had sobered up all of a sudden.

'You should probably head back. I can call you an Uber,' he said, without looking at me.

I wondered if he was having mixed feelings about us. I wondered if he'd realised Marc wasn't the one, but I was. My mind was racing. I was imagining moving back into my flat, being together, being with Squall. I'd be better this time around. I'd clean more, I'd shower every day, I'd be more romantic. I'd do everything to make him happy. But his eyes weren't imagining that. He wasn't lying next to me thinking about me.

'Is everything alright?' I asked, trying to make eye contact.

'We shouldn't have done this.'

'What do you mean?'

'This was just sex, Leo.'

I was taken aback. 'It wasn't just sex. How can you say that? I am sure even Marc would feel very differently about that.'

'Marc and I have an open relationship. I can have sex with just about anyone. Doing it with you was clearly a mistake, though.'

I was speechless. I was so upset I couldn't say anything. I felt worthless. Disposable.

'I see,' I said while trying to stop my tears. I grabbed my clothes and started putting them on.

'I am not what you want, Leo. I know I said in the past that I deserved better, but you do too,' he said while grabbing my hand.

'Yeah, I do. Please, just call the car,' I ordered, while heading to the living room.

He grabbed his phone and started typing.

'It's on its way,' he said.

Tears were running down my cheeks. I could barely breathe. I couldn't leave quickly enough.

I was done waiting for Jake to notice me.

I was done trying to be better *for him.*

CHAPTER 11

£1701.45

NOVEMBER WAS COMING TO AN END. Daylight was getting scarcer and scarcer, customers at work were becoming more and more annoying, but one thing that was improving week by week, was my "second job." It took a few weeks of chatting endlessly and getting nowhere, but between the shorter Grindr dates and the much more involved *Seeking Arrangement* trips, I was looking at a semi-steady source of income. I had something planned for almost every evening after work. I did realise I was neglecting friends in favour of weird strangers that liked feet or spandex, but I thought it would be worth it in the long run. I had already saved enough for the engagement party in Ibiza and it was only a matter of time when that would be booked. I hadn't spoken to Jake in weeks. I ignored his calls, and I even avoided visiting Squall. I had even missed his birthday, which was something I never thought I would do. I was still hurt by the way I was treated, but I managed to channel that into something more productive. I started keeping some sort of diary of the men I was meeting. They all had such different stories and odd behaviours, that I thought maybe one day I could group them into a novel or something like that. Even after all those years, a tiny, minuscule part of me still had the fantasy of becoming an author. I was fully aware nothing positive would ever happen to me, hence why I'd drink constantly; however, maybe this time I had a special story to tell. Maybe.

I was heading towards a pub near work. Both Dominic and I had the early shift, so I thought we could catch up on our personal lives without actually being at work.

It was a dry, cold evening. Christmas lights were lit up all the way to Sloane Square. All the designer shops were about to close and everyone was frantic about coming home.

As soon as I opened the pub door, a wave of intense heat slapped my face. It was one of those pubs that had an actual fire going on. Brilliant for people that are cold all the time, but I was the kind of person that always dressed in layers, in case I couldn't escape the heat source. As such, I stripped down to a short-sleeved t-shirt as soon as I walked in. Dominic was sitting at a tiny table. He was also wearing just a vest, presumably for his following activities that evening.

'Took you long enough!' he shouted at me, while standing up to give me a hug.

'There's no need for hugs. I literally just left you fifteen minutes ago.'

'Yeah, but this is the outside world. It's a new me,' he smiled, while giving me a hug. Frankly, it was just an excuse to give me a little touch. I didn't mind, since apart from random men who just wanted to fuck me, my only interaction was with Jake, who tossed me aside like the trash human being I felt.

'I'm getting a bottle,' I announced, while heading towards the counter.

'A bottle? Thought that would never happen the week before payday,' he said, suspiciously.

'I have managed to save some this month, I guess.'

'Interesting,' he said, while trying to figure out what was happening.

I was given my bottle by the bartender and I brought it to the table, along with two glasses.

'Look, you always get me drinks. Let me do something nice for once,' I commanded.

'Okay, I am not complaining. And don't get snappy.'

I poured us both two hefty glasses, and I leaned back on my chair. The pub was full. It was mostly people who worked around Knightsbridge, all trying to vent to each other about the horrors of retail. I could relate.

'What are you doing later, by the way?' I asked.

'I am actually seeing Owen for dinner.'

Owen was Dominic's ex-boyfriend. Unlike Jake and I, they'd actually do things together maybe every other week. Dominic decided to end things with Owen after a long year of not having sex with each other and increasingly growing apart.

'What's he been up to?' I asked, while sipping my lovely dry wine.

'Well, he was recently admitted to a hospital, and I have a vague feeling he overdosed on something.'

'Shit, are you sure?' I asked.

'It wouldn't be the first time! We will see. Hopefully he won't lie straight to my face.'

He probably will, I thought.

He gulped down his wine, wiping his lips and beard with a paper napkin.

'What are you doing tonight?' he asked.

'Nothing, actually. I think I'll go to bed early.'

'That's unlike you. What's happening?'

'Sara is going to try some wedding dresses on in the morning, so I have to be there to judge.'

'Weddings suck,' he said with a disgusted face.

'Don't tell me. I don't want to ruin it for her.'

'Are you okay otherwise? You seem a bit different lately.'

'What do you mean?' I asked, off put.

'I don't know, you just seem more on edge. Have you been seeing your therapist more often? Is that why you had to do all those changes to your days off?'

'What? No!'

'Okay, I am just trying to make sure you're fine,' he justified, while putting his hands up.

I scratched my head and pulled my hair back. Maybe telling Dominic about what I had actually been doing would help me gain an extra perspective.

'Alright, it's nothing hugely interesting, but I have been going on a few dates with different men.'

'That's what every non-disfigured gay guy does. Why the secrecy?'

'...for money.'

His face turned sour. 'You're doing *what*?'

'You know those people on Grindr that ask you to give them a blow job for a certain amount of money?'

'Yes. Disgusting ones.'

'Well, I said yes to a few and here I am, able to buy a bottle of wine a week before payday.'

'You're whoring yourself to strangers for pub wine?'

'Of course not. But it has definitely helped with expenses and stuff.'

'I'm sure there are better ways for you to do that. I really don't know how I feel about this, sweetie.'

I was surprised. I was not expecting such a judgemental tone from him, the queen of raves and MDMA.

'Of course, you don't know how you feel. You can't relate, because you don't *need* the money.' I poured myself another glass.

'Hey, don't do that. My concern is valid. Don't turn it into me not being able to relate because my stupid parents send me money,' he said while touching my hand on the table.

'Sorry, I just thought this would be a girly conversation on the people I had met, but it clearly took a weird turn.'

'I just want to make sure you're not doing anything dumb.'

I grabbed my jacket and put it back on. 'I'm going to go now. I have to get up early to be with my friend tomorrow. Have fun with Owen.'

Dominic got up as well. 'Leo, calm down. I just—'

'It's alright. I'll see you at work,' I said, while leaving.

I regretted telling him instantly. I couldn't believe the

way he acted, like the situation was beneath him.

Was it?

Was I really doing something so despicable that my friend who most definitely had a drug problem, along with some serious depressive behaviour, felt like I was doing something stupid?

One thing was certain: I certainly couldn't tell any of my other friends at that point.

I turned my phone off and went straight home to bed. Didn't even exchange a word with Andrew. I just wanted to sleep and see some dresses in the morning.

Fuck everyone else.

———————•———————●———————•———————

I woke up feeling better than I had in weeks. Going to bed early really helped with the getting up part. It was a bright, sunny, cold morning. I was wearing my favourite aubergine jumper and my Chelsea boots, coincidentally walking the streets of Chelsea. I was also surprised I had managed to sleep well without my pills. I hadn't taken any since my return from Paris, and I felt overall better. My energy levels, albeit spiked with my daily Monster Energy, were just off the charts. I was genuinely, fucking looking forward to a fun morning with my best friend.

Sara asked me to meet her at a small boutique in Mayfair. I was carrying a box of vegan donuts, just in case there wouldn't be food there. I also had a very good workout in the morning, so I thought I could splurge a little on the calories. I doubt she'd feel the same, though.

'What the fuck are those?' she shouted from a distance.

'Food, woman. Food.'

'Don't make me see them. I am so fat this morning.'

She'd always say that. I could probably wrap my hands around her waist, and they'd touch. That's how skinny she was.

'Obese, I'd say.'

'Yeah, look,' she said, while opening her jacket and showing me a big fat nothing. Made of bones.

'Alright, yes, Shrek. Who else is coming?'

'Abigail, my sister and my assistant.'

'You invited Duncan to this?'

'Yeah, why not? He's funny, and he had nothing to do. And there he is,' she said while pointing behind me.

Duncan appeared behind me and put a hand on my shoulder.

'Hello, you two. Nice to see you again,' he said while giving me a hug.

'The girls are already inside, arguing on who has the most power in this wedding. It's hilarious to watch.'

'I cannot wait to see that,' I said. 'There will be champagne, right? I had to wake up early for this.'

'Of course, there will be champagne. I'm not a savage, Leo,' she said while grabbing me to go inside.

I tendered my hand to grab Duncan as well. He smiled and held on to me.

It was just us in the shop. I had frankly never even thought how this ordeal would work. I had bought my wedding suit from Topman.

'Hi, girls,' I said while doing a big wave with my hand and giving them both kisses. Sara's sister Emma looked radiant.

'Good to see you, Leo,' she said, smiling through her big doe eyes.

'How's the publishing world treating you, miss?'

'There's a lot of dark fantasy out there! I am a little tired of reading it, to be honest.'

'Are you a writer?' asked Duncan.

'Literary agent. I help writers get published,' she explained.

'Cool,' he said. 'At least you have someone to send your stuff to, Leo.'

'Yeah, one day, maybe.'

I waved at Abigail.

'Hello, handsome,' Abigail exclaimed, while giving me a big hug.

'Please hand Duncan a glass of champagne or whiskey so he can forget he's going to see me having a fucking meltdown,' Sara said while looking around for a shop assistant.

'Oh, I am actually trying not to drink for a while,' he said, slightly embarrassed.

I looked at him as if he had announced a sex change.

'But hey, what the hell,' he said while taking the glass. 'You can take the man out of Scotland...'

'I feel like you should also chug one down, quickly,' said Abigail to Sara, who was fidgeting.

'I don't want to be bloated.'

'You can't be this nervous when you start trying things on,' said Emma.

'Oh, fuck it. Just hand it over,' Sara ordered, while reaching for a glass and chugging it down straight after. 'If I burp loudly, you have no one to blame but yourself.'

'Just go grab a couple, otherwise we'll be here all day,' I said.

'Do I just try on shit? Where the fuck is David Emanuel telling me I look great?'

'I'll do that,' said Duncan while sitting on a big white chair and biting into a donut.

'Hello Ms Langaard,' said a short, ginger girl wearing a tight black dress. 'I am here to help you get into some of our most fabulous dresses.'

'Oh, praise Jesus,' said Sara.

The shop was all kinds of bridal. There were orchids on every single surface. I was walking on the softest beige carpet. I nearly took my shoes off to experience it fully. The room smelled sweet, like the kind of perfumed soft toys you'd gift to new-born babies. I sat next to Duncan and grabbed a flute.

'I love weddings,' he said. 'My sister got married last year, and it was so, so much fun.'

'Did you wear a kilt?' I asked.

'I actually did! Want to see a photo?' he said, smiling.

'I do!'

He went through his Instagram and popped a group photo up.

'Nice legs,' I said, while giving him a flirty smile.

'Thanks, it was so comfy. I'd wear it all the time if I could.'

'I'd be happy with that.'

Calm down, Leo. Quit your predatory ways.

'I'll show you one day,' he said.

Maybe he was into it just as I was.

'Sara, I have to pop out for a second to do a phone call,'

Abigail announced. 'It's for the podcast tour. I'll be quick.'

'Abigail's podcast has taken over the nation!' said Emma.

'I went to see her live, and she was incredible. She's probably made a fortune from her tour alone,' I said. I didn't consider her a 'rich friend' when I first met her, but I think she had become the richest of them all.

Bitch.

Sara went into the changing room with the short shop assistant and I was left alone with Emma and Duncan. I kept sipping my champagne and tapping my leg on the floor.

'So, Leo. Are you still working in Knightsbridge?' she asked, making eye contact with her big green eyes, same as Sara's.

'Yeah. It's a nightmare this time of year.'

'I hate going around there. I can't afford anything,' said Duncan.

'You and I both,' I replied.

'But you're always wearing designer clothes!' said Emma, with a little giggle.

'We do staff sales sometimes and I can get away with buying things with a 90 percent discount.'

Sometimes I'd play with the discount code, just so I'd get something for cheap. Huge sackable offence.

'That's a perk!' exclaimed Duncan. 'I am still waiting for the perks of my job that don't involve being ordered around for over eight hours a day.'

'Oh, don't be envious. It's a tiny droplet of a perk in an ocean of melted crap.'

'Well, remember that working with books is what I do,

so if you ever want me to take a look...'

Before I could say anything back to Emma, Sara opened the changing room curtains all of a sudden, appearing as a white blob, wearing an ill-fitting bunch of lace and silk. She obviously hated it. You could tell her 'feeling fat' was taking over her mood.

'Obviously not this,' she said, annoyed. 'I really don't know.'

'You have tried one. There's about three hundred in this room alone. Try a bunch and we will decide,' said Emma, trying to be the voice of reason.

'This is a waste of time,' Sara said, while closing the curtains and being the opposite of reason.

I decided to walk into the changing room to see what was going on.

'Oi, are you okay, woman?'

'I'm feeling overwhelmed,' she said while sitting down with an unzipped wedding dress on. 'I don't know if I want to do this.'

'Jesus, what the fuck? One dress down and you're having an existential crisis already?'

'Alfie and I have only been living together for a year. I don't know.'

'You'll live together for another few months before you actually tie the knot. You're going to love these months. You'll have crazy monkey sex and shout at each other because of stupid wedding planning shit. But eventually it'll be worth it.'

'He still watches Sunday cartoons!'

'Yeah, so do I!'

'He votes conservative, Leo.'

'I don't know how to respond to that.'

'I just don't want to ruin everything. Look at you and Jake. You don't even speak anymore.'

'Jake and I didn't speak for a great deal of our last year together. Don't take that as an example.'

'Uhm, maybe,' she mumbled, while looking at a rack of dresses with a disgusted face.

'Have you really not found anything that you actually like?'

'There's this one,' she said while grabbing a long-sleeved piece. 'But I'm scared I'll sweat off my tits in Greece if I wear this.'

'Just give it a try and shut the hell up. I'm going to go for a wee. You better be wearing some bridal shit when I get back,' I said while leaving the changing room and heading for the toilet.

My blood was rushing to my head. I wasn't feeling good. All I wanted was to kneel and to hurl everything that was in my body. I vomited loudly and for a prolonged period of time. I couldn't put a stop to it. I wasn't sure why I was feeling like this. Perhaps I was somewhat triggered by the wedding talk? Or maybe the champagne in the morning wasn't an optimal choice. Either way, my head was completely inside a toilet, and that was not where I wanted to be.

The *Bridesmaids* irony was obviously not lost on me.

CHAPTER 12

£1602.56

'*CAN WE PLEASE TALK SOON?*'
I had been ignoring Jake's calls and texts for days. I'd read the text, let him know I had read it and never reply. It was a chilly morning of mid-November.

'Coming to London for a weekend. Keen to have dinner together?'

I wasn't sure if Jimmy wanted to set up a 'paid' meeting, but I was pleased to see him, even if it was just lunch and a fuck. I'd throw that for free, if there was no reward included. I had the day off, so I decided to accept Andrew's invitation to hang out together for lunch. I hadn't seen him in a few days. Lately he had been working late, so I'd hardly see him come home.

I had just left Victoria Station, walked through the hordes of tourists and white collars wandering around, and crossed the main road to get to a small Italian restaurant close to Andrew's workplace. He was already waiting there, which was unusual for any of my friends. My face felt overtaken with the worry he had something serious to share that he couldn't tell me via text.

The restaurant was just hidden in a corner, with bright red checkerboard tablecloths. It looked family run. It was cosy, with mood lighting on. If I didn't know better, this looked like a date place. Andrew was sitting at a table at the back, going through stuff on his iPad. He was wearing a baby-blue shirt worn under a V-neck navy jumper. That was pretty much his work uniform, just different colours of shirts and jumpers each day.

'I gather you didn't want to sit by the window?' I asked to gain his attention.

'You know I hate those seats,' he said. 'I don't want weird people walking by watching me eat.'

'Of course,' I said while sitting down and putting my jacket behind my chair. 'So, what kind of lunch is this? The one where we can or cannot drink wine?'

'Yeah, go for it. I have no meetings later.' He got the waiter's attention and ordered a bottle of red. I was unsure of which one, as Andrew was a bit of a wine snob and would actually spend time picking one. He'd probably scouted the menu beforehand.

'This is so nice!' I said, while looking around.

'Yeah, I eat here a little too often. But it's so damn good.'

'Be careful with that pasta,' I said while tapping on my stomach. 'It's deadly.'

'Tell me about it.'

The waiter came with the bottle of wine, ready to pour it out.

'Would you like to try it...?' he asked.

'Yes,' said Andrew.

'Nah, it's fine,' I said at the same time. 'Oh, come on. I am sure it will be fine.'

The waiter proceeded to pour out the wine. We both cheered and drank a few sips.

'See? It is nice!' I said.

'I know it's nice, I picked it! I just wanted to make sure it wasn't spoiled or something.'

'You know who's being spoiled, right?' I said, smiling. 'So, not that I don't appreciate a spontaneous lunch with my favourite flatmate, but was there something you wanted to tell me?'

Andrew's eyes were avoiding contact with me and he kept going through the menu.

'We have time, let's just order something first,' he commanded. 'How are you feeling anyway? You've been poorly for some time now.'

'Yeah, I don't know, maybe I should just spend more time in bed.'

'Sure, by yourself, though. Skank.'

'Hey!' I said while pointing a finger at him. He didn't even know half of what I was doing. Skank was uncalled for!

'I think I'll just have a pizza. I'm starving.'

'If you're having one, I'll have one too. Then we can both be fat bastards.'

He smiled at me, took another sip of wine and grabbed the waiter's attention once again. We put our orders in, and I couldn't wait to stuff my face.

'How's work, by the way?' I asked, noticing his somewhat defeated look.

'Right. Here's the thing...'

Uh-oh.

'...It is very possible I will get a huge promotion soon,' he said without any enthusiasm whatsoever. '...I'll know for sure by the end of the week.'

'That's amazing! So, we are celebrating? Why do you look that serious then?'

'If I do get it, it means I'll have to relocate for an extended time, probably a few years.'

I was confused. Why was I only hearing about it so late?

'Relocate where?' I asked, now worried about the outcome.

'New York,' he said.

Shit.

'...nothing is set in stone yet,' he added. 'But it would mean I'd have to sell the flat.'

'Fuck.'

'I am so sorry. It's happening all so quickly and I didn't want to alarm you,' he reassured me, while rubbing my hand on the table.

I wasn't sure what to think. I was not expecting such shitty news.

'I am obviously ecstatic for you. I am just a teeny tiny worried I'll be sleeping rough very soon.'

'Like I'd allow that,' he said.

'Do you think it'll sell quickly?'

'I want it to. The quicker I sort things out here, the

quicker I can get settled over there. I am really sorry, Leo.'

'No. Don't be stupid. It's a great, incredible thing that has happened to you. Do not spoil it thinking about your flatmate.' I attempted a smile. 'You should be very proud of yourself. I know I am.'

'I will, of course, help you find a place and everything. I'll be there for you.'

'I know.'

'You could also come with me. That's a very viable option.'

Viable? Was there anthrax in the wine? How did one of my wiser friends start chatting such shit?

'Oh, absolutely,' I said, sarcastically.

'I'm serious. You hate your job, you're depressed all the time, and Jake is out of the picture. You could start anew in a pretty cool city.'

He wasn't wrong.

'So far, I have been counting my friends as a pretty big reason to stay in London, but you are all just moving on with your lives. Sara is about to get married, John is hardly around and I often wonder whether Dominic is just a coworker.'

What would I have in a few months' time? An ex-husband who was trying everything in his power to hurt me and to get rid of me? Even my dog was better off.

Maybe it was a viable option.

Maybe I did need to think about it.

———•——————●————————•———

As soon as I left Andrew to go back to work, I headed

to the nearest gay bar to get unbelievably steaming drunk in the fastest way possible. It was 3 p.m.

I had decided to go to a bar near Sara's workplace, so she could come join me as soon as she finished with work, but luck was just not on my side. It was one of those days where no one was available to do anything. All of my friends were busy, and I was in no mood to see any gross man trying to get into my pants over dinner, while I was feeling down.

The bar was very stereotypically gay. Circular booths with leather seaters were all around the borders of the bar, with a few tables scattered around the middle. Screens were playing music videos by the world's favourite divas. It was early afternoon, so there were only old men drinking by themselves, or sitting together, gossiping about the good ol' times. I was sitting at one of the booths, right in front of the bar counter, so I could make quick eye contact with the shirtless guys serving drinks. Also, it was so that I didn't have to face the old men. I wasn't in the mood to entertain anybody, apart from my dumb sorrows.

Then I did something quite unlike me. I texted someone I didn't know so well. I was already near Sara's workplace, may as well ask him. He accepted, and only an hour later, Duncan came through the door to keep me company.

'You are really ruining my resolution to quit drinking,' he said while coming towards me.

'I'm a bad guy. What you drinking? I'll get it,' I said, mimicking what most of my friends would say to me. Perhaps I was trying not to look like the poor loser all my friends saw me as.

'I'll drink what you're drinking,' he said, in what sounded a much thicker Scottish accent than I had heard him speak before.

'Can we have two more of these?' I asked the bartender, while pointing at my empty vodka and diet Coke.

Duncan sat in front of me. He was wearing a Vans t-shirt and his iconic blue denim jacket. His hair was fluffier than last time I had seen him.

'I'm so glad you asked me to come. I have never been here,' he said, enthusiastically. 'It's cool!'

'Oh, it's super cool.' I laughed. 'There are a few men behind you that are about to eat you up.'

'I don't mind that. I have a low self-esteem!' His grin made me smile, slightly. 'What's going on with you? I'm glad you texted, but you've been waiting for over an hour.'

'I'm fine; it's just one of those days.'

'Don't I know. My boss is away and being an absolute fanny with everyone via e-mail.'

'I hear he's not the most pleasant to work with.'

'Yeah, no. He has mood swings all the time. I thought he was hot the first time I saw him, and now I literally shit myself when he tells me off for whatever reason.'

One day I truly needed to investigate why Jake found Marc so compelling, considering that every single person who met him pretty much called him a cunt soon after. Then again, my friends were probably lying to make me feel better.

'Don't be scared of him. He's just a little raging homo,' I said while gulping my drink.

'You know him?' he asked.

'Sort of. He's my ex-husband's boyfriend.'

'Oh, shit,' he said, knowing he stepped into bad territory. 'I had no idea.'

'I'm surprised Sara hasn't said anything.'

'She only talks nicely of you. She has actually shown me a lot of photos of you asking me if I found you attractive,' he said while smiling.

'Oh, my god. What?' I laughed as well.

'Yeah, don't tell her I told you. I don't want her to stop.'

'What kind of photos?' I was fake-outraged.

'The good kind!' His eyes were shining.

I wasn't sure what was going on, but he was the exact person I needed to see that evening. Gone were my issues, gone was my incoming doom of being homeless. I was just sitting in front of a handsome, funny, genuinely nice guy and it felt great.

'I'll make sure I only send her good ones from now on. And I'm going to demand some of you. What's fair is fair,' I said.

He laughed once again. I didn't think this guy had any other expression, but as the alcohol started having an effect, we started tackling more personal issues, such as my home situation.

'I hate moving. Looking for a place to live in London is fucking awful,' I complained.

'I've recently had to move. It was tough. I was living with my ex-boyfriend and one day I realised it wasn't right.'

'He wasn't right?'

'For me. He wasn't right for me. We would argue all the time, and it was just toxic all around,' he confessed in a much more serious tone.

'I'm sorry,' I said.

'It's okay. It's been tough at the beginning, but I know it was the right choice. I just wish I didn't feel so fucking lonely all the time.'

'I can relate.'

Soon we both realised how depressing the evening was turning out, so we drank the last of our drinks and tried to cheer each other up.

'Hey, do you maybe want to come back to mine?' I asked. 'We could get another bottle, but we could wear sweatpants and listen to music that doesn't have a cheesy chorus?'

'I quite like that idea,' he said while getting up and putting his denim jacket back on. 'Where do you live?'

'Streatham.'

'That's actually not too far from me. At least I can get home quickly if you decide to kick me out because you're bored.'

'I doubt that.'

We walked close to each other, waited for an Uber together and jumped in it. I wasn't sure what was going to happen once we got home, but I was pleased to spend more time with him alone. I was curious to know the kind of guy he was behind his cute crooked smile. Our conversation never got stale, even during the half hour car ride.

Once we arrived at the destination, all we had to do was cross the street and finally get inside. I wanted to drink more, but above all, I had a tub of hummus that was just begging me to eat it.

I kept looking at Duncan, rather than the way ahead, so I had completely missed the giant man sitting by my front door.

'Can we talk now?' said Jake, probably waiting there for hours.

'Jake. What the fuck are you doing here?' I said, with a vein popping in my forehead.

I couldn't believe he decided to show up like that. My whole cosy mood with Duncan was officially ruined.

'I'm going to go, Leo,' said Duncan, while patting my shoulder. 'I'll see you soon.'

He turned around and left me, in front of Jake.

I was fuming.

CHAPTER 13

£1457.82

I T WAS WINDY AND COLD. My hair was slightly damp from sweat, probably due to the amount of alcohol I had ingested that evening. I was so angry. I felt shakes, all throughout my body. My heart was pounding like the door knock of a bailiff; my blood was rushing through every part of me. I looked at him like he was garbage. I wanted him to vanish.

Jake was just standing there, towering over me.

'Who was that?' he asked.

'I asked you what the fuck you are doing here. Why are you here?'

'You haven't been taking my calls or responding to my texts.'

'I didn't want to talk to you.'

'Can we go inside, please?'

I rolled my eyes and opened the door. The flat was

lit by only one table lamp at the entrance. Andrew was probably in bed already, so I walked into the living room with Jake and closed the door behind us. He sat down on the sofa, moving a cushion to the side of it. I was standing up, restless.

'What do you want?'

'Leo, I'm sorry about what happened.'

'Sorry about what? About the fact you fucked me in so many ways that our last encounter doesn't even count as fucking? The fact that you've become a god-awful person?'

'I missed you. I saw you doing much better and...'

'You think I'm *much* better?' I interrupted. 'You think you can dump me bang on in the middle of severe depression and then come back to pick up the prize when things get slightly better?'

'No.'

'Let me tell you one thing. I am not better. In fact, life fucking sucks. Life for Leo Cotton fucking sucks a hundred percent of the time. I want to die, all the time. I have no reason to keep on living this hurtful, pathetic existence I keep waking up to every morning.'

'Don't say that.'

'Let me finish,' I commanded, while staring into his eyes. 'I was drowning. I was suffering because I couldn't measure up to the standard I had set myself to. I knew that, but at least I had you, and Squall. You ignored me. You saw my pain and looked the other way. You had your eyes on another guy, because suddenly your younger husband wasn't acting so young anymore. He had fucking layers and a fucking illness that prevented him to ever be happy. And you kicked me out. You didn't want to deal with me. I was damaged goods, and you fucking kicked me to the curb, because I had changed and wasn't giving you my ass anymore.'

'You know that's not what happened.' He stood up. 'I was also going through a difficult time, and I just needed space.'

'Space? You got it. You took it. You went with someone else. Someone that could make you feel things. Someone that wasn't so complicated. I had to leave my home and my dog, for you to go through your god damn mid-life crisis. I had to take a job I despise in order to support myself, and now, one year later, you're here at my door, ruining an otherwise pleasant evening, so I have to ask again, Jake. Why the fuck are you here?'

'I'm not sure. I just wanted to see you, make sure you're okay after last time.'

Andrew suddenly stormed into the living room.

'Get out, Jake,' he demanded.

I couldn't say anything. I was drained. I was never the person to say what they thought. I'd always keep things to myself. Just not that night.

'Please leave. It's late,' Andrew reiterated.

'Okay,' Jake said, while leaving the room and the house soon after.

I was staring at the wall, tired, spent. Andrew gave me a hug. I knelt and cried. I sobbed, loudly, angrily.

'We won't be able to do this for much longer, Andrew,' I said, detaching myself.

'Leo...'

'I'm going to bed.'

Soon I'd lose that too.

It had been an overall shit week. The store was getting busier and busier, with more and more douchebags trying to buy expensive crap for their unloved ones and demanding the impossible on a daily basis. Moreover, I worked really hard to make sure I'd be scouting the whole of London for horny men who looked like Quasimodo and needed to pay to ever experience the touch of another human being. My next victim was called Phil, and he was a CFO of a company in the States. The man sent quite a few disclaimers on his physical shape. He was apparently obese, but also very tall. His photo was a typical work portrait, with a dashing suit and combed hair. Yes, the guy had hair, which made for a nice change. He was in London for business and only free for a few days. According to him, he enjoyed the company of 'young' Englishmen for dinner. A dinner I was going to be paid £250 for. No mention of sex or any odd kink, so this was going to turn out to be an incredibly easy job.

I was walking toward the entrance of the Waldorf Hotel in Covent Garden when I realised how tired I was from work and all the emotional bullshit I had faced in the previous couple of days. I was still mad at Dominic for his insensitive judging. I was mad at Jake for both screwing me and ruining my evening with Duncan. I was mad at Andrew for leaving me for New York and overall I was mad at the world for making my brain not produce enough happy goo. It was nearing Christmas time and everyone walking around me were seemingly glad and cheery. When would I get to do a happy dance about something?

I looked at my phone to check the time, and I noticed a text from Abigail, asking for the deposit for the engagement party in Ibiza. My heart started racing. It was time to part with some of the money I had made being a hooker and rip the plaster off. As soon as I was about to get to my banking app, Duncan texted me.

'When are we getting together for another drink?'

And then for a second I forgot how mad I was at everyone. I even cracked a little smile. I couldn't wait to see him again. I loved my group of friends, but sometimes it was hard to complain about the same things over and over to them. I did not appreciate Sara's look when I'd vocalise my hatred for my job, but at the same time not apply for anything else. She was a doer, while I was a fuck-my-lifer.

I put my phone back in my pocket and realised I was standing at the entrance of the hotel. Phil was waiting in front of the main door, hands in his pockets and a big American smile that greeted me with an enthusiastic 'hello' and a big bear hug. He was huge. He was about 6'4' and probably weighed twenty-four stone, but his mannerisms made him incredibly cute and cuddly.

'Hello, sir,' I said. 'Nice to finally see you.'

'Pleasure is mine,' he said, in a bubbly American accent. 'Would you like to get inside? It's freezing.'

'In your room?' I asked, perplexed.

'Oh, no,' he cackled. 'To the restaurant. It's really nice there.'

'Of course.'

A porter opened the door for us and we both walked in, with me going first. The entrance hall was magnificent.

Marble floors, accents of gold just about everywhere. Huge vases on top of Greek-style columns brimming with flowers cascading their leaves over them. Everyone working at the hotel looked distinct and elegant, and for a second I truly felt like I was entering Buckingham Palace albeit severely underdressed. Phil was wearing a grey suit. The jacket fit him perfectly, probably made to measure considering how big he was, but the trousers were slightly ill fitting, like most of the 'slacks' in America. They were a straight fit, falling over the slightly square-toed black shoes he was wearing. It was like the States were about a decade behind when it came to skinny or slim fit. Overall, he looked dashing. His hair was perfectly styled, and his face looked freshly shaven. I, on the other hand, hadn't even trimmed my beard or washed my hair. It was parted in the middle and fell over the two sides of my face, an homage to the esteemed teenage actors of the 90s, I thought. Honestly, I was just too lazy to go get it cut, and I had to make it work somehow. My chunky brown boots were making noise on the shiny marble floors. I felt out of place, but Phil walked beside me, continuously smiling at me and making sure I was at ease.

'Is it your first time here?' he asked.

I was unsure whether he was being serious or not. But I had been here before. I'd came to the hotel for one of Sara's work parties. I'd snuck into most parties that had an open bar and a gift bag.

'I have once, I think,' I replied. 'Although I haven't had the pleasure to dine here with a CFO yet.'

'Oh, please.' He started laughing. He was loud, but not obnoxious.

We were seated at a corner table. The napkins were made of cotton and a bottle of champagne in an ice bucket was waiting for us. A bunch of English roses were placed in the middle of the table.

'I actually don't drink, but I absolutely want you to have some champagne or wine if you want,' he declared, while laying his napkin on his lap.

I wasn't sure if it was some sort of test or trap. But there was no way I was going to say no to a bottle of champagne standing right in front of me. That'd just be rude.

'You don't like drinking?' I asked, while the waiter was filling up my glass.

'My mom was an alcoholic. So, I never really liked it, I guess.'

'I'm sorry to hear that.'

'That's fine. There are worse things about her. She's a republican.'

'Oh, I'd take alcoholic any day then.' I giggled, soon realising it may have been an ill joke.

He smiled, so hopefully he didn't take offense.

'My father was a drug addict,' I said.

'That must have been tough,' he commented.

'My mother would drive past him unconscious on the street, on our way to school.'

'I'm sorry, Leo.'

'It's okay. He's dead now.'

I looked into his eyes and realised I was dragging down the mood of the evening. He didn't give a fuck about my family history. He was paying me for a damn good time.

'Let's pick some food! I am famished,' I exclaimed.

'What do you feel like eating this evening?'

I quickly glimpsed at the menu for a vegan option, but unfortunately it was the kind of place where I'd have to combine different things to make a dish. I hated being that person.

'Not too sure,' I said. 'I just need to ask for a bit of guidance.' I tried to grab the waiter's attention, and he swiftly came to our table.

'Are you ready to order, sir?' he asked.

Ha ha. Sir.

I tried to speak with a low tone, as I didn't want to put a spotlight on myself while I desperately tried to get a course that wasn't 100 percent potatoes.

'Would it be possible to make the vegetarian pasta vegan? Maybe doing without the cream?'

'We can absolutely accommodate for that. Any other allergies?'

'No, just no animal secretions and I'll be dandy,' I said, with a smile on my face, like vegans weren't hated enough.

'And for you, sir?' he asked Phil.

'I'll have the same, please,' he said, while closing the menu and handing it to the waiter.

The waiter took our orders and left us be.

'You didn't have to do that,' I said, slightly embarrassed.

'I am a big fan of vegetables. So, what kind of vegan are you? Health conscious?'

'Oh, god no,' I said, while nearly spitting the champagne. 'I just don't think animals deserve what we do to them for something stupid like food. I have a dog who is full of personality and sass, and I couldn't imagine him being exploited or killed. It's not right.'

'You seem passionate about it.'

'I find the world very unjust. I don't want to be grouped with the oppressors that make it even more unjust. Also, cows and pigs are some of the greatest creatures.'

'I agree. I grew up on a farm and made a lot of them my friends.'

He seemed relaxed, like he did this all the time. I couldn't quite get used to it, because every man I had met wanted a different experience. This felt particularly pleasant, because as far as we had discussed, there wasn't going to be any sex involved, although I was cautiously sceptical. Not sure what kind of man would pay £250 to hear my blabbering for an hour.

'So, do you like London?' I asked, trying to change the subject to something that wouldn't put me on the spot so much.

'I love it. But I like living in Boston as well. London just feels different. More refined.'

'Really?'

Images of the average Londoner puking their guts out on the pavement, while having one of their tits out and hair on their face, waiting for an Uber Pool, were flashing through my head. I had been that Londoner. I had been that Londoner many times.

'Yes, and I love this area, with all the theatres and musicals. It's fascinating.'

'I do love London.'

'So, tell me about yourself. What do you do for a living?' he asked, while pouring himself a glass of water.

'I work at a department store that sells designer clothes. Not the most fun job in the world.'

'You listed 'writing' as one of your hobbies. What kind

of writing?' His expression looked genuinely curious.

'Oh, it's nothing. Sometimes I just write my thoughts, or experiences. But it's mostly awful.'

'That's how majority of artists feels. If you don't doubt your skill, you're probably doing something wrong,' he said while making eye contact. 'If it's something that makes you feel good, it's worth pursuing just for that reason alone.'

'I am not sure if it does anymore,' I said, while staring at my glass and rubbing my fingers up and down the stem. 'I don't know. I think I'm too old to have that dream.'

'What's the dream?' he asked, trying to capture my eye gaze again.

'I don't know. Honestly.'

'You realise you just said you're too old in front of someone who's almost double your age?' he asked, with his big bright American smile.

'I know, sorry.' I pulled my hair back, out of awkwardness. 'I wanted to be a writer since I was a child. But I am lazy. I don't want to sit down and write something that's just going to be garbage. Does that make sense?'

'No, I get that,' he said. 'That's a very common feeling that afflicts the vast majority of people that have a passion. You wouldn't be the first writer to feel that way.'

I gave him a half-smile. I knew what he was saying, but at the same time he didn't know me, or anything about me.

'Can I ask you a personal question?' he asked, out of nowhere.

'Of course,' I said, curiously.

'How long have you been doing...this?'

'Whining?'

'No,' he cackled. 'The means by which we met each

other and the whole reason you're sitting in front of me this evening.'

Ah, the escorting. Obviously.

'A few months, I reckon.'

'I am only asking because you don't appear to be like any other I have met through that app.'

'In what way?' I asked, concerned.

'Just different. You seem very smart, like you could do other things.'

'I'm not sure a smart person would put themselves in this position.'

'So why do you do this?'

I was starting to get annoyed by the stream of personal questions. I didn't want to think about what I was doing, because the moment I did, I would probably rationalise how stupid I was being.

'I will be thirty years old very soon and I am the only one within my group of friends who hasn't done anything decent with their lives,' I confessed, while staring at my glass. 'My best friend is getting married soon, and for once in our lives, I want to have some disposable money. I want to be carefree and just think about celebrating her. I don't want to come up with excuses as to why I can't go to the expensive club, or why my present might be the cheapest of the pile. I just want to slap my debit card onto a till with conviction, without the fear of it being declined at any given time.'

Saying some things out loud can really do a number on you if you're the kind of person who keeps all this shit to themselves. All the time.

'I see,' he said. 'But as someone who is watching from

the outside, it's very possible your friends want to be with you because of *you*, and not because of silly nonsense about money.'

'Will you tell me that money doesn't equal happiness?' I challenged, while taking another sip at my glass of champagne, which probably cost as much as my food budget for the month.

'There are certainly more important things than money. Trust me when I say money can't buy you company when you're feeling lonely in a big house and all you want is to speak to another human being.'

'You can always *rent* company, I guess.'

I didn't think he found my remark funny. I could be quite cunning sometimes. We had a few seconds of silence and before I could say anything, the waiter came with our plates. Phil's eyes were still gentle, but I was scared I had fucked up our evening.

Shit.

CHAPTER 14

£2457.82

PHIL AND I HAD A GREAT DINNER. I stumbled a few times on inappropriateness, but I really enjoyed his company.

Phil was a self-made man. He was born into a relatively poor family, and grew up with a single, alcoholic mother and two younger sisters. When he came out as gay, his mother hit him and threw him out of their home.

When I came out, my father punched me in the face. My mother kicked *him* out instead.

I had just sipped the last of the wine bottle, and we were both completely finished with dinner.

'It's still a bit early. Did you by any chance want to hang out together a little longer?' he asked, timidly.

'Definitely,' I said. 'What did you have in mind?'

'Well, I have a really big room upstairs. I could order us something to drink, we could watch some TV. Did I mention the room has a Jacuzzi?'

'That sounds lovely, Phil.'

It really did.

'Obviously, I am aware this was not part of our original agreement, but don't worry, you'll definitely be—'

'Let's just go,' I interrupted. 'It'll be nice to relax a little.'

We both got up, and he started walking in front of me to make way. I brushed my hand against his huge back. I wanted to let him know I was actually having a good time.

Phil was staying in the King Astor Suite, one of the biggest hotel rooms I had ever seen. The décor was white, blue and cream. It had a living room, with a sixty-inch television and a gramophone. Everywhere I looked there was something that screamed luxury. There was a basket full of goodies on the bed with Phil's name on it. There were chocolates, pastries and a trolley full of bottles. I was in awe.

'Would you like a drink? I believe there's just about everything here, but we can always ask reception to bring whatever you want.'

My stupid face was still looking around the freaking five hundred square foot room, when I realised he was talking to me.

'I'll have a bourbon with ice if it's there,' I said, while scouting the trolley for a bottle of bourbon. It was there.

'At your service,' he said, while pouring it into a glass. 'Get comfortable. There are slippers, or even a bathrobe if you want.'

'I am actually dying to see the Jacuzzi,' I said, with my eyes lighting up, like a child.

'The bathroom is down there,' he said, while pointing at a semi-closed door next to the gigantic bed.

I entered the room, and everything was bright and white. There was a TV in the bathroom, but the most impressive thing was that the hot tub itself was humongous. I appreciated the fact that Phil was a big man, but I was not expecting for us both to fit in it comfortably. The tub was controlled electronically, and you could just press a few buttons for it to fill up in the exact temperature you wanted it to be. As soon as I activated it, the tub didn't take much time to be filled.

I stripped naked and put a bath towel around my waist. I popped my head out of the bathroom and called Phil.

'So, are we trying this thing together or...?' I asked, in a flirty way.

Phil was removing his jacket and tie.

'Together...?' he stuttered, while looking at my bare chest.

'Yeah, I thought the whole point was to continue talking,' I said, giving him a big smile.

'I didn't pack any swim shorts.'

'I didn't either, just get in.'

I grabbed my bourbon and put it on the side of the tub. I got in it and it was steaming hot. It felt incredibly good. Phil walked into the bathroom soon after, covered by his bathrobe. He took it off slowly, as if he was really conscious of stripping naked in front of me.

He quickly made his way down into the tub to minimise

the time I could potentially stare at him.

'Isn't it nice?' I asked, while extending my legs.

'It is!' he responded, with enthusiasm.

Phil didn't have one single hair on his body. I couldn't see his nether regions as a big flap of belly fat was covering them, but as far as I could see, the guy was as smooth as a dolphin. The bubbles were noisy, but unbelievably relaxing. I hadn't planned an evening like that, but it certainly surpassed my expectations.

'You have a really great body,' Phil said, while looking at my chest area.

I was flattered, even though I knew I suffered from some form of body dysmorphia that would make it impossible for me to accept such compliments. However, I was aware I was bathing with a morbidly obese person and saying shit like, '*Stop it, I'm so fat,*' wouldn't be well received, so I thanked him, like the much more adjusted person I strived to be.

'You know, you're very different from what I expected,' he confessed.

'What do you mean?'

'Well, it's embarrassing to admit, but I have done this before...with others.'

'I imagined that.'

'But it's never been like this. I know what 'paying for company' sounds like, but I do get lonely during work trips. I'm always by myself, and it's nice to just unplug and hear someone's story. Perhaps someone I wouldn't have had the chance to meet otherwise.'

'I can get behind that,' I said, while staring at the bubbles. 'It started as a thing I'd do to stroke my ego. It was almost a way to prove to myself that my ex wasn't right. It was a way to tell myself that people would even *pay* to be with me. It was going to be some easy money and I could finally get over the velvet rope and get to where my friends are...feel like them for once.'

'Have you ever thought you may be a lot more than a pretty face and a good body?'

'No.'

'You're well-spoken, you're kind, you're interesting, and I got this just by being with you for an hour.'

My eyes were getting glossy. I hardly ever got gratuitous compliments. I'd usually get those from a very drunken night with Sara, where we'd tell each other how pretty and how amazing we were.

'Thanks, Phil.'

'If writing is what you want to do, just give that a try. No one is going to believe a writer with nothing written,' he said while tucking my hair behind my ear. 'And your friends are your friends because of who you are. They don't need you to be rich or to be spending like crazy. It's all in your head.'

'Yeah, maybe.'

The conversation was getting a tad too personal for hot tub banter. I needed for it to steer into much lighter territory, so I sat closer to him.

'Now I'll hear you better,' I said, while putting my hand on his naked thigh.

'Fine by me,' he stuttered, nervously.

'So why do you feel lonely, Phil?'

'I live by myself, I work in a big private office, and I travel by myself. There isn't much room to make friends. I always assume people want something from me.'

'I understand. I can be your friend.'

'Ha, you'll be running away from here afflicted by boredom if you become my friend.'

'I am not bored, Phil,' I whispered, while giving him a soft, tender kiss on the lips.

I knew what I was doing. I was conflicted about making a physical move. He didn't request it, but I knew he wanted it. I knew I had to give him something for us to cultivate this 'relationship,' but at the same time I was scared he was going to misinterpret my intentions.

He closed his eyes and kissed me back, with his big, doughy lips.

'Leo, please don't feel like you have to...'

I interrupted him by putting my tongue into his mouth. His hands were placed behind my thighs. My cock was surprisingly getting really hard over it. I guided his hands to grab it, so he could feel it, and he sighed. I was trying to find his, but I couldn't get to it easily.

'Let's get out of this tub,' I murmured.

He consented, like a little obedient puppy. We dried quickly, and I moved him onto the bed. He was lying on his back and I was on top of him. His hands were on my chest, slowly descending around my hips. His penis was minuscule. I couldn't even tell if it was hard or not, but I grabbed it with my two fingers, until he started moaning in pleasure. Then I grabbed one of his nipples, first softly, then much harder.

'Yes, master,' he whimpered.

It was clear the famed CFO was actually a sub in bed. I was about to have way too much fun with this scenario.

I held his head so I could put my cock on his face, and he hoovered it into his mouth like he was eating ramen noodles. I pushed it hard, and he choked on it until he relaxed his throat and allowed me for deep throat action. It was sloppy and wet, but it felt god damn good.

Phil was touching himself and rubbing his left nipple. That's when I sat on his face and made him lick my arsehole. His warm tongue went everywhere, like he was licking a plate. I really wanted to try to fuck him, but I wasn't sure how to stick it in with all the excess flab, so I decided to put two fingers down his throat, to get them drizzly with saliva and to then put them inside his hole. He screamed in pleasure.

He wanted for me to get further, harder. I put another finger in it, and next thing I knew, my thumb was the only one left out. His arsehole was making the same noise as his throat when I was face fucking him. I had never fisted anyone before, but judging by how sweaty and horny Phil was, I could tell that's what he wanted from me. I looked around the room to see if I could spot any sort of fisting lube, but I couldn't see anything. It barely looked like he had unpacked. My four fingers were still inside him, but I could tell I wouldn't be able to get to the next step without some seriously thick Crisco-like lube. I didn't want to kill the atmosphere with me asking where the lube was, so I tried to stick my very dry thumb in, to see if he'd vocalise the location of our secret ingredient.

He screamed louder and pointed at the bedside table. I opened the drawer and voila—a small bucket that looked like it stored DIY paint, rather than anything remotely sexual.

I managed to open it with my left hand, while my other hand was still very much inside Phil.

The whole time he was whinging like a little girl. The power rush was exhilarating. Think of me, a guy riddled by anxiety and doubts, now about to get elbow-deep into a gigantic American man. I was ecstatic.

I grabbed a fistful of the product and smeared all over my wrist and my arm, adding more and more and getting my hand to move inside him, in circular motion. When both his hole and my entire arm were covered in the stuff, it made it incredibly easy for me to add the thumb in and completely get my fist and part of my arm inside him. His screams sounded like he was getting murdered, but I kept going. He could stop me at any time, but he kept begging for more.

My hand kept coming out clean, which was surprising. I wondered whether he had somewhat planned this beforehand. I didn't think anyone could be fisting-ready just like that. Not that I was complaining, considering I wasn't wearing any gloves.

I found the whole process very erotic. I felt like a porn actor, making grunting noises and calling him names. It was like I had forgotten how sweet our conversation was throughout dinner and now my only goal was to get deeper and make this man cream himself from pleasure.

He kept masturbating his tiny dick, and all of a sudden, he did just what I was expecting: shot a load all over himself. His final moan was louder than any sound he had made throughout the session.

I slowly removed my arm from him and left his gaping hole breathing on the ruined sheets.

I was panting; my heart was thumping out of my chest. I wasn't sure what had gotten into me. I never thought I could be that person.

I also didn't cum, which wasn't surprising, considering my favourite hand wasn't available for work. I didn't mind. I'd have a hell of a wank once I got home.

I got into the toilet and washed my arm off. That stuff really gets stuck to you. Everything was slippery and with a very distinct smell of chemicals and some sort of lavender.

That's when I looked at myself in the mirror, my forehead dripping with sweat and my hair all over my face. I felt like a stud.

I came out of the bathroom and Phil was wearing his bathrobe. I was expecting him to feel awkward, but he was just as smiley as he was before we even started doing anything remotely sexual.

'You are exceptional,' he said. Like I had just aced an essay.

'It was fun,' I responded, trying to sound cool and detached. I was putting my jeans back on and trying to get dressed as soon as possible. I was not a fan of the moment after. I wasn't much of a cuddler and I could really do with some sleep.

'You can stay here if you want,' he said, being conscious it was quite late.

'I have to get up early for work, but thanks for a lovely, lovely evening.' I grabbed my jacket and gave him a kiss on the lips. I was about to leave, when he called me.

'Don't forget this,' he said, handing me an envelope.

I trusted him, so I didn't even open it there and then.

'Goodnight, Leo.'

I smiled at him and waved goodbye.

I checked the envelope in the lift, and big fucking whoop, there was a thousand pounds in it. All in fifty-pound notes. I couldn't believe my eyes, but it appeared Phil really, *really* appreciated my company.

Well done, Leo.

———•————————•————————•———

My flat was silent. It was late, and I wasn't sleepy at all. It was probably the adrenaline from the sex acts of the evening, but my brain felt wired. I sat in front of my laptop updating my profile on *Seeking Arrangement* to add more risqué bits to my sexual biography. I didn't want to miss out on extra money. I had also added some of the photos Petar took of me in Sofia. Something about the black and white nude added a tad of professionalism to my profile.

The wedding was only a few months away, and I felt like I was already in a good place to treat myself a little.

I wanted to do what my friends did: go to a roof top bar, give my card away to open a tab, order bottles and bottles of expensive bubbly and maybe even say yes to that jacked weirdo that always shows up at straight clubs with cocaine and bitches.

Why the hell not?

CHAPTER 15

£2455.90

ECEMBER HAD CREPT IN and my job was officially turning into a nightmare with every passing day. I had been rearranging the stockroom since early morning, so luckily I was spared from interacting with awful customers, but there was something else I was dreading. It was Dominic's first shift back since he went on holiday to Berlin. He'd do that around three times a year. He'd spend nearly twelve hours dancing and doing drugs at a club called Berghain. It was the kind of club where you could just wear a jockstrap and a pair of leather boots and be fucked in the middle of the dance floor by some sweaty, long-haired, dressed in rubber wear bloke, and no one would bat an eye. In fact, it would be encouraged.

I was organising coats by size and colour when I finally heard his bubbly voice.

'Sweetie?' he screamed from the stock room entrance.

'I'm here,' I shouted.

He gave me a huge crotches-touching hug. It felt nice. I had been a dick to him.

'I wanted to apologise for how we left things last time,' he said.

'Don't worry; I think I was on edge or something.'

'You know I'm not actually in the position to judge anybody.'

I smiled.

'However, I do have some news,' he said with a dark face.

'Oh no, what's happening to you now?'

'Well,' he said, while scratching his bald head. 'I am going to give my notice period to Katherine.'

'You're doing what?'

'Yeah, I got approached for another job and I think it's time for me to take it.'

'You got a job offer while wearing a leather harness at a techno club?'

'No,' he laughed. 'But I did meet some cool people that wanted me to interview at a record company, to work with music. That's what I have always wanted.'

I took a second of silence. It was Andrew's news all over again. I needed to stop being so conceited about how the news affected me and start being happy for my friends.

I gave Dominic another hug and kissed him on the cheek.

'Well done, you.'

'Now we just need you to get the fuck out of here.'

I wondered if I ever could.

'I am just going to have a look around on the shop

floor. I'll see you in a bit,' he announced, while leaving me alone with a pile of shirts to fold. Funny enough, it was the very same cherry blossom shirt Marc wanted to buy.

I was folding my third or fourth shirt, when I realised one of them didn't have a security tag on. I looked around to see if there was anyone around and put it inside my pants.

I knew there weren't any security cameras in that stock room, so it would be impossible to get caught. Also, I needed something to wear for the evening. I was going to see a German guy named Stefan for dinner, and I wanted to look hot.

With all the saving I was doing, I really didn't want to spend my hard-earned money on overpriced clothes, not to mention I enjoyed the thrill of stealing it when Marc wanted it so much. It was extremely satisfying to take something from him for once. He had easy access to Jake, Sara and, heck, even my Squall. Just not this damn cherry-blossom shirt.

Stefan's house was right around the corner from work. All I had to do was walk down Sloane Street and follow the smell of success and pretension all the way to Chelsea.

I had met him on *Grindr*, while using my usual technique of finding the profile with the most *LinkedIn*-esque air to it. He worked in finance, but he was an art "enthusiast" as he so-called himself and enjoyed cooking and drinking fine wine. He sounded really good on paper, except his face looked like a flounder, and his body had never seen the inside of a gym in its life. His naked photos showed his skin covered in freckles, even his arse, which was prominent in all the photos sent. I was starting to see a pattern in older successful men wanting to get fucked hard by someone younger and far less successful than them.

This job was only going to get me £150, but I had nothing else to do, other than perhaps meet Sara afterwards to go for a dance or something. This would pay for entrance and drinks. I also hadn't masturbated in a few days, so why not empty my balls into a very keen German?

I walked into his building and it was enormous. The main door opened to a vast space where in the middle you could find reception and a dapper-looking old porter.

I greeted him and asked for directions to reach flat 32, and I made my way to a tiny, wooden lift that could fit three people at the very most.

I quickly chewed and swallowed a piece of gum to refresh my breath and pushed my hair to the sides. I looked at myself in the lift mirror, and my new shirt looked great. I unbuttoned it a bit to show a hint of chest hair and put my hand in my pants to adjust my junk. The lift opened up on the third floor and I was ready.

A really hyper man opened the door.

'Hello!' I said, trying to find a way not to sound like a dork.

'Hey there, beautiful!' he shouted, while giving me a big hug. Music was pumping out of the flat, loud. 'I am cooking some quick dinner. Tell me you're hungry!'

Stefan was nothing like what I was expecting. There was some shyness to him when we texted, but this fast-talking individual was completely different. He reminded me of Dominic on a night out.

I walked inside the flat and it was a loft-looking flat spanning two levels. I entered into the huge living room, which took a majority of the ground floor. The walls were full of character and personality. The guy was positively obsessed with purple and colourful woollen rugs hanging at every corner. Photos of him taken on trips around the world were perfectly framed around the room. There were disco lights flashing in rhythm with the electronic music. I couldn't even hear myself think. I removed my shoes and walked about.

'There isn't too much to show. This is the living room, bathroom is down there in the corner,' he said while pointing at it. '...and that upstairs is the bedroom. I'll show you later.' He winked.

Gross. But I'd play along. The bedroom was actually more of a mezzanine floor, and you could actually see the bed from the living room sofa. It was an interesting layout, but I couldn't shake the feeling he was an eighteen-year-old trapped in the body of a forty-seven-year-old man.

'Would you like a drink?' he asked in a thick German accent. 'I have just about anything. I have made us a cocktail if you want. G&T?'

I looked at him with large, wide eyes. He was going at a thousand miles per hour and I wasn't anywhere near drunk enough to follow the same pace.

'Yes, please,' I implored, while grabbing a huge glass filled with ice, lemon and what seemed like a litre of gin.

'Did you find the place alright?' he asked, while chugging about half of it.

'Yeah, I work around the corner, so it wasn't too hard.'

'You're fucking hot, by the way,' he said, while scouting me up and down. 'Really lovely eyes and thick hair.'

There was something about his ways that I found very off-putting, but I did enjoy his forwardness.

'Come closer,' he said, inviting me to come to him in the kitchen. I obeyed and walked to where he was. That's when he put his hands right above my arse cheeks and looked at me. His light blue eyes were surrounded by a reddish hue. The guy had either not slept the night before, or smoked hella weed.

'That's better,' he said. Then he proceeded to give me a hard, intense kiss. His tongue immediately made its way down my throat and I could feel his cock getting hard from that alone.

'Wow,' I said, panting and detaching from him. 'You don't waste time.'

'Sorry, I just wanted to say hi properly,' he said while going back to cutting some tomatoes to make bruschetta.

His breath revealed he was a smoker which I wasn't a big fan of, but the kiss was alright. Sometimes I'd forget these men had full VIP access to my body, as long as I was there with them. I took the wooden cutting board where the bruschetta were placed to the main coffee table in the living room. Stefan followed me with two bottles of wine and popped them both open.

'I like how you do things,' I said to him, with admiration.

'Yeah, why waste time?' He smiled, while sitting next to me. 'You're okay with the music? I can put on something more chill now.'

'That'd be great, actually.'

A shout to Alexa later and we were listening to much

more appropriate music.

'That's better. Now I can hear your voice,' he said. 'Tell me about you. Do you like to travel?'

'Yeah, I do. I love travelling.'

'What's your favourite part about it?'

Weird fucking question.

'Uhm, it's actually going to a supermarket.' I giggled. 'I know it's kind of weird.'

'No, I get that. It's quite fun.'

'What about you? You seem to have travelled quite a lot.'

'Yeah, I took a sabbatical and travelled all over the place. I really enjoy connecting with other people,' he said, while crunching on a bruschetta. 'Do you meditate?'

'God, no,' I replied, quite abruptly. 'I mean, I don't think it's for me.'

'Why not?'

'The inside of my head is screaming all the time. I'd have to shush that bitch first.'

He laughed, quite loudly, then he grabbed a metal box on the table, just by the wine.

'I may have the solution to that.'

I was intrigued and also confused. He took a smaller round box and opened it in front of me. 'Want to relax that screaming for a bit?' he asked, while showing me the content of it.

'I'm not sure if I can do weed.'

'Oh, come on,' he said, while lighting up a joint. 'This is going to blow your mind.'

'Alright,' I said, while reaching for it and having a puff. I thought I had become a pro since Paris. I coughed way less than that time.

'It's nice, huh?' He smiled, while stretching his arms and legs.

'Yeah, it's...punchy.'

Stefan also lit his own joint. Apparently, he didn't want to share. I wasn't sure I could do a whole one, but it seemed mellow so far.

'What do you like to do in terms of sex, Leo?' he asked, while blowing a big cloud of smoke.

'I don't think there is much I wouldn't do. Depends more on what you like.'

'Very nice,' he said, while giving me a flirty look. 'Can I see your cock?'

I was now used to his demeanour, so I realised I just had to play along. I unzipped my jeans and showed him my pants filled by my semi-hard cock.

'Take the jeans off,' he ordered, while smoking his doobie and blowing smoke at the ceiling.

I took them off. Left my sport socks on. I was comfortable.

'You should do the same,' I said.

'Why don't you help me take them off?'

I went over to him and helped him out of his acid-washed boot-cut jeans. He was completely naked underneath.

'I don't really wear underwear,' he said while adjusting his penis and stroking it. 'Why don't you come here and give it a little lick?'

I didn't really want to, but my head was starting to relax from the weed, so I thought I'd suck it up. Literally, I guess. I knelt in front of him, while he was sitting with his legs spread open. I held his dick gently, giving it a soft lick all down his shaft. He then pressed my head against his balls, and I put them both in my mouth, licking them softly.

'That's nice,' he said. 'Look at me.'

I raised my eyes to look at him, while my mouth was busy sucking the tip of his cock.

'That's good,' he said, while caressing my chin. 'Let me taste you now.'

I stood up and pulled my pants just under my balls. My rock-hard cock was staring at him straight into his face. He smoked the last of his joint and proceeded to suck me off, deep. There was no gag. Just a very smooth blow job. I wasn't sure if it was him, or the weed, but I could feel a tingle all throughout my body.

'Okay,' he said, stopping all of a sudden. 'Time for a break.'

I reached for my glass and finished my G&T. Stefan grabbed one of the bottles of wine and poured us two big glasses.

'Turn around now,' he ordered.

'Huh?'

He wanted me to lie on my stomach on the sofa. I obeyed, and then he took my pants down. My arse completely exposed. Did he want to fuck me?

'You'll love this,' he claimed.

That's when he carefully made the wine drip from his glass onto the lower end of my back, making it flow all the way down to my crack and successfully sucked it all up with his mouth.

I was impressed. And aroused. His tongue kept

making its way into my hole. My head was pushing against a cushion. I felt like the lower part of my body was completely disconnected from the rest of me.

'Fuck, yes,' I moaned.

'You're so hot!' he screamed, like a psychopath. Then he spanked me, quite hard. Reminded me of the weird professor man who wouldn't stop doing that to me. I guess it was Stefan's way to tell me he was done with my anus.

I pulled my pants back up, and he kept playing with his dick and smoking another joint.

'What zodiac sign are you?' he asked, out of nowhere.

I gave him a side eye, as I wasn't sure if he was being serious or not. Then I remembered I was in a flat covered in random crystals and shit, so I figured this was the kind of homo who would make real judgments based on zodiac signs.

'Aquarius,' I said, timidly.

'Ha, I knew it!' he said while pointing at me. 'Me too.'

'Wow. Cool.' I wasn't sure what the fuck was going on.

'You know, Aquarians are a special breed. We are creative, unchained. We are wired differently.'

I really wanted to tell him that zodiac signs had been found to be completely wrong and pretty much any horoscope could be applied to just about anyone, but he seemed very happy to live in his bullshit bubble.

'We are the best,' I said, throwing a fist up in the air, like an idiot.

'The very fucking best,' he said with the joint between his lips and looking for something else in his box of fun. 'I'm not sure how you're going to feel about this, but I'd love the company.'

He took a piece of paper, all folded into itself. It was a piece of newspaper and I had no idea what Stefan was about to do. Then he unwrapped it, and I realised what it contained. Mister German was a cokehead. That really explained his over the top performance throughout the evening.

I had never done cocaine. Ever. I was terrified of it. I had seen so many films in which someone would snort a line too many and start convulsing and foaming at the mouth before dropping dead.

'Do you want to?' he offered, while handing me a short paper straw with green stripes.

'You start,' I said, actually unaware of how to do it.

He proceeded to snort two of the four lines he had arranged on the table. He sighed and rolled his eyes to the ceiling, while stretching his arms.

'You know, I have never even tried it before,' I confessed.

'It's easy. Just breathe in through your nose as much air as you can, then push it all out.'

Seemed easy enough.

'Then close one of your nostrils and sniff the whole line through the straw.'

Weird feeling. The whole powder ended up into my nose, but I could also taste it through my mouth. It felt like it was all over my teeth. I drank some wine to wash off the taste.

'You've done it right!' he shouted again, like a football fan in heat. 'Do the other one, and I'll prepare some more. I am so happy you came tonight!'

I did the same with the other line, and it was a

much more pleasant experience, although my teeth felt somewhat weak. I felt heat rushing into my brain. I was hot, all over my body. I grabbed Stefan's joint and did a few more puffs. The music got louder and sexier, and after lining up the cocaine, he stood up to dance, stiff dick in the air, while smoking the rest of the weed.

'Dance with me,' he said.

I stood and danced next to him. We were hugging, kissing, touching each other's backs. He put his hand through my hair and then lowered my head so I could suck him off again. Now his cock wasn't hard anymore, but he could still feel the heat of my tongue.

'Do another line,' he said.

I turned to the coffee table and snorted two more.

'Good boy,' he said.

I never felt so great. It was the first time in months and months where my brain wasn't saying anything. Gone were all my issues. Gone were all those doubts and all those thoughts I deemed so dangerous. I thought for a second about the meds Dr Grey prescribed and how little effect they had compared to what I was feeling with Stefan. I felt like an entity was taking over me. My whole body was moving with the music. I could hear every single beat. My heart was pulsing with it. I could feel it through my chest.

'Fuck me,' he said all of a sudden. I hadn't even realised my cock was still hard. I had no feeling. Just a hard cock facing the ceiling. He handed me a condom, and I quickly put it on. I'd usually have trouble putting one on, but not that night.

I slid it right into Stefan. It fit perfectly. I started gentle and then fucked him hard. I had a hunch he wasn't feeling much of anything either. We managed to do a few more lines throughout the evening, and I even got to do one just above his arse crack. We fucked and we danced and we laughed and we laid down, while the entire room was spinning and lights were getting blurry.

All until Stefan fell asleep, exhausted, with my cum all over his body. But I wasn't sleepy. I wasn't tired. I wanted to go out still. It was only ten o'clock, after all.

I took my money off the dresser, put my clothes back on and went out without him realising. It would have been a good idea to go home, but I wanted to dance some more.

I knew Sara was out, so I decided to go see her. She was in Shoreditch, at a club with Alfie and Abigail.

'Yes, come see us!' she texted.

I called an Uber and patiently waited to get my dance on with my best friend.

I felt incredible.

———•————————●————————•———

It didn't take long for me to reach the entrance of the club, and I was facing a long queue.

I didn't have the patience to wait. Luckily, she came out, looking amazing. She was wearing an orange crop top and tight ripped jeans. Her hair was in a high ponytail, with big earrings jangling from her ears.

'Hello, my angel!' she shouted while giving me a hug. 'I am so happy we are out together. You never want to go out!'

She wasn't wrong. I actively despised clubs. I hated dancing, I hated being around sweaty people and I especially hated straight clubs. But hey, I didn't feel like myself then, so everything was game.

'I wanted to see you!' I shouted. 'Do I have to wait in the queue?'

'Oh, fuck that,' she said while holding my hand. 'He's with me, Clinton,' she said to the bouncer while walking in.

'One moment,' he interrupted.

I was shitting myself thinking he was going to say something about the coke I had done, but it was clear it was just in my head. He simply wanted to check my pockets.

Soon after we descended into a dark club, full of smoke and women wearing insanely short dresses, dancing on each other to get the attention of men hosting tables. We had our own table, apparently. Alfie was sitting, drinking a beer with some other male friends, while Abigail was drinking and dancing away.

'Hi everyone!' I shouted, without being heard much.

Sara offered me a glass of Crystal and it tasted like heaven. I was dancing like I was in a music video. I felt hot, and the soundwas deafening.

'What were you up to this evening?' Sara asked.

'I was on a date,' I said, making air quotes.

'Why the quotation marks?'

'Oh, it doesn't matter. It was fun though!'

'Why didn't he come with?'

'I just wanted to have fun with you, that's all!'

We hugged and danced together. Then I noticed a guy staring at me. This would happen quite often at a straight club. Gays would scout each other for help. I moved onto him and danced with him. I was rubbing myself all over him, like a slutty pop star.

I was having a good time, when he suddenly put his hands inside my pants to look for a cock to grab.

Something got into me and I didn't appreciate that at all. I pushed him away from me, quite abruptly.

'What the fuck is your problem?' he shouted, while pushing me back.

'Get your hands off me.'

Then Sara got involved.

'Go somewhere else!' she shouted at him. He then moved to another part of the dance floor.

'Are you okay?' she asked me.

'Yeah, he just really fucking annoyed me,' I said, while pulling my sweaty hair back.

'You sure you're not ill or something? How much did you drink?'

'I'm fine, Sara!' I shouted. Loud enough for the others to hear me.

'I think you've had a tad too much to drink tonight, mate,' Alfie said, while putting his arm around my neck.

Maybe I was acting like a dick. If Alfie took notice, then I must have been a wreck.

However, I can't forget Sara's eyes that evening. The look on her face. She knew something was up.

And then I forgot the rest of the evening. I know I ran to the bathroom to throw up. Then not much else. Did I pass out into the toilet? Did Sara leave without me because I was such a dick?

What in the living fuck was happening to me?

CHAPTER 16

£2455.90

WAKING UP THE NEXT MORNING was the opposite of fun. I had been sleeping on my side, and I had drooled an embarrassing amount. There was a huge wet patch on my pillow. My hair was on my face, damp, sweaty. I had fallen asleep with my contacts still in—they were stuck to my eyeballs. I looked around. My eyes hurt; everything was blurry. Then I realised I wasn't in my bed. I was at Sara's. I was sleeping on her emerald velvet sofa. I was wearing a t-shirt that wasn't mine. I still had my own jeans on. They probably weren't able to remove them because of how skinny they were. I wasn't wearing socks, and I had a puke bucket on the wooden floor, right next to my head. There was a tiny bit of vomit, mostly spit.

I couldn't remember getting there, or much at all, really. It was the first time, in a very long time, that I couldn't remember what I did the night before. Then I recalled a few bits. I had seen Stefan, the crazy German who couldn't act his own age. I had drunk wine and spirits, I had smoked marijuana, and I had done multiple lines of cocaine. I still couldn't believe I had done that. I managed to live for twenty-nine years without ever doing drugs, and now I had succumbed to a stranger's peer pressure. That was so dumb. My insides felt like they were burning. My whole body felt like that. Weak, exhausted. Every bit of breeze coming in from the cracked open window felt like a blade running down my spine. I wanted to get up, but every muscle in my body felt like lying down. I was hungry, thirsty, nauseous and on edge. I remembered faintly an altercation at the club. Did I punch someone? Did I act like a tit?

It took all the strength I had to get up. I sat down on the sofa. My head was spinning. Vomit was coming up again. I grabbed the bucket and threw up. Hard. I hoped no one was still in bed.

I got up, walked around, and looked at myself in the mirror. My hair was all tangled up and wet. I must have sweated like a motherfucker.

'You're up!' Sara said while entering the room. She sounded loud. Not sure if she actually was.

'Hey,' I muttered, with a pasty mouth.

'It sounded like you murdered a dinosaur just now.'

I wasn't sure what time it was, but it looked like she had time to shower, do her hair and makeup and actually get dressed. I mean, who would wear jeans in the house? Voluntarily?

'I must be catching a cold.'

'Oh, please. Here,' she said, while passing me a glass of effervescent orange stuff. Probably a *Berocca*.

'Thanks,' I murmured, while sipping it gently. Any wrong move and I'd be heaving again, this time in front of the angel that took care of me all night. 'What happened? Why am I here?'

'You were in no capacity to look after yourself last night,' she explained, while sitting down next to me. 'What happened?'

'I think I had too much to drink.'

'You always have too much to drink. Like, since I've known you.'

'The first time we went out together *you* got me way too much to drink.'

'I know, but it was always fun. Last night didn't look like fun. Are you okay?'

'What do you mean?'

'Well, if I didn't know any better, I'd think you were on drugs.'

I had forgotten Sara had far more experience than I did. All throughout her teenage years she had smoked and snorted pretty much every substance in existence.

'Of course not.'

'Are you sure? Because this looks more like a comedown, rather than a hangover.'

'Oh, my god, woman. I just mixed things and now feel like shit.'

'Did you take your meds last night?'

Shit. I couldn't even remember the last time I had taken them. A week? A month? It's like I completely removed them from my daily routine, and now who knew how long it had been.

'I don't think so,' I said, trying to be vague.

'That's really stupid. Take them as soon as you get home. There's no telling how bad you'd feel if you stopped taking them all of a sudden. You don't want to trigger another episode of hypomania where you max out all of your credit cards and get into crazy debt.'

'This is a very aggressive awakening, just so you know.'

'Be thankful I didn't leave you there. You were insufferable,' she said with a little smile, although I could tell she was being truthful.

'Thanks.'

'So where were you before you came to us? You never liked clubbing.'

'I know. I suppose I was in a very good mood.'

'Okay, I'll stop pestering. I actually prepared you a bath.'

'Oh!'

That sounded amazing. I didn't deserve her.

'Go in. And wash your hair please. I'm positive you have vomit in it.'

'Fuck, what a catch.'

'You're obviously still very sexy,' she said while getting up and giving me a small kiss on the forehead. 'Yeah, please get into the tub as soon as possible.'

I did just that. I stumbled on my own steps and got into the bathroom. The mirror there revealed even more how disgusting I looked. I stripped naked and looked at my chest and back. I had scratches all over it. My arms and my legs were covered in bruises. Hopefully from the fall and not for getting beaten up by some bloke at the club.

Fucking hell, Leo.

I put a leg inside the bath, and it was scorching. Bubbles were thick and smelled like coconut. I put some relaxing music on my phone and slowly descended into the water.

My skin felt raw, abused. Everything hurt. Was this what drug addicts had to go through? I didn't want another dose; I didn't want to feel like this. I just wanted to be in my own bed and sleep.

I put my head underwater and looked up. What would happen if I just stayed like that? Never coming up for air. Would just stay there, still.

No.

Not today.

I got back up. I breathed.

'When do we get to finish our evening, Mister Cotton?'

I couldn't believe I had such a nice guy like Duncan still potentially interested in me. I was sure that if he knew more about me and my fucked-up life, he'd run away as far as possible.

I had completely forgotten I had to see Jimmy, as he was in London for the weekend. I was still feeling crap from the night before. Even after the bath. Even after the nap. I had to run home to get changed, as my brand spanking new shirt smelled like sewage and was essentially ruined, and my jeans were covered in questionable stains. I put on the first jumper I found and immediately changed into some comfy trousers. It was just Jimmy after all. He wouldn't care. He'd just want my cock. He was already waiting for me at a French restaurant. I was late. That is what happens when you spend the night before acting like a twat.

I entered the restaurant. A gentleman with a waistcoat opened the door for me. It was one of those places that didn't look particularly fancy, but the menu wouldn't have anything below thirty quid. Luckily, I wasn't paying.

Jimmy was sitting at a corner table. Having a cocktail from what I could see.

'Sorry I'm late!' I said.

'No worries,' he said while standing up.

I wasn't sure what our dynamic was in terms of salutations. I went for a hug. I didn't know whether a kiss would be appropriate. Thinking about it, I didn't remember kissing him at all in Paris. It mainly happened in the genitals area.

A hug worked.

'You look very nice,' he said, while looking straight into my eyes.

'Really? I feel awful.'

'You're always handsome. How are you? What have you been up to this weekend?'

As soon as he said the word weekend, a little gulp of vomit made its way up my throat.

'Just had a few drinks with friends. Nothing major. How's London been treating you?'

'Yeah, not too bad. It's cold, though. Colder than Germany.'

Germany. A little more vomit.

'Oh, you know me. I am always hot.'

The waiter came to the table with a bottle of red. I wasn't sure if I could stomach it.

'I took the liberty to order beforehand. Is red alright?'

'Yeah, sure.'

I looked at the wine being poured into my glass. Maybe I'd have a sip. Wouldn't want to be rude.

'We should go on a weekend away again,' he said, while scouting the menu. 'It's been too long. I miss your nice cock.'

He did not whisper whatsoever. I was positive the table next to us had heard him. I looked around, but no sour faces.

'Sorry, was that loud?' He giggled.

'A little, but yeah, I'd love to go away again.'

'I was thinking Prague. Ever been to Prague?'

'No, Prague sounds great. Same deal as last time?' I asked.

'Yes, of course. I may be coming with a friend again and sharing an *Airbnb* this time.'

Sure, as long as they are as hot as Nicolas, I thought.

'I'm down for that.'

'I was thinking January? After Christmas and all?'

'Yeah, I can definitely do that. Sorry, I need to go to the loo for a second.'

'Sure, go ahead.'

I got up and looked for the Gents sign. There was no one in. I felt like I wanted to throw up but didn't have the courage to do so. I wished I could go home there and then. I washed my face with cold water and dried it with some paper towels.

Much better.

Then the door opened. Jimmy came in.

'Oh hey,' I said, confused.

'Can I have a little taste?' he asked, cheekily, while pointing at the accessible toilet.

I couldn't think of anything worse.

But sure, whatever.

We got into the toilet. He was as excited as a little schoolgirl. He unzipped my trousers as fast as Superman. My dick looked like it had worked overtime for weeks. I was surprised it even managed to get itself hard. I knew it wasn't my doing. My brain was fried.

He started sucking me off. I wasn't feeling much. Maybe I was very nervous that a disabled person may have needed to come in and I was going to get arrested, or something.

I started fucking his face fast. I wanted to be out as soon as possible.

He didn't.

He spat on his two fingers and lubricated his arse. He wanted me to fuck him. Bare. At a restaurant toilet.

'Maybe we shouldn't...' I said, worried.

'Oh, come on. It's hot,' he begged. 'We'll be quick.'

It hurt. It was tight. There wasn't enough spit. I entered him hard. I put my hand on his mouth so he couldn't make a noise.

The tightness felt good. My throbbing cock was going in and out of his perky arse.

'Sit down,' he said.

I think I rolled my eyes up. I sat down on the toilet and he rode my cock. I was in deep. He was riding me like a cowboy. His hole was warm. He was going back and forth, while I was grabbing his bum cheeks to fuck him harder.

'I'm about to cum,' I whispered.

'Do it.'

Good thing we had the STI talk already.

I loved shooting my load inside guys, but London was such a fucking landmine when it came to gays, I wouldn't have trusted doing that with many.

I grabbed the lower part of his back and bred him with my semen.

'So hot,' he said, while getting up and putting his pants back on. 'See you at the table.'

He had managed to leave unnoticed. Thank fuck.

I grabbed a piece of toilet paper to clean up my cock from the sex. I was expecting some blotches of poo on it, but my whole head was actually covered in blood.

Ouch for him, I thought.

I pulled my trousers up, flushed and went back to the table.

I could cross this off my bucket list now.

CHAPTER 17

£2877.90

CHRISTMAS TIME CAME ALONG. It has been a few weeks of alternating rigorous paid sexual intercourse with strangers hitting their fifties and ignoring my closest friends. I was trying to actively avoid Sara until the new year, as I was terrified to confess my extra-curricular activities to her. I had taken a few days off work. It was the only time of the year where I could pretend to have a normal office job and spend time home during the festivities. Andrew went to his parents' house in Brighton, so I would be stuck at home by myself with Squall. I had decided he would be the perfect companion to my second 'lonely' Christmas. I had a yearly tradition to spend Christmas drinking with John, who despised his own family, and would try to stay as far as possible from them. This year word got around, and Abigail asked to join us. The woman was great at her podcast, but drinking was her true talent.

I left them both at home to wait for Jake to come with Squall, so hopefully I wouldn't have to see him. I, in the meantime, proceeded to hit our local Tesco's. An idiot move, as anyone going to the shops on the 24th of December would be classed as a moron.

I was going to try to find anything for us to eat. I was a vegan, John was a vegetarian and Abigail would put just about anything in her mouth. My bar was very low.

I hit the alcohol aisle first, grabbing as many bottles of wine and vodka I could find. I stood up after putting as many £5 bottles of red wine as my trolley could fit, then I noticed him. He was kneeling, probably checking the label of different wines to find the one with the most alcohol content.

'Hi,' I said, gently tapping on his shoulder.

'Hello you!' Duncan smiled big time and gave me a hug.

He was wearing his signature denim jacket, but this time it was paired with a forest green Christmas jumper featuring Rudolph and a pompom red nose. His hair was messy as always, with his adorable loose curls.

'I'd ask what you're doing, but it's pretty clear.'

'Yeah, I decided last minute not to go to Edinburgh this year, so I am piling on Christmas food.'

'That's just a gin bottle and a sad cabernet, Duncan.'

'Yeah, that's all I need.' He smiled, while fixing his denim collar. 'What are you doing?'

'Well, I am attempting a decent vegan dinner for my friend John and Abigail. Are you alone?'

'Of course not.'

'Ah.'

'I have Netflix.'

'Oh, my god,' I chortled. 'How would you feel about combining forces and coming to mine? Everyone loves a foursome.'

'Really?'

'I have a very good-looking dog.'

'Oh well, I am sold then!'

I was happy and terrified at the same time. John was notoriously the better-looking guy between the two of us, and I swear I'd murder him point-blank if he made a move on Duncan.

'So, where have you been all this time?' he asked.

'I just have been stupid busy with my dumb job. I really wanted to see you again, though.'

We started walking towards a till together. He looked incredibly cute. I had forgotten how much.

'Why didn't you ask me then?'

'I don't know.' I pulled my hair back and looked at him. 'I think I was embarrassed at my ex coming over and making a scene.'

'I used to be an ex making a scene, so I completely relate. He probably really missed you.'

'Oh, ha. Fuck no,' I laughed. Hard. 'Sorry. No. He despises me.'

'I doubt that.'

'I just want to tell you beforehand. We share custody of my beautiful dog Squall. That's all. He is spending the holidays god fuck knows where with your dumb boss Marc.'

'Oh yeah, I forgot about that.'

'We will have fun.'

'Really?'

'We will get drunk.'

'That'll do,' he said while putting his arm around me.

———•————————•————————•———

The flat was toasty. I would never put the heat on if Andrew wasn't home. He'd like it hot and I liked it glacial. But I appreciated not many other people would feel like that.

'Duncan!' Abigail shouted, while peeling potatoes in the kitchen.

'Hiya!' he saluted.

'I believe you haven't met John. He's a dick, don't listen to a word he says,' I said.

'Hey. Mean. Pleasure to meet you,' he said while tending his tattooed hand to Duncan.

'Do not put your claws on him,' I whispered into John's ear.

'Okay, okay, Jesus,' he said. 'Duncan, what brings you here?'

'The promise I'd go blackout drunk. Hopefully before midnight.'

'I think we did a one o'clock last year, Leo, didn't we?' John asked.

'We fell asleep for an hour and then came back for the rest of the vodka. Dumb idea.'

'Yeah, it was,' John said. 'Hey, what did you buy? Did you get ice cream?'

'Nah. All that was left were a few bottles of booze

and frozen peas,' I responded. 'We really ought to do this earlier next year.'

'Christ, you're hoping to be in this same depressing situation next year?' Abigail asked.

'You're damn fucking right,' said John while raising a glass.

Then the doorbell rang.

'Are you waiting for anyone else?' Duncan asked.

'No, it's Squall and his handler, I assume,' said John. He was sitting on the sofa drinking bourbon, like a villain in a mafia film.

I went to open the main door. He was standing there, in his tall-ass 6'4'-ness.

'Hey,' I said unenthusiastically.

Squall immediately jumped on me. I gave him head scratches.

'Merry Christmas!' Jake said.

I nodded.

'Do you have company?' he asked. 'I wouldn't really want you to be alone on Christmas.'

'I do. Don't worry.'

'Okay. What do you have planned?'

'You're not asking to join, are you?' I asked, slightly confused.

'No, of course not,' he said while rubbing his arms from the cold wind that was howling throughout the day.

He was wearing a new coat, with a faux-shearling collar, all black. His beard was freshly trimmed. He looked tired.

'I got you a little something,' he said, while handing me a wrapped up packet.

'You really didn't have to.'

'It's nothing.'

'Is everything alright?' said Duncan, while kneeling and giving Squall a cuddle. 'Oh, my goodness. You're gorgeous!'

Jake looked at him, confused. He was frowning, almost as if he was trying to grasp who the guy was.

Duncan stood back up and offered his hand to shake Jake's.

'Hi, I'm Duncan, how are you?'

'This is Jake,' I anticipated, but purposefully didn't share any more details about him.

'Of course,' Duncan said, while putting his hand on my shoulder.

Sweet.

'Alright, I better go now. Bye little Squally,' he said, while giving him a pet. 'I'll see you in a few days.'

'Have a nice Christmas, Jake,' I said, while closing the door.

Duncan took Squall out of the harness, so he could go around the house freely.

'You okay?' he asked.

'Yeah, absolutely. Let's have some dinner, shall we?' I said, making air quotes.

———— · ——————— ● ——————— · ————

We had a glorious feast of a few slightly spent root vegetables and a *Linda McCartney* roast, all showered in plenty of alcohol. We were all merry, taking jabs at each other, but that Christmas felt so special because I realised

I wasn't alone. Even if things weren't going my way, and I was feeling as if I was losing my mind and myself, those people would always bring me back to a nice safe space.

My mother loved Christmas; she would try her absolute best to make it as special as she could with her limited funds. I appreciated my new Christmas tradition with my friends, but my heart would always ache whenever I'd stop to think about my mother and how much I missed her. I wondered what she'd think of me, of the kind of person I had become. She would be incredibly disappointed, just like my friends, if they really knew.

⸻

I was washing the dishes with John, while Abigail and Duncan were sitting on the sofa, going to town on yet another bottle of wine.

'I can barely stand up, mate,' John said, while drying a plate. 'Have I become a lightweight?'

'I am shocked. With all the travelling you do for work, I'd expect you to have a drip of fancy bubbly going straight to your veins,' I said, while pulling my shirt sleeves higher.

'It's not really as fun as it sounds. I am basically alone in a hotel room one hundred days a year, if not more.'

'But you still love your job. You have an amazing career.'

I was surrounded by friends who were knee-deep into creative industries, and I was just the poor friend who would tag along and stress over every little expense to barely keep up with their lifestyle. I felt like such a fraud. Even when I had money, I felt like I was stealing it, like

I was conning the gay community to exploit its weakest, most emotionally insecure men for something that I wasn't even sure was worth it.

'Can I tell you something?' I asked, with a serious tone.

'Yeah, of course, you can tell me anything,' said John, while sitting on the counter next to the kitchen sink.

'You know, I have been using the app you suggested a few months ago.'

'Yeah, I had no doubt you lied to me when I asked you about it.'

'Really?'

'Really.'

I stood quiet for a second. I watched the running water hit the thousand plates we had used throughout dinner.

'How's it been?' he asked.

'Sometimes it's been fun.'

'Did you have to do anything you didn't feel comfortable doing?'

'It's always a bit uncomfortable.'

'Then why don't you stop? I mean, I know you do enjoy sex, but if you needed another source of income—'

'I have no other talents,' I interrupted.

'Oh, fuck off.'

'I swear.'

'Look,' he said while getting off the counter. 'There are plenty of things you can do. I think sometimes your negative thinking really gets in your way. It's like you have taken the worst qualities of a writer, without actually writing anything.'

'The tortured, drunken arsehole?'

'Exactly.' He put his hands on my shoulders. 'You

know what you want to do. You just think it's impossible because not many succeed. But guess what?'

'What?'

'Every time you go inside a book shop, those objects you see stacked or standing vertically one next to the other? Those have been written by real people.'

'I just don't know if anyone would want to read my crap.'

'I am dying to read your crap.' He smiled. His whole chiselled face shined when he smiled. His light blue eyes and his freckles made him so handsome. 'Quit the bullshit. And quit having sex with gross men. You're better than that.'

'Thanks,' I said while closing the tap. 'We really never talk like this.'

'It's the bourbon. It makes me wise. Now get the fuck away and call Abigail over. We'll take the dishes from here, so you can chat with the guy you've been staring at all evening.'

'You were that guy.'

'Fuck off, Leo,' he said while bumping my hip with his. 'Go away.'

———•———————●———————•———

Duncan was in the living room rubbing Squall's belly. He was having a full-on conversation with him, so I was sure he was crazy drunk.

'I want one of those too, please.'

'Take your shirt off and I will,' he said, laughing.

I sat down on the sofa next to him. Our legs softly

touched, but neither moved theirs away.

'I am happy you didn't want to go to Scotland for Christmas.'

'I am happy my mother is crazy judgemental, and I didn't have the energy to go see her.'

I cackled. 'What do you mean?'

'Last time I went home I had gained a few pounds because I eat like shit in London and she wouldn't let it go. For the whole time I was there.'

'Isn't that what mothers are for?'

'No, I just wanted the cheap drinks!' he shouted. 'Ever been to Scotland?'

'No, never,' I said, slightly disappointed in myself.

'You should. I'd show you around.'

'Oh, is it a scenario where we go together?'

'Absolutely. Wouldn't want you to be harassed by those pesky Scots.'

'Aren't you one?'

'I'm a gentleman.'

I smiled at him. His stupid reindeer jumper was staring back at me.

'You want to squeeze his nose, don't you?' he asked, while staring at me.

'I think I do,' I said, fully engaging in the gazing contest.

I squeezed the pompom slowly.

'Now this feels weird,' I said, trying to break the tension. My heart was racing; my blood was flowing to each part of my body. I felt the heat rising. I hadn't felt that feeling in a very long time.

'Were you expecting for it to light up or something?'

he asked.

'Just anything, I guess.'

'Okay,' he said. He moved closer to me. We moved slowly towards each other. Our noses slightly touched, and then our lips made contact. Our eyes were closed. Kissing his lips made me feel like it was only the two of us, sharing a moment. Brushing mine against him, I softly bit his bottom lip. He smiled while the heat rose in his cheeks. It felt electric, but sweet. Then he placed both his hands around my head, slowly tending his tongue to meet mine. I could feel his warm breath, shallow, dictated by his heartbeat. I used my hands to pull his head closer to mine. I couldn't get enough of kissing him, and every second that went past, I wanted more and more.

Then we realised we weren't alone in the house, looked at each other and smiled.

We both wanted more, but for now, it was a perfect first kiss.

CHAPTER 18

£2619.40

URING THE HOLIDAY SEASON, it wasn't so uncommon for me to miss my mother more than the rest of the year. It was a time where I really struggled being by myself, but luckily it wasn't something I'd have to worry about. Every Boxing Day I'd share a lovely festive meal with Sara's parents: Sven and Danielle.

It was another morning of sunshine and brisk breezes. Rays were beaming through the main boulevard in Richmond. I was walking with two bottles of champagne inside my backpack.

Actual expensive champagne. I could afford it now.

The road was silent, as if people were still at home, having a late breakfast.

Sara's parents' house was located in a quiet cul-de-sac, surrounded by a gigantic garden. I quickly entered through the black and copper gate and knocked on the main door. The wreath was as gorgeous as ever. A pine needle circle of white and red flowers, glitter and a giant silver bow. Danielle would go extremely over the top when it came to Christmas decorations.

Sven opened the door with a big, bright smile on his face. He was wearing a Santa hat, along with a lovely grey Christmas jumper. His cheeks had a red hue, most likely due to the heat being blasted inside the house. Sara would get cold easily.

'Hello, mister Leo!' he said with enthusiasm.

'Sven!' I exclaimed.

He hugged me tightly. 'So good to see you. You look good.'

'You too! Do you even age?'

'Constantly, I'm afraid. Come in!' he said, while closing the door behind me. He grabbed my coat and hung it by the entrance. 'Everyone is in the kitchen already. Go ahead and get yourself a drink!'

The house was so big. I couldn't even fathom growing up inside such a huge place. Decorating it must have taken an eternity. Every corner was carefully designed to warm my cold, lonely heart.

'Is that you, my love?' Sara shouted, while sitting on a stool, drinking champagne in the kitchen.

'Hello, gorgeous,' I said, while giving her a kiss on the cheek.

'Leo, you made it!' said Danielle, who was wearing a Christmas apron and working hard on our meal.

I gave her a hug. 'It smells incredible in here.'

'Oh, thank you. I think I have gotten the hang of this whole vegan business.'

'You are really too kind to me,' I said, with a smile.

'Hey, we could do with less cholesterol in our lives,' said Sven, tapping his hand on his belly.

'Speak for yourself,' said Sara. 'Can't believe my food wishes come after Leo's!'

'Yep,' said Sven, messing her hair up.

'These are for you, guys,' I said, while handing out the two bottles.

'You really didn't have to,' said Danielle. 'Thank you, dear.'

'Did you rob a bank on your way here?' asked Sara, suspicious.

'Shush, you,' I dismissed, quickly.

Emma entered the kitchen while speaking on the phone, but she quickly ended the call. Work related, by the sounds of it.

'Hey, book nerd,' I said to her.

'Leo, my dear,' she said while giving me two kisses on the cheeks.

'Are the presses going crazy?' I asked.

'It's a busy time of year, for sure.'

I sat down next to Sara, sipping the champagne she poured me. Being all together in the kitchen felt remarkably cosy. I was lucky to have this 'adopted' family in my life.

'Has Alfie gone to see his parents?' I asked Sara.

'Yeah, he flew to Santorini early this morning,' she said.

'Did you guys have a nice Christmas?'

'It was fine.'

I didn't want to push for more information. Sara's wedding stress was probably making her a little snappy.

'So...when will you be bringing a new boyfriend, Leo?' asked Sven.

'Whenever I get rid of this 666 written on my forehead, I guess?'

Sven laughed out loud. 'A handsome man like you should really not have this much trouble finding someone!'

'Ah, Sven, if only the world agreed with you...'

'Oh, here,' he said, while handing me a small wrapped gift.

'What is this?'

'It's Christmas, Leo. What do you think it is?' Danielle said.

'It's only a little something,' said Sven.

I quickly opened it. It was a *Montblanc* pen. I never thought I'd own one in my lifetime. The card inside said, *'For your first autograph. Love, Sven and Danielle.'*

'Wow. This is gorgeous,' I said, slightly emotional. 'Although I don't have much to autograph.'

'...yet,' said Sven. 'Something tells me this won't be the case next year.'

'Do you know something I don't?' I asked.

'I believe in you,' he said, while giving me a pat on the back.

'Jesus Lord, what is this cheese-fest you two?' said Sara, poking fun.

I laughed, then looked around myself. I was surrounded by people who genuinely loved me. My father never accepted me, but these people welcomed me with open arms and supported me throughout some difficult years.

I was the lucky one.

Shopping after Christmas was a little ritual of mine. I was a firm people hater, but nothing would get me hyped up as much as pushing a little bitchy gay from the thirty-inch waist section of the sales corner at Topman. Sara had fought hard for over an hour in the ladies' department. We were both Internet shoppers, but I was in need of an outfit for New Year's Eve. Sara and I had planned to go to one of those swanky Essex-like parties on a boat in Canary Wharf. It was organised by a client at her firm, so we would hopefully receive some perks, because so far it cost me £100 just to be able to get in. I wasn't mad. I had raised enough funds to be able to have at least a little fun. My tickets for both Ibiza and Santorini were booked. I only had to get a hotel room for the wedding. I'd wait until my trip to Prague with Jimmy. Also, I wasn't sure whether Duncan would want to perhaps share a room. We had messaged each day since Christmas. I wanted to kiss him again. One wasn't enough. I wanted to do it all the time.

Jimmy would be my last job. I was sick and tired of being other men's property, no matter the price. I wanted to go on a normal date; I wanted to offer to pay for dinner. I wanted to put my arm over my man with pride. I wanted to have selfies of us on my phone, which I'd look at during my work commute, and smile. I wanted all that, and it wouldn't have been possible with my whoring around the city of London on my days off.

Duncan was going to be there. He would be flying back from Edinburgh and coming directly to the party. I was excited to see him. I was excited to kiss him at midnight.

Sara finally found me in the sea of last-minute suit shoppers.

'There you are,' she panted. 'There's no signal here, and I couldn't find you. I thought you had left!'

'I can't leave until I find something decent.'

'How hard can it be? It's a suit. They're hardly different from each other.'

'What about colour?'

'It's going to be fucking dark. Just pick one.'

'I want something festive!' I said, while doing jazz hands.

'Why do you do that? It creeps me out.'

'Sorry.'

'Plus, knowing you, you'll be out of it before you know it, as soon as Duncan shows up.'

'Ha, I'm a slut. How funny.'

'No, I think he is.'

'Oh, don't tell me that.'

'I'm joking,' she said. Then she grabbed a midnight blue jacket, with a satin lapel. 'What's wrong with this?'

'Nothing?' I said, while touching it sensually.

'Do you want two minutes alone with it?'

'No, it's perfect. How did I not see it?'

'I find perfection amongst trash. It's what I do.'

'Is that why you don't have a wedding dress yet?'

'It's all trash, hun. Fucking trash all around. I'll get married in jeans.'

'I think your Catholic mum would have a stroke.'

'Yeah, but think of all the jewellery I'd have access to.'

'Don't joke about that,' I chortled.

'I kid, I kid,' she said while looking at her phone. 'Crap.

I forgot I had a nail appointment.'

'Are you going to be late?' I asked, still holding the jacket.

'Not if I leave now. Will you be alright on your own? And you should get that.'

'I'll be fine, go.'

'Okay, I love you,' she said while giving me a kiss on the cheek. 'I will see you later all dolled up.'

She left in a hurry, and I was stuck by myself in the store. I checked the price tag, and it was still £200. Would it be worth buying it? I'd probably only wear it once. It also reminded me of a Dior suit we carried at work. Maybe I could get that one. The shirt was extremely easy to get out.

I could probably work in the store for a few hours with the excuse of helping them out with the mob of people last-minute shopping for New Year's Eve.

How would I get a suit out, though?

I was pondering.

I was scheming.

It didn't take long for me to make that decision. The shop was starving for help, especially at the back of the house where everything was a mess. That was exactly where I wanted to go. I was surrounded by clothes that didn't have security tags, thanks to my meticulous work. I had to be quick, but also act as nonchalant as possible. People do not normally think that others who are perfectly calm and confident are doing anything wrong. The suit I had chosen was beautiful. This one had a satin lapel, but it also had a silver line underneath, so it would shine when reflecting light. The suit was nearly two grand. I couldn't even remotely imagine spending that. Ever.

The jacket fit me divinely.

There were still a few people in the shop, but it was already closing time. I quickly hung the suit in a fitting room and closed the door. That was the first step. I power walked to the managers' office to grab my backpack and my winter coat.

'Leo, you're still here!' Katherine blurted as soon as I got into the office.

'Yeah, I got sucked in with all the people buying stuff and I had to stay extra.'

'Thank you for coming in today! It actually helped us so much.'

And, of course, this would be the only time in over a year that I would receive some sort of gratitude for doing my job. The day I had decided to jeopardise it and get arrested.

'No worries. Hey, I'm running a bit late for the party I am going to tonight. Do you mind if I get changed into my outfit in a fitting room? I have no time to get home.'

'Yeah, absolutely,' she said with an uncharacteristic smile. 'I'll be doing the same. And my hair and make-up. It's the retail life.'

'Thank you. And Happy New Year!' I said with a big fake smile.

I quickly got into the fitting room with my suit and put it on as quickly as possible. I was shitting myself. My face felt like it was on fire and my whole body was shaking.

Too late to go back.

I put my winter coat over the suit and quickly left the then empty shop floor.

I walked up the stairs to reach the employee exit. I quickly clocked out and greeted the security guards. I was almost out of the building.

Then the horror.

The alarm was triggered as soon as I walked past the detectors.

Fuck.

Once again, I was internally screaming, all while my whole skin felt like it was getting barbecued.

'Was it me?' I asked, trying to play dumb.

'I think so, walk back...?' asked the security guard.

The alarm was triggered again.

Shit. Fuck.

The security guards and I were on very friendly terms. We liked each other. I couldn't imagine pissing them off with such a bullshit act. Maybe I needed to come clean?

No, it was too late.

One of them used a portable detector and hovered it over my body. It didn't take too long to find the rogue security tag. Behind my fucking collar.

Some dick in my team had put more than one security tag on the jacket. I couldn't believe my dumb employees had managed to screw up the simplest of tasks.

'There it is!' he said.

I needed to remain calm. Panic would only make it worse.

'That's so weird. It definitely didn't beep on my way in. I bought this from Selfridges earlier, before coming here.'

'These security tags are really stupid sometimes. I

swear they work half the time. Do you have a receipt?'

I opened my backpack to pretend to look for the receipt. My head was on fire.

'I can't find it. I may have left it in the store. I didn't get a bag because I had my backpack. And you know me and the environment!'

'That sucks. Good thing it fits!'

'Exactly.'

'I'll just remove it. Those people are idiots.'

My whole body felt like collapsing. I couldn't believe it. The guard used a portable tag remover and even commented how good I looked in the suit.

'Good to go. Have fun tonight.'

I smiled. Nervously.

I left immediately and ran to the tube station. That evening I was a lucky motherfucker.

I started laughing by myself loudly. I had left the store with a two grand suit and they even helped me out in the process.

What a rush.

Fuck the Topman suit. Leo would be entering the New Year in Dior.

Fuck yes.

CHAPTER 19

£2389.09

THE SHIP WAS IMMENSE. It lit up the entire area surrounding it, mainly huge city buildings that sprouted with chaos and loud white collars during the day, but at night were dark and quiet. Beautiful people wearing beautiful clothes and adorned masks were eager to spend an unforgettable evening drinking champagne and putting this year behind them. I also would have liked to put the year behind me. My life had taken such a turn. Being single for the first time in years, finding myself sharing a flat with a friend, going back to a job I despised, but more than anything, putting my body at other people's sexual mercy for money. What a rollercoaster.

I wasn't sure where my mental health was. I wasn't sure how those events would affect me.

I was standing outside the entrance to the ship, walking in circles in very painful patent black faux leather shoes.

I was wearing my shiny new suit with a crisp white shirt underneath. My hands felt like icicles. I had been waiting for more than fifteen minutes and had zero alcohol in my body. The product keeping my hair pushed back also felt like ice. I was ready to go in and scout for canapes that didn't have animals in them and shove as many as possible into my mouth, to then go to town on the open bar.

I was wearing a black mask, with gold leaf details on it, something I had bought on a romantic trip to Venice with Jake. This was the first time wearing it outside the house. It was now just a simple mask. Gone were all the happy memories with Jake. I really felt like a prince for the evening—a feeling particularly special, considering I'd usually play the role of the pauper millennial, counting pennies to buy bread.

'Hey, good looking!' an incredibly stunning Sara shouted from afar. Her hair was wavy, all placed on the side, with a small, striking black mask covering her eyes.

Alfie was his usual cute self. No trace of beard, tidy hair and a Zorro-style of mask. His suit was simple, but he paired it with some fancy loafers.

'Hi, princess,' I said while kissing her hand. 'Mr Holland, always a pleasure to see you.'

We gave each other a solid, manly hug.

'Where's your date?' she asked, looking around.

'Duncan is going to be late. He's flying back from Edinburgh and his flight has been delayed. He's on an *Easyjet* plane wearing a tux. Bless him.'

'Oh, that's a shame,' she said. 'Luckily you're in the company of the best people.'

'Yeah, I'll be your man for the time being,' said Alfie,

cracking a smile.

'I am the only man he'll be with, thank you very much,' said a probably already tipsy Sara.

'What do you say we go in and drink our sorrows away?' I proposed.

They both nodded and made way.

The ship's interiors were magnificent. Red velvet all around, details in mahogany wood adorned every corner. Sophisticated arrangements of flowers inebriated the air. Everything looked luxurious, and everyone's masks made the whole gathering quite Marie Antoinette-esque.

I had never been inside a ship. For once in my life, I wasn't feeling out of place, even though I was wearing a stolen suit.

'What is this incredible suit you're wearing?' asked Sara, while having a really close look.

'I found it after you left. Thought it'd be more festive.'

'Wow,' she said, with big, shocked eyes.

'It looks really expensive, mate,' said a surprised Alfie.

'Nah, I got it on sale. Nothing major.'

'Shit, well done,' she commented. 'I should take a photo of you and send it to Duncan, so he can hurry the fuck up.'

'I'll wait for him to see me in real life.'

'When you're going to be sweaty and wasted?' she asked.

'Yeah, that's my sexiest.'

We walked towards the main hall, and it was gigantic. Tables for people to sit, a huge dance floor, but most importantly, an army of waiters with glasses of champagne on silver trays. So far, so good. I grabbed two, so I could down one at once, and keep the other one to sip on.

'That's my boy,' she said.

I smiled and pushed my back against a wall.

'I think I'll stay here for a second to ease myself into the huge crowd. It's okay if you guys want to have a look around. I'll be here having a few pre-drinks.'

'Alright, I do have to have a look around because I think there's some people from work, and I want to make sure I know what they look like, so I don't make an absolute twat of myself,' she said, while fixing her dress. 'We'll be right back.'

I grabbed another glass and looked at my phone. Duncan's plane had finally taken off. I didn't have to wait too long.

Then I got another text.

'Is that you in the black and gold mask, looking moody and mysterious?'

I looked around. Why the fuck would Stefan be at this party? I couldn't see him.

'I'm waving.'

I looked up, and there he was. Wearing a tux with a purple bowtie and a disco-ball effect mask. His silver hair shined bright in the light.

'Hi there,' I said, nervously.

He didn't waste any time and kissed me, grabbing me by the waist.

'You're so hot!' he shouted.

'Thanks,' I said, looking around, making sure Sara wasn't anywhere near. 'What are you doing here?'

'What do you mean? I am one of the organisers!' he said while raising his glass.

'You've organised this?'

'Nah, just put some money into it and showed up tonight.'

'Convenient!'

'I hope you didn't buy a ticket for this.'

'I did! Full price and everything.'

'Nonsense,' he said, while putting a couple of notes into my jacket's inside pocket. Probably a few hundred. It felt weird. 'Oh, Dior. Look at you!' he said, while reading the label inside. 'There's clearly someone out there treating you better than I am.'

'Oh no, nobody does it like you do, Stefan,' I said, while pinching his right cheek.

'Look what else I found in my pocket!' he said, while shaking a small plastic bag containing a few pills.

'What the hell are those? Put them away!'

'Oh, it's fine. Just take two. It'll make your evening more fun.'

'Oh no, thanks.'

'Please? For daddy?'

Ew.

It was in that moment I saw Sara and Alfie walking towards me.

'Okay, if I take them would you please leave right now? My friends are coming here and have no idea of the kind of activities that got us together,' I said quickly, panicking a little.

'Alright, but I will see you later when they kick in!'

I took them both with the rest of the champagne in my glass and gave him a nervous smile. Then he blew an air kiss and left.

Fuck.

It had been over an hour since I had taken the pills and didn't feel any difference. I felt more energetic, if anything. Everyone looked amazing, the music was loud, the drinks were constant, and I was, overall, having an absolute blast. Sara and Alfie were dancing, while I was, once again, leaning against a wall. I wasn't sure what I had taken, and the last thing I wanted was to make a dickhead out of myself. My heart rate was certainly accelerated; I was getting very, *very* hot. I wanted to remove my blazer and shirt and be free to dance half naked. In fact, I wanted everyone to be half naked. It was so hot and sticky. Everyone would have loved it. Duncan would come to the party and immediately take his clothes off. We'd dance together and wait for midnight to give each other a slow, passionate kiss.

Suddenly I couldn't see Sara anymore. Everything was somewhat blurry. I was sipping more champagne, in an attempt to rehydrate myself from the heat. My hair felt wet. Not damp, full on wet. I hoped my friends would be drunk enough not to notice.

I saw Stefan walking and dancing around from afar. I started thinking about the hot sex we had together, with me fucking him hard and him screaming and moaning in pleasure. I felt more heat. I was certain something was happening in my body. I wondered if I had taken a safe dose. I wondered if I had taken something that would interact horribly with alcohol. I wondered how I'd get home. My mind was speculating, questioning, panicking. All of a sudden, I wanted to write. I wanted to write my novel, I wanted to talk about all of my feelings, all of my problems, all of my stupid decisions. I wanted to talk and talk and talk about how angry I was at Jake, or how smitten I was about the sweetest Scottish guy. I wanted to do all these things. I was relaxed, but excited. Maybe I needed to get some fresh air, maybe I needed to jot down some sentences for a potential novel, or maybe I just needed to throw up. What I needed wasn't exactly clear.

I stopped leaning on the wall and started walking. I did want to get on the deck where the pool was, where people would be smoking, so I could be alone in my thoughts.

Yes, great idea.

I moved, and someone very familiar started walking towards me. I couldn't tell who it was. It was like I was trying to tap on a database in my brain, but the battery was low. My brain felt foggy, but then his voice ricocheted all around the walls of my head. It was a voice I didn't like. A voice I didn't think I'd encounter that evening.

'Leo, is that you?' he asked, with a Mean Girl-esque tone.

This was by far worse than my Stefan encounter.

'Marc.'

Why was he there? Why did he greet me? We would try the impossible to avoid each other, and now he was coming to see me? What the fuck did he want?

'I love what you're wearing!' he said, scanning my whole ensemble.

He had his hair all poofed up perfectly with a shimmering shine. He was wearing eyeliner and glitter on his face as well, just in case the Phantom of the Opera mask wasn't gay enough. I could see him wearing a sheer shirt under a deconstructed velvet jacket. I wondered if this guy owned any non-see-through clothes at all.

'Thanks,' I said. 'I didn't think you'd be here.'

'Yeah, some of the organisers are my clients.'

'Of course.'

I didn't know what to say. Part of me thought it was a hallucination. I didn't think I had taken hallucinogens though. The situation was bizarre.

'I saw you earlier at your workplace actually, running into a fitting room. Don't think you saw me,' he said.

Shit, did he see me stealing the suit? Of all people, he would be the one to bust me?

'I didn't see you.'

'Well, I can see you made the right choice. Wasn't this really expensive?'

'It was a bargain, really.'

'I didn't think Dior was on sale. I wish I knew.'

'Yeah, should have asked someone!'

'I did.'

Why was he still talking to me?

'When they said Dior wasn't on sale, I just assumed you were trying it on to post on Instagram or something,' he said.

'I'm not that pathetic.'

'Yeah, look at you wearing it. It's fabulous!'

'Hey, where's Jake?'

'He's home with the dog.'

With *my* dog.

'I'm surprised he didn't come. He's always loved New

Year's Eve.'

'I don't think he does much,' he said with a smile.

That's funny, because I'd always be called an old lady for fucking hating it. He'd even do his own firework display. Maybe the shitty tattoos he had gotten made him forgo his damn personality.

'I'm shocked,' I said.

'Are you okay? You seem a bit...' he said, while moving his hand side to side, near his head.

'Positively not...' I proceeded to make the same gesture. 'Have a nice evening, Marc.'

I finally got to move away from him. I found it laughable that the guy was literally sleeping in my bed, on my side, and still felt the need to piss all over me to *Marc* his territory.

The cold air of the deck felt great on my skin. I was roasting; my back was completely sweaty.

I'm on my way! Duncan texted.

My heart was beating fast, with excitement.

Sara and Alfie found me near the smokers.

'There you are, mate!' he said, while patting my back.

'What are you doing here?' Sara asked, with a hint of confusion.

'It's so hot downstairs; I really needed to breathe out here.'

'How much did you have to drink?' she asked.

'A fair bit, but I don't think it's that, no, really, I am great, I'm loving everything: the music, the people, the masks, it's all fabulous,' I said, really quickly.

'Did you have a Jägerbomb?' he asked.

'No, why?'

'You sound like you just had a massive energy drink!'

'I don't think so.'

'Did I see you speak to Marc earlier? Or am I really drunk?' Sara asked.

'He came to me. I don't know what his problem is.'

'Maybe he just wants to be nice?' she said, without much conviction.

'Yeah, right!'

'Okay, how about we go for a dance?' she asked, excited.

'Sounds good, just let me go for a wee first.'

'Fine, we'll see you there!'

I walked back down, looking for a toilet. I asked a few crew members and got sent to one that was at a lower desk. Hopefully it was going to be the one with less people. It seemed like no one was around. Good for me. I opened the door to the gents and there was nobody, then all of a sudden, I heard the door behind me open.

'Hello, stud!'

I turned around, and it was a jacketless Stefan.

'Did you follow me here?' I asked, creeped out.

'I just saw you and thought I'd accompany you wherever you were going! Also, my room is down here.'

'You have a room?'

'Of course! Why wouldn't I?'

'Okay.'

'Come, I'll show you,' he said while grabbing my hand and taking me outside the bathroom.

'My friends are actually—'

'They'll be fine, it'll be quick.'

I was dragged down the corridor into his huge room with a window facing the big city buildings. The bed was covered in red velvet sheets. Everything was as luxurious as the main hall, if not more. If I didn't know any better, I would have thought I had just entered the Titanic.

'Drink?' he asked, while opening the mini fridge.

'Sure. Bourbon there?'

'Of course,' he said while pouring down a glass. 'Here.'

I grabbed the glass and sat on the bed. My head was spinning slightly.

'This is nice.'

'It is,' he said while grabbing a black tray with cocaine on it. 'Want some?'

'What did you give me earlier by the way?'

'Just something to get you relaxed!' he said, while placing the tray on the bed next to me. Then he proceeded to kneel down and to unbutton my trousers.

'No, I'm not really...'

Then he stopped for a second.

'Ah, is it because you're not being paid? Cheeky. How much for me to suck you off?'

'I'm not really in the mood for—'

'Come on,' he took my hard dick out of my trousers. 'Very nice!'

'Stefan, really.'

He started checking his pockets for money and took out another two hundred.

'Here,' he handed me the money and started licking my cock, which at that point, didn't even feel like part of my body.

'Fine,' I said, while falling with my back on the bed. I was staring at the ceiling, while I was receiving a sloppy blow job by a drug/sex addict. It felt good. I wasn't sure if it was due to lying down, or the drugs hitting my brain. Either way I had no idea what was going on.

'Do a line, we still have lots of time to have fun,' he said.

It seemed like a terrible idea, but I chugged the whole glass of bourbon and snorted a line straight afterwards. Stefan howled.

Actually howled.

'Let's finish later,' he said, while zipping my trousers back up.

'Okay,' I said, while getting up. 'I'll see you later.'

'See you later, sexy.'

I closed the door behind me, and everything just got blurrier and hotter. It felt like I was walking into a sauna fully clothed. I stumbled upon walking up the stairs and made my way to the dance hall. The music was deafening.

It took some trial and error, but I eventually spotted Sara.

She was with Alfie.

And Duncan.

Finally.

I walked towards them with a big smile.

'Where the heck have you been? You've been gone for an hour!' said Sara.

An hour. Weird. She was wrong. I was gone for no more than ten minutes.

'I've made it!' Duncan said, looking dapper.

I wanted to kiss him, and to dance with him, but then all the lights went off, and the music stopped.

I wasn't sure what had happened, but then everyone was gone too. Then everything started spinning around, and I fell.

Then blackout.

———•——————●——————•———

I opened my eyes slowly. I was on a bed. My head hurt. Everything hurt. I was on a bed in just my pants. Had I been raped? Did Stefan take me somewhere? I was incredibly confused.

Then I looked up. Duncan was sitting on a chair next to the bed.

'Hi,' he said. Softly.

'Where am I?'

'My room. I told Sara it would be better for you to come here, since we don't live too far from each other.'

'I don't understand,' I said, while slowly sitting up.

'Hey, easy!' he said, while helping me stabilise.

'What happened?'

'Well, I am not sure. I went to the party, but you weren't there. But then you finally came and then passed out. Straight away. It looked painful.'

'Oh, god.'

'Did you take anything odd?' he asked.

'No, I don't think so. What time is it?'

'It's five in the morning.'

'You stayed awake for me?'

'Yeah, I was worried,' he said, while caressing my

drenched hair.

'I am so sorry.'

'About what?'

'About all of this. I ruined our evening. I was really looking forward to dancing and kissing and whatever.'

'It's fine. New Year's is overrated anyway.'

'I'm really embarrassed.'

'Don't be. I was more worried than anything. I wasn't sure if you needed a hospital!'

'You made the right call. Thank you.'

He smiled tenderly.

'Are you okay, Leo?'

I sighed and took a break.

'I'm not sure.'

'You know, you can talk to me.'

'I just ruined everything.'

He gave me a soft, tiny kiss on the lips.

'Happy New Year, Leo,' he smiled. 'You didn't ruin anything.'

I smiled slightly, but I felt incredibly guilty.

'I think I should go.'

'Don't be silly. Go back to bed!' he said, with a worried face.

'I need to go,' I said while getting up and putting my trousers back on. 'I am so sorry you had to do this.'

'Leo, seriously. I just wanted you to be okay. I wasn't thinking about anything else.' He stood up in front of me. 'I just came for you.'

'And I fucking passed out,' I interrupted, while putting my shirt back on. 'I am mortified.'

'Why are you being so apologetic? It wasn't your fault!'

'I don't know what happened. I just know it wasn't supposed to happen.' I put my hands on his shoulders. 'I really like you, Duncan. I really, really do. When we kissed, it was magical. And I know it's god-awfully cheesy to say so, but it's how I felt. What you have in front of you isn't the best version of myself, but if you're patient, if you wait for just a little longer, I will be.'

Duncan's face scrunched up. His eyes were still gentle. 'Leo—'

'I'm going to go now. Again, I am so sorry about this.'

I left in a rush. I felt like shit.

As I left his flat, I was surrounded by other drunk, drugged up Londoners all around me. All laughing, all still having fun, while I felt like a poor excuse of a human being. The roads were wet; the wind was cooling my skin, still damp and raw. My eyes were burning, and all I wanted was to disappear. I put my hands in my jacket pocket and found the cash Stefan had put in there, all scrunched up, like I was some sort of gross vending machine.

Duncan should have just left me there.

He deserved better.

What the fuck was I becoming?

CHAPTER 20

£2165.90

IT HAD BEEN A FEW DAYS INTO THE NEW YEAR, and so far I wasn't particularly impressed. It rained every single day, and I refrained from speaking to any of my friends. I still felt like a joke of a human being, and all I wanted to do was to be by myself. I was sitting at the gate of my flight to Prague, tired and restless. I didn't want to go. I was over this charade of me pretending to control men for my gain. I was the puppet, the one being controlled, the one being used. They had nothing to lose. They just wanted to have a little fun, pay for it and toss me aside.

I was one of the last people in the queue to get onto the plane. I wasn't feeling very festive; I wasn't feeling very whore-y either. I had my passport in my hand, and I wanted to shred it to pieces. I could have just left and gone home. I could change my telephone number and forget about all these people that would book me, like I was an object.

Instead I queued.

I presented my boarding pass.

I showed my passport.

I said thank you.

I walked towards the entrance of the plane. I said hi to the flight crew. They were all smiling, showing teeth. They were trained in pretending genuine joy. I wished I knew how to do that. I worked in customer service and couldn't fake it the way they did.

I walked all the way until the end of the aisle. I was seated at the very back end of the plane. No one was sitting next to me. I sat by the window and looked at the wet tarmac, watching the drops falling onto the glass, right next to my face. I was tired. I wanted to sleep, but I knew I couldn't sleep on a plane. I physically couldn't.

We were about to depart. The crew members were doing their thing.

I took my phone out to put it on airplane mode, and there were multiple texts from Sara. I thought she wanted to check up on me, but it seemed a lot more serious.

She'd never ask me to 'call her.' She hated speaking on the phone. And yet, I had three missed calls, all from a few minutes earlier.

I called her back. I was worried. She said it was an emergency.

What the fuck?

It rang for a few seconds.

'Hey,' I said.

'Leo, where the fuck have you been?!' she shouted. Her breath sounded shallow. Her voice was raised as if she was distressed, or panicking.

'I had my phone on silent. What's going on?'

She was sobbing, loudly.

'Sara, what's happening?'

'My dad!' she paused, she sobbed. 'He had a heart attack. I'm at the hospital. My sister isn't here yet. Alfie is at work. I am so fucking scared!'

'Oh my god.' I was speechless.

Then a flight attendant came over.

'I am sorry sir, but you really ought to turn your phone off now.'

'Where are you?' she asked, still sounding confused and upset.

'I am sorry, I have to go now, but I will call you super soon.' I turned my phone off.

What the hell was I doing?

My best friend needed me, and I completely checked out. I was going on a fucking holiday.

Fuck.

I was an arsehole.

The plane started its departure, and I had never felt worse.

———•————— ● —————•———

The journey wasn't particularly long, although I had managed to drink a few small bottles of wine and write a few thoughts down on paper. Once I arrived at the destination, I turned my phone on. There were no messages from Sara. I didn't know what to do. I wanted to call her, but I wouldn't have known what to say. I couldn't be there for her, physically. I wished she called me earlier. I wouldn't have boarded the flight. I wished I never started travelling for those men. I wished I didn't need that money. Just as I was about to call Sara, my phone battery died. A sign, I thought. Maybe I would have upset her even more.

I looked around the airport for Jimmy, but he wasn't there. I started getting nervous, as I couldn't use my phone to contact him.

I looked around some more, and then I finally saw a man in a suit holding a sign with my name.

Thank fuck. He had sent a car to pick me up.

So far, I hadn't loved anything about that day. The air felt cold on my face. My jaw was clenched. I wasn't wearing gloves or a beanie. My jacket wasn't even thick enough for that weather. I immediately jumped into the backseat of the car and enjoyed whatever song was playing on the radio. I was only going to be there for two-and-a-half days. I was doing this for Sara. I was doing it to make her day special.

The trip to the Airbnb was under twenty minutes. I got out of the car with my weekender bag and looked around. All the buildings were a shade of grey and beige. They all looked the same, with imposing main gates. I vaguely remembered the flat was number six. Luckily the main door was already open, so I just made my way upstairs. The staircase smelled of tomato sauce and garlic. It was pungent. I could smell basil too. Someone was getting ready for some delicious lunch. I knocked on the door and waited a minute. I was worried they had gone out. Maybe they texted me, but I was never able to see it. I knocked again, then heard a noise inside. Someone was definitely there.

The door was opened by a tall, lanky fella. Dark skin, curly hair, buzzed around the sides, bushy eyebrows and big brown eyes.

'Hi, you must be Leo?' he asked. His accent was English, southern maybe.

'Yes, hi. You must be Jimmy's friend?'

'Yeah, I'm Eddie. Come in!'

I walked in, and the flat was huge. Spacious living room with marble tiles, a rustic, wooden kitchen and a large sofa. I placed my bag on it.

'Is Jimmy here?' I asked, looking around.

'I'm here, I'm here,' he said, while coming out of the bathroom. 'So good to see you, Leo.' He went for a kiss on the cheek.

'Is that all?' Eddie asked. 'Thought I'd see more passion!'

'Maybe later,' Jimmy said.

Weird thing to say, but I wasn't really in the mood for much anyway.

'Shall we have a drink before we go out and explore the city?' Eddie proposed.

'I'd love one,' I said. 'Also, if I could find a plug to charge my phone?'

'Yeah, absolutely. There's one right next to the sofa,' said Jimmy.

'What would you like to drink, Leo? We have beer, cider, wine, and a bottle of scotch,' Eddie said while scouting the inside of the massive grey fridge.

'Scotch is fine.'

'Oh, a scotch man. That's sexy,' he said, while taking the bottle out and pouring it into glasses.

'I think I'll just have a cider,' said Jimmy.

The scotch tasted beautifully bitter. It warmed my whole body with just one sip. I could relax for a second. Forget the shit storm that was happening back home.

'How was your flight?' Jimmy asked, while putting his hand on my thigh.

'It was alright. I had plenty of fun being in a row by myself.'

'That's always the best,' Eddie said. 'Where are you based in London?'

'Streatham, but I may be moving out soon.'

'How come?' Jimmy asked.

'Well, my flatmate is planning to move to New York, so he wants to sell the flat. He still has time, but it's something I am going to have to deal with at some point.'

'Is he letting you stay until he sells it?' Jimmy asked.

'Yeah, he still needs to work through his notice period, but he's travelling there often for the time being.'

'Good for him!' Eddie said, while raising a glass. 'I love New York.'

'I have never been,' I confessed.

'Maybe we can go for a longer holiday,' Jimmy said, while putting his arm around me.

'Yeah, maybe,' I said, while smiling at him. 'So, what's the plan for this holiday?'

'Well, we are going to the city centre to see the big square and have a look around,' said Jimmy.

'...and then in the evening, we must go out,' Eddie quickly interrupted.

'The whole reason we are here is for Eddie to go crazy with some boys,' Jimmy explained.

'Yeah, I get to do what I want on holiday,' he said, giggling.

'He has a boyfriend back at home, so this is his way to get loose.'

'Fair enough,' I said. 'Sounds good. I could do with a good night out.'

'Clubs here are really fucking cool,' Eddie said. 'Nothing like the clubs in England. Guys are hotter too.'

I was into it. I'd use the trip as a goodbye to this part of my life. I would take Jimmy's money and delete all those dangerous apps that had become such a huge part of my existence.

'Eddie and I were planning to get some groceries for the flat, in case we get hungry at random hours. Would you like to come with, or do you maybe want to take a power nap?'

'A nap sounds great actually, if you don't mind? I'll be far more energetic later.'

'Sure, I'll try to find some vegan stuff for you to eat. We are in the land of sausages and beer, so hopefully you'll be able not to starve,' Jimmy said, while slightly laughing.

'Thank you,' I said, yawning.

'See you later.' He kissed me on the lips.

I went into the bedroom and threw myself onto the mattress. The room was quite basic. High ceilings, with a long door leading to a balcony. The duvet was soft and thick. I took off my jumper and jeans and got under it. I was knackered.

I'd call Sara after my sleep.

I had to.

———•———————•———————•———

I wasn't sure how much I had slept, but it was enough for me to wake up and not understand where I was or what fucking year it was. That was usually what would happen to me when I'd take an afternoon nap.

I got woken up by Jimmy sucking my dick under the covers. I wasn't sure how I felt about it, as he had definitely started while I was sleeping, but I guess there could be worse ways to be woken.

I wasn't exactly in the mood. My cock was hard, though, so maybe my bottom half was feeling it.

'I have missed this,' he said.

I didn't miss that at all. I would have loved to sleep for another hour, if anything.

'Can I sit on it?' he asked.

'Sure,' I said.

I had little to no intention of interacting much with it. I'd let him do the work.

He quickly managed to fit my entire dong inside him. I wasn't sure if he was pre-lubed, but I was certainly impressed. He was warm, smooth. His eyes were glowing. His head was tilted backwards, and he was thrusting his waist, to really give me pleasure.

He was going fast; he just wanted me to come inside him.

'I love your big cock,' he said.

'He loves you too,' I said, giving him a smirk.

He went faster and faster, until I could no longer hold it.

I didn't even warn him, I just grabbed him by his waist and shot my load deep inside him. I even lifted him with my own pelvis, I was that relieved.

He kept me inside him for a bit.

'I'll never get tired of this,' he said, with his whole body dripping with sweat.

I was fully awake then.

'Are you guys ready?' Eddie said, opening the door to the bedroom. 'Oh, you fucking?'

I was mortified.

'Just finished, actually.' Jimmy got my cock out of his hole and walked out of the bedroom, butt-naked, towards Eddie who spanked him as soon as he walked past.

Weird dynamic.

'I am just going to take a shower and then I'll be ready,' I said to Eddie.

'Cool. Feel free to walk naked too!' he said, with a cheeky look.

'Imma need a few more drinks, Eddie.'

'Oh, don't worry. There will be.'

He left the room, and I put a pillow on my face.

I was hungry.

I needed to get my arse moving.

———•———————•———————•———

The city looked stunning. Sun rays were shining through the clouds, making a mix of dark and cyan sky. It reflected perfectly onto the gothic architecture of Prague. Buildings had black details, and Wenceslas Square was beaming with tourists taking photos at every corner. I was eating a plain pretzel, while Eddie and Jimmy were munching on sausages. I also got used to the temperature. My hands felt frozen, but I was able to regulate myself in the cold, kind of like Squall would do in the middle of winter. My baby.

We walked and walked. It was truly spectacular. I looked around myself, reminiscing about the times I'd go travelling with Jake and we would spend our time bickering. I made myself so small for so long...I had gone on holiday with Sara once, and she'd want to stop every ten minutes for a drink. I'd be wasted by the time we'd reach our initial destination, if we ever managed to get there.

Eddie had already been to Prague. It was his favourite city to have a lost weekend. I hadn't even checked my Grindr yet. I didn't know what kind of guys would be interested in me here. Perhaps it would be like Sofia, where I got bombarded with messages by horny, muscly, handsome men.

'So where are we going this evening, Eddie?' I asked.

'There's a really cool place called Max. It's got bright lights and lots of people go there.'

'I can see you've done your research,' I said.

'Oh, I always go there. They are open til late too,' he said while raising both of his eyebrows.

'Eddie has pretty much the whole of Europe mapped out with the places he likes to perv on guys,' Jimmy explained.

'That's handy!' I exclaimed.

'What about you, Leo? Do you have a boyfriend back at home you leave alone to have fun with Jimmy?'

I wanted to. I wished I had my shit together enough to have a boyfriend. Single life was sucking major arse recently.

'No,' I said. 'I am completely at Jimmy's disposal.' I looked at him and ran my hand through his hair.

'That's promising!' Jimmy said, giving me a wink.

I smiled a little. I walked through a few breath-taking bridges looking onto the Vltava River. The city truly felt like a fairy-tale setting. I was just with the wrong people to experience it.

'Did you guys have enough time to see the city? Because I could really do with going back to the flat and doing a few drinks and other stuff,' Eddie said, making a 'smoking' gesture.

'Oh, is it that kind of evening?' I asked.

'You okay with it?' asked Jimmy, while brushing his hand gently on my back.

'Yeah, of course,' I said. 'It's our fun weekend after all.'

'Amazing, because I really want to get fucked this evening. Literally,' said Eddie, while dancing and walking.

I wondered how my liver was doing.

———•———————•———————•———

We left the flat quite late. It was around eleven and the roads were booming with life. I, of course, didn't pack any clothing particularly club appropriate, as I didn't actually own any. I was wearing a tight t-shirt that would give the illusion of bigger triceps. Jimmy was wearing his usual attire: a short-sleeved polo and slim grey jeans. Eddie, however, was rave-ready. He was wearing a bright neon green string vest under a black coat. It looked fine on him; he was really skinny, like a grown-up twink. He was trotting around, flushed from drunkenness, singing, pirouetting and being a tit. Jimmy seemed much more of an introvert, so it made sense for him to surround himself with people that would pull him out of his shell. It explained why he was friends with Nicolas or Eddie. Both huge personalities, both slags.

We reached the club after a five-minute walk. It seemed like the Airbnb was booked based on the club distance alone. I removed my jacket and gave it to the cloakroom attendant. Cheap as fuck.

'What are we drinking?' Eddie shouted, over the loud music.

'Double whiskey and Coke for me,' Jimmy ordered.

'I'll have the same,' I said. 'Thanks.'

The club was very fun. Eddie wasn't lying, there were neon signs all over the place. If it wasn't such a sketchy place, I would have deemed it as pretty Instagrammable.

'Here we go,' said Eddie with our drinks. Then he was served nine shots of Jägermeister.

'What the hell are those?' Jimmy said, giggling.

'Pure fun,' Eddie said. 'Come on. Just do three in a row and then have your cocktail.'

I wasn't thrilled. I couldn't exactly do shots. The idea was making me want to throw up already.

I couldn't. I had to pursue this image of "cool guy". So, I did. One down, two down and the third may have come back up slightly, but eventually went down. All washed up with the whiskey and Coke. I felt like I had reached alcohol capacity within minutes of being at Max.

We moved on to the dance floor, where we really had fun dancing with each other. The music was dated, European, but hilarious. It was so loud I couldn't hear anything else, or think for that matter. Then I needed the loo. All that drinking was bound to come out at some point.

I told Jimmy, who decided to follow me. Eddie kept on dancing with strangers.

The toilets were very dark. It would be the last place you'd want to wipe your arse at. Luckily, I only needed a long piss, so I opted for the urinals.

They were packed with men. It was just one of those long ones, where you'd touch legs with your fellow pissers. It was a gay club, so no one minded.

I finally found myself a spot, and I immediately went in. I could barely hold it anymore. Jimmy managed to get himself next to me although he wasn't interested in relieving himself. He was just there to watch my penis do its thing. I couldn't entertain him until I was absolutely done with the stream of urine coming out of me. I really couldn't deal with an erection there and then. As soon as I was done, he started touching it, stroking it gently to make it hard. He went down and sucked it, like a feeding bottle. No one around us minded. In fact many of them just plain stared at us and wanked themselves. It was hot, in a dirty, porn-scenario kind of way.

When more people started queueing to use the urinals, I pulled my trousers back up. I didn't want to put myself between those poor queens and their piss relief.

Jimmy stood back up and we left the area.

'Come with me,' he said, holding my hand.

I wasn't sure what he wanted me to see, but we went through a very dark corridor with only a small source of light, where there were a few guys having a circle jerk.

'What's this?' I asked.

'Look!' he said while pointing at the light.

It was a glass panel where you could see men peeing or sucking each other off. Turns out, that was the other side of the urinal. People in the toilet couldn't see behind as it was dark glass. Eddie was there with the other guys, with his cock out.

'Hello,' Jimmy said.

Eddie continued, completely unbothered by the fact we were there.

'You guys just missed someone getting his dick sucked off,' he said, enthusiastically.

'I think that was us,' I said.

'Oh, nice cock, then!' he said while looking at my crotch area.

'What are you doing?' I asked.

'I'm into watching guys piss. It's hot.'

Jimmy grabbed Eddie's cock for a little rub. Weird friendship, I thought, but we were all pretty wasted.

Eddie put everything back in his jeans and walked away.

'Let's have a browse,' he said.

We followed him through more dark places. The club had a lot more to offer than a dance floor and a bar. Room after room of guys fucking each other, rooms with swings, rooms with mirrors and a dark labyrinth. We walked into a small corner one. The light was scarce, and we could barely see each other.

Jimmy quickly pulled my jeans and pants down to my ankles. He started sucking my cock, making it drip with saliva. Eddie, in the meantime, was behind me with his hands inside my t-shirt, touching my chest and nipples. He started kissing my neck, and then turned my face towards him, so we could make out.

Jimmy was sucking hard on my dick, while grabbing Eddie's arse behind me. Then he stood up, unzipped his trousers, pulled them down and rubbed his arse cheeks on me. He was begging me to fuck him, in front of Eddie.

I obliged and quickly made my way inside him. I grabbed him by his waist and fucked him hard, with my balls slapping his skin. Eddie was watching, touching himself. He'd touch our bodies and walk around us. He'd talk dirty; he'd entice me to fuck Jimmy harder and harder. Then he decided he wanted to take part in the action. He lubricated his cock and tried to put it inside me. I wasn't sure I wanted him to do that. I wasn't sure he had a condom on. I was uncomfortable. The fumes of alcohol were clouding my judgement, though, so after a few minutes, Eddie was inside me, while I was still pounding Jimmy. We were all sweating on each other; I could feel Eddie's warm breath on my neck.

But it wouldn't last long. I didn't want Eddie's spunk in me. Lord knows where that cock had been.

'I'll be right back,' I said, pulling myself out of the situation.

'We'll wait here,' Eddie said, giving me a pat on my

arse.

I walked out and got into the accessible toilet. The only one which could be locked. I washed my face with cold water and looked at myself in the mirror. I was incredibly drunk, and I wasn't too sure I was having fun. I kept thinking about poor Sven at the hospital. I should have been there. My hands and legs were shaking at the thought he could die from a heart attack. I wouldn't have been able to ever forgive myself.

I dried my face with a paper towel and walked back to the guys. I was feeling a bit dizzy from the heat and the darkness, but I found them eventually. Jimmy was sucking Eddie off. I guess he trusted him more than I did.

'Welcome back!' Eddie said. 'Want to put your mouth on it too? Please?'

I didn't really want to, so I just pushed Jimmy's head harder, while I bit Eddie's bottom lip.

They were surrounded by two other guys pleasuring themselves watching us. That's when Jimmy stopped with Eddie and started sucking one of those guys, while the other was preparing Jimmy's arse to get fucked once again.

I watched them while Eddie was jerking me off and licking my neck.

All of a sudden Jimmy was being fucked raw and the other guy was about to cum into his mouth.

Jimmy didn't know these people. He just gave them his arse. Just like that. How many guys would get to dump their semen into him?

I felt sick to my stomach.

'I'm heading out,' I said to Jimmy.

I put my clothes back on and left the room. I had made it to the cloakroom, and I was being handed my jacket when Jimmy ran to me.

'What's going on?' he asked.

'I just had enough. I need to leave.'

'Okay, I'll go with you.'

'What about Eddie?'

'Oh, he's going to stay here for a while.'

'Cool,' I said, while making my way to the exit.

The outside freezing air slapping my skin was the perfect sobering method I needed. My blood was rushing through my veins. I was shaking with rage. Part of me couldn't find words.

How could I have been so fucking stupid? How could I have dropped the ball so damn hard?

Fuck that evening.

'Are you sure everything is alright?' Jimmy asked, while trying to catch up with my fast pace.

I couldn't look at him. But I needed to ask.

'Is this something you do often?'

'What?'

'Getting fucked bare by whomever.'

'No, of course not.'

I started raising my voice. I could barely control myself.

'So, was today a special occasion? You're meaning to tell me that between our meetings, you swear you wear a condom with everyone?'

'Well...'

I suddenly stopped. I still couldn't look at him.

'How can you be so sure you're clean, if this is what you do?'

'Okay, I didn't know how to tell you...'

'Tell me what, Jimmy?'

Anxiety was taking over my whole body. All of a sudden, my heartbeat was screaming into my ears. I was terrified. I didn't want him to tell me.

'I am HIV positive.'

'You are what?'

Tears started streaming down my cheeks. I couldn't breathe.

'I am sorry I didn't say anything.'

'You fucking piece of shit!' I shouted.

'Wait, wait. Let me explain, please.'

'I asked you.' My voice was loud, but stern. I looked at him straight into his pitiful eyes. 'I asked you, point blank. I asked you if you were clean, and what did you say to me?'

'I'm sorry.'

'You fucking said yes. Between the three times we saw each other we had unprotected sex over thirty times. You didn't think you maybe needed to tell me after Paris? You could have said, '*Sorry I couldn't tell you before, but please go to a clinic and get PEP.*' But no. You lied straight to my face and told me you were clean.'

'Look, it's not how you think. I am on medication.'

I started walking again towards the flat.

'Do you know how stupid I feel now? Trusting you? I'm a fucking idiot! Is this your thing? You pay guys to convert them so that you don't feel so alone?'

'No.'

'Then what is it, Jimmy?'

'I'm undetectable; I take my medication every day.'

'And I am supposed to trust you on that because…?'

'It would be stupid for me not to do it. I'd feel ill.'

'How do I know you're not lying to me right now? Is Eddie's status disclosed, or should I have this conversation with him as well?'

'He is also positive.'

I couldn't believe what I was hearing. I put my hands on my head. Everything was so confusing. I felt dizzy, lost and furious. I wanted to scream, cry, punch someone in the face. I turned around and put my hand around his neck. I had learnt how to press hard, having experience with all these dickheads in my life.

'Leo, stop.'

'You allowed your fucking moron of a friend to fuck me and you didn't think of warning me?'

'I was really drunk; I wasn't sure what was happening. We were having fun!'

I pushed him. I pushed him hard enough to make him fall on his arse.

'You have ruined my life. And what really fucking sucks, is that I have no one to blame but myself.'

'Leo, look. People with HIV live a normal life. It's far safer for you to have unprotected sex with someone on medication than it is for you to have sex with someone who's unsure on their status.'

'I can't believe what I'm hearing.'

Jimmy got back up. I wanted to spit on his face, but I

knew he'd probably enjoy it.

'My best friend's father is at the hospital fighting for his life and I couldn't be there for her. I came on this fucking trip thinking the money I'd get to spend to have fun with her would make it all better. I fucked up so badly.'

I started crying. My emotions were taking over; the alcohol was leaving my body and all I could feel was sadness and anger.

'I really want you to document yourself, Leo. I am serious.'

My whole face hardened. I was grinding my teeth.

'Honestly, we can talk at home; I can tell you my experience. I also reacted badly when I first found out. It's normal, but in some ways, I get to live better now, because I know I already have it. It's almost liberating.'

I couldn't hold it anymore. I punched him as hard as I could in his stupid whiny face. He fell, once again.

I had never hit anyone. My fist was in incredible pain. I clutched my hand under my armpit. It hurt so much. My whole body was shaking, and I could barely speak.

'Here's what's going to happen. You're going to give me my money, and you're going to book me on the next flight to London. Book a fucking car, so I can leave right away and wait at the airport until it's time for me to fucking leave.'

'I can do that.'

'Then I'll get tested, and I swear to god, if you gave me HIV, I'll take your stupid fucking face to court and get your arse served.'

'Okay, but really,' he tapped his lip with his shirt, to

dab the blood. 'I am pretty confident you will be fine.'

'After that, I never want to see you or hear from you ever again. Is that clear?'

'Leo, I am really sorry.'

'I can't even look at you. How could you? Fuck. Fuck! Who does that?!'

He started crying and sobbing.

'Whenever I have been upfront, people can be horrible. They judge you; they think you don't matter, that you're diseased. You didn't look at me like that.'

'Jimmy, find me a flight. I don't want to hear your life story. I don't give a fuck, frankly.'

'Leo, please. Once you get to London, do some research. You'll discover I am right. You have nothing to worry about.'

'You know what? I have to take meds every single fucking day and I haven't done so since I went to Paris with you. I know how easy it is to forget. I am not going to trust you or your fucking dickhead friend. You fucked up. We are done.'

We walked back to the flat in silence.

I threw my things in my bag. I dried my tears.

'Why don't you sleep here tonight?' he asked.

I looked at him as if he was completely insane. Sleeping there? With him? Deluded fucker.

'Is my car downstairs?'

'Yeah. Here's your money as well.' He gently put the notes on a table.

I grabbed them immediately and just gave him a look of despise.

'Please let me know if you land and get home safe.'

'Go to hell, Jimmy.'

I walked out and slammed the door behind me. I started crying again.

I was fucked.

My life was fucked.

CHAPTER 21

£2987.84

COULDN'T SHUT MY BRAIN UP. I couldn't stop thinking where I could have prevented this situation. I couldn't stop thinking about how stupid I had been. I couldn't blame anyone other than myself. I was staring at the window of my seat. I was in business class. Remorse is a bitch. He had even given me more money than promised. What would my life with HIV be like? How many people would I need to call, to prompt them to get tested? How would I tell my friends? I felt like my heart had been stabbed with a thousand needles.

I was the only person on the plane chugging straight bourbon at such an early hour of the day. I couldn't eat. I hadn't eaten in over twelve hours and I didn't care. I hadn't slept at all during my wait at the airport or during the flight. My anger was keeping me awake.

I was going to live with the disease for the rest of my

already miserable life. I was thankful for not having slept with Duncan.

Imagine that. Imagine having to tell the sweetest guy in the world that I had fucked up so badly. That I was so fucked up.

I wanted a hot shower. Boiling, even. I'd get home, get changed and immediately go to see Sara. I could bet she was mad. Angry at me for not being there, when she had always been there for me. Every single time I needed support.

I didn't deserve her.

I was no best man. I was the worst man.

The plane started its descent into London. For the first time I wasn't nervous about turbulence or the plane making sudden movements. I couldn't care less if we crashed.

I had hit rock bottom.

The flat felt different. There was a coldness to it. Flat boxes were scattered around the rooms. Andrew wasn't home. I couldn't even remember if he was in the country. That's how little I had paid attention to other people around me. I put down my weekender bag. I felt weak.

I dragged my feet towards the bathroom and opened the shower tap. I wanted it to be boiling. I hadn't slept all night, so I felt exhausted, but incapable to rest. I took off my clothes. I had every intention to throw them away. I didn't need any more reminders of what had happened in Prague.

I felt dirty.

I put my naked body under the running water. I put my head under it. I had a headache. I felt feverish. I put my face under the burning water. Images of the night before kept flashing through my mind. Would things have been different if I hadn't gone there? I would have been with Sara straight away; I could have picked up the pieces. I could have been the friend she thought I was.

Instead I was out and about, testing my luck.

It took me twenty minutes to leave the shower. The bathroom was engulfed in steam. I couldn't see anything. I wrapped myself in a bath towel and left the room. I was cold; my hair was still dripping onto my shoulders. I'd shiver at each drop. My eyes were about to burst into tears.

The thought alone of going to the hospital and getting tested scared the hell out of me. Reading those pamphlets in the waiting room, the ones that would tell you how much easier life with HIV was now, compared to fifty years prior. There would be happy, empowered gays telling you how they do it. There would be information on the kind of meds you'd have to take for the rest of your life. They'd never tell you you'd get to live for as long as a person that didn't have the virus. They'd say, 'a fairly long life.' Whatever that meant.

My father didn't live a long life.

I didn't bother drying my hair properly, so I just put a beanie on. I put on a white shirt and a pair of slim trousers. I didn't care about looking good. I just wanted to see her.

Apologise to her.

I was sitting in the back of a car taking me to St. Pancras Hospital. I had a bunch of flowers in my hand. I wasn't even sure if that would be an appropriate gift for a sick man. I didn't know. I never visited anyone at the hospital. We were nearly there.

I was trying to think of what to say to her. I needed to tell her the truth. I needed to stop hiding stuff from people.

I got out of the car and walked through the hospital's main entrance. My pace was slow. I wanted to drag the walk. I walked towards reception. There was a bubbly woman who called me 'darling.' I asked her where they'd keep a man who had a heart attack the day before. It wasn't too far from where I was.

I walked towards cardiology. The hospital was clean, cyan walls and yellow accents. There were signs everywhere; they made it difficult for you to get lost. The hospital smell was harsh, sterile. I had goose bumps just being there. I was terrified of doctors, needles and everything that happened within those walls.

I still remember those times when my dad would take me to the hospital to beg for used needles and would leave me sitting in the waiting room for what felt like hours.

Then a familiar face appeared, as smooth as a child's with eyes that hadn't seen sleep for quite a few hours. Alfie yawned his way to me.

'Hey,' I said. 'Where is she? What's been going on?'

'She is very upset. I just left her, as I have to go to work, but she's in the waiting room with her mum and sister.'

'Where is it?'

'Just straight down there,' he said while pointing at

the corridor behind him. 'You can't miss it.'

'Okay, thank you.'

'Please make sure she eats something. I don't want her to pass out.'

'Will do, thanks.'

We gave each other a hug, and I watched him until he disappeared behind the door.

I turned around and made my way to the waiting room. My heart was beating so fast, I was glad I was in cardiology. I wondered if anxiety could cause me to have a heart attack.

God, I wished.

I opened a set of doors and she was there, on her phone. Probably trying to read a book. She was by herself, wearing tight sweatpants and a hoodie. Not an ounce of make-up and hair tied up in a messy bun.

'Hey,' I said.

She lifted her eyes up from her phone and gave me a look. She was surprised to see me, although in a somewhat angry way.

'Where have you been?'

'I am so sorry.'

'Leo, I honestly can't deal with you right now.'

The way she said my name sounded like a blade. A scalpel thrown and shoved into my chest.

'I was out of town, and I couldn't be on the phone, but I came as soon as I could.'

'Really?'

'Absolutely.'

'So, where did you go?' she said, while putting her phone down and standing up in front of me with crossed arms.

'It's a long story and I don't think this is the place to—'

'I have been here all night. You'd be surprised by how much time I have to listen to your bullshit excuses.'

'I was away, with a guy.'

'A guy?'

'Yeah,' I said, while trying to look anywhere but her eyes. Her sad, angry, giant eyes. 'I have been really stupid.'

'So, this is what you've been up to? Fucking off away with 'guys'? Is that why you've been so odd for the last couple of months?'

'What do you mean 'odd'?'

'Oh, I don't know. The fact you never reply to calls or texts anymore, or the fact you were fucked on drugs on New Year's Eve and passed out?'

'Maybe.'

'Who even are these guys?'

'I don't really want to have this conversation here.'

'Then leave. I don't need you. I can't fix you right now,' she said with near crying eyes.

'I don't need fixing. I am here for you.'

'You're here for me? What are you exactly doing for me? Am I wrong to think you're here only because you realised how shit you've been? Has your 'hyper' mode run out?'

'What are you talking about?'

'Leo, have you been taking your meds?'

'I...'

I wasn't.

'Is it possible you've stopped all of a sudden, let's say, four months ago? And you've been going through yet another long episode of mania and doing all kinds of stupid irresponsible shit?'

'Gaslighting? Seriously?'

'Am I wrong?'

'I don't know,' I said. Suddenly I realised what was really happening within me.

'I can't believe you.'

'Jesus Christ, Sara. Maybe, just maybe I have been busy trying to make money to be able to attend your ridiculous events that cost a fucking fortune!'

'What are you even talking about?'

'I had to have sex for money, so that I could pay for the fucking Ibiza trip, or get to fucking Greece for your goddamn wedding!'

'That's what you did?! What the hell, Leo? Are you out of your mind? Who even were these people?'

I was getting angry. I was tired, and I was upset. I could barely control my words.

'Fucking rich men who had money to throw away. Kind of like you and everyone fucking around me. You have no idea of the things I had to do. No fucking clue.'

'Are you blaming me for your poor money management and the fact that your mind goes to 'prostitute' before doing, I don't know, a fucking normal weekend job? Or, since you've been telling me about it for years, a fucking writing job?'

'I am not like you. I don't have opportunities falling onto my doorstep.'

'Oh, fuck off. You haven't written in nearly a decade. Don't give me that shit. You stopped taking your meds, because you most likely enjoyed what you were doing and now it has finally bitten you in the ass!'

'You have no idea what you're talking about. You're so wrapped up in your own world that you can't even imagine or relate to how someone who wasn't born with a mother fucking silver spoon in their mouth feels on a daily basis. You go around parading all the free things you get through your job and all the shit you buy with your parents' money and all your friends do the fucking same.'

'You're walking on mighty thin ice.'

'I feel so stupid. I did all this for you. I should have known.'

'You didn't do this for me. You did it because it felt good. That's why you haven't gone to therapy. You were 'fixed,' but you weren't. You were just replacing therapy with sex and alcohol. As you always fucking do.'

'I did it so I could catch up with you all! I don't know how many times I have to repeat I cannot afford to live your fucking lifestyle.'

'Then grow a pair and speak up.' Her voice was getting higher and higher. 'I am so fucking tired of picking you up. You don't care about anyone other than yourself. All you've done this past year is blame Jake and money for every single problem you've had. You had a part in that breakup. You had a part in choosing the stupidest way for you to make money and you had a fucking part when you decided to forgo therapy. Go home, Leo. I don't want to see you.'

'Fine. You won't see me at your hen do either.'

'Good fucking riddance. I'll get your money back. I wouldn't want you to go in the streets and jump into a stranger's car to make up the loss.'

'Keep it,' I said, while leaving.

'Don't come to the wedding either while you're at it!' she shouted.

I took a deep breath and kept walking.

Tears were streaming down my face.

CHAPTER 22

£3233.78

W HEN BAD THINGS HAPPENED IN MY LIFE, they happened all at once. Like an avalanche of steaming shit covering my whole body. I felt like I was standing still, and the whole world around me was running at the speed of light. I wasn't sure what to do with my life. I had lost everything.

For once in my existence, I had cash at my disposal in my bank account and it didn't make me happy. I didn't know what to do with it. It was stained. I lost myself while trying to earn it, and for what? Being shouted at? Being given HIV? Being left alone?

I was sitting at work. I wasn't in the managers' office. I was sitting in a private room in Human Resources. I thought people had noticed that I wasn't feeling well, and maybe they were taking steps to support me in the struggle. Katherine walked in, along with an HR representative, ready to take notes. This wasn't a support meeting. This was trouble.

I didn't care anymore.

'Hello, Leo. Thanks for coming in,' Paula from HR said.

Katherine wasn't even looking at me. I was also staring at nothing.

'This is only a preliminary informal meeting,' she added.

I had no idea where this was going. It wasn't informal. She was writing notes. What had happened?

'Could you retell the events that happened on the 31st of December?' Katherine asked.

Then I knew. 'We have reason to believe...' echoed through my ears. I wasn't sure who was talking. I wasn't sure how long I was there for.

A customer had seen me going inside a fitting room and leaving with a suit on.

A customer.

I thought I had hit my all-time low but being blasted for shop lifting was rock-bottom. Again, something that was completely my fault.

It had to be Marc.

Marc was the fucking snake who meddled in crap that didn't concern him.

Of course.

It wasn't enough to take my husband, my flat, my dog, my best friend and even the guy I thought I could be with. He had to take my job away too.

I was escorted outside the building by security. The same guy I had looked straight in the face and lied to. I was suspended for a month.

I was going to miss Dominic's last day at work, and I'd have all the time in the world to revel in my own fucked up mistakes at home. Alone.

As soon as I stepped outside, I got caught in the worst rainstorm I had ever experienced. Typical.

I grabbed two bottles of bourbon on my way home. That's all I could do. I deleted all hook-up apps from my phone, all social media. I had no friends. I just wanted to get in bed and sleep all day.

That's exactly what I ended up doing for the following two days.

I was wrapped in my duvet, lying on my side, staring at the wall in my room. I heard a knock. Andrew walked in.

'Hey,' he said in a worried voice. 'I came as soon as possible. How are you?'

I couldn't respond. My eyes were just an unstoppable flow of tears. I didn't have the strength to get up, eat, shower or anything at all. I just wanted to be left alone, with my thoughts. I longed for my pills, the ones that would put me to sleep. I didn't want to see Doctor Grey, though. I'd have to admit how much I had fucked up. She'd judge me. Everyone judged me.

Andrew knelt next to me and caressed my hair, most likely greasy and disgusting.

'I heard about work, and Sara,' he said. 'I'm sorry.'

'I messed up so badly, Andrew.'

'It's okay. I'm here.'

'...for now.'

'For as long as it's needed. I'll go get some food.'

'I'm not hungry.'

'Well, make yourself hungry, because you're eating soon.'

'Don't bother.'

'I'm serious, Leo.'

'Don't bother with me. I'll just go to sleep,' I said, while putting the duvet over my head.

———•——————————●——————————•———

Eventually, I managed to get up. I had to wait for Jake to come over. He'd bring Squall for me to look after, while he'd fuck off to Japan with Satan's spawn himself. One more thing he had taken from me. I didn't care anymore. I didn't care about Japan. I didn't care about Marc opening his big whore mouth and making me lose my job.

I wasn't sure if I wanted Squall with me. He was an energetic dog, and that meant taking him outside for walks. I hadn't been outside in days. I hadn't been in contact with anyone in days.

———•——————————●——————————•———

I was glad I had deleted all social media. I probably wouldn't have been able to handle seeing Jake going to all the places I had imagined seeing with him or seeing how Sara's posse would be having the greatest time at her hen do.

Squall knew I was depressed. He only required a short walk per day. He didn't hold that against me. I was grateful. I could tell he understood. As soon as I'd start crying, he'd try to get me up. He'd lick me; he'd give me small bites.

I talked to him sometimes. I told him what a great friend he had been to me. I told him it wasn't his fault things between Jake and I didn't work. I told him I never intended to abandon him. I ran my hand through his thick fur and gave him cuddles.

I grabbed my laptop. I needed to look for a new job. There was no way I'd be able to go back to my old one. Once the suspension would be over, I'd be sacked, and I'd be sitting on the pavement, begging for attention and pennies.

It's what I'd do best, clearly.

I opened a few websites. I had no strength. I couldn't write a convincing cover letter. I couldn't convince anyone to give me a chance. I looked a wreck and felt even worse. Imagine that at a job interview.

Instead I opened Word. I needed to channel the darkness I was feeling inside. And words started writing themselves.

Once upon a time, there was a village where all its inhabitants lived happily and in harmony with each other. The villagers worked together and would sing happy songs all day, every day. No one would ever cry, because their hearts were stored safely inside them, and there was no way anyone could get their hands on them.

But there was one boy living at the edge of the village. His heart was not inside him. He'd have to hold it with his hands, exposing it to the outside elements. The boy was not like the other villagers. He wouldn't sing happy songs or become friends with the others. The boy had two entities inside him that would fight constantly to take control of his heart. One entity was called Blue, and if it took over the boy's heart, he'd be sad all the time. The other entity was called Red, and if it took over the boy's heart, he'd get to have energy all the time, but he'd be completely uncontrollable. The boy would stay indoors, as he didn't want the other villagers to notice he wasn't like them. He didn't want Blue or Red to control him. He just wanted to have his heart inside him, like everyone else.

So, he embarked on a quest to meet a wizard who could help him make Red and Blue work together, so he too could be as happy as the rest of the villagers.

The wizard, however, wouldn't be cheap, and he required a payment. The little boy didn't have any gold coins on him.

'What can I do?' he asked, desperately.

The wizard pointed him to the next village over, where people didn't have hearts, but they each owned plenty of gold.

So the little boy walked and walked, with his heart in his hands, fighting Blue's urge to go back and stay in bed, and Red's voice who'd tell him to run and steal all the gold from the villagers.

After an arduous walk, the boy found himself in the village, but he noticed that no one was as happy as the villagers he knew growing up. They looked malicious.

One of them came over to the boy and offered him gold for a small piece of his heart.

The boy agreed and received a few coins for a piece of his heart. More and more evil villagers found out about *the heart and took pieces for themselves and filled the boy's pockets with gold.*

'Brilliant!' Red thought. 'We will be rich, and we will be kings of our village!'

Blue's voice was faint, as it suffered greatly from the boy's heart being taken piece by piece.

The boy was weaker, but he didn't realise because Red's voice urged him to continue. Red's voice would tell him this was the right thing to do. It told the boy he didn't need to rest, he needed to keep walking and find more gold. The boy started becoming Red, and he was filled with energy. He could even run, run as fast as possible. He wanted to go to the next village over to see if there was more gold to be had, even though the boy had enough to get back to the wizard and finally be able to have his heart inside, like everyone else.

But one day the boy found himself in a forest just outside the village. Alone once more, with little to no heart left to give. Blue was able to speak again, in the quietness of the woods. 'You need to go back and rest. No one wants that little heart you have left. Let's go back to bed.'

The boy started becoming Blue, as he had no more strength to go on, or to go back to the wizard. So, he sat under a tree and started crying. Nothing could console him, and Red's voice became fainter and fainter.

I never pictured myself as a writer of a children's book. There was no way I could relive the filthy and disgusting acts I had to do in the previous months. I felt like the little boy. I was sitting under the tree by myself, crying, with nowhere to go. Squall was sitting next to me on the sofa. His head was close to me. I could feel his warmth. I wondered how Sara was. I wondered if her dad started feeling better. I wondered if we'd ever be friends again.

I wondered if she'd go on her trip in Ibiza and have an amazing time without me.

Of course, she would. I wondered how better her life had become without me to constantly worry about. The tiny fragment of heart I had left within me was in pain.

As cheesy as that sounded.

I eventually ran out of booze, so I had to go to the nearest off-licence to stock up. I left Squall at home with Andrew. He had a day off. In a different reality and timeline, he would have taken me to the airport to have an incredible time with Sara and the others. Instead, I was carrying two bottles of wine in a paper bag, about to grab my keys and open the front door, when a voice got my attention.

'Hey.'

I turned around as fast as I could. She was standing next to a car with the engine still on.

'What are you doing here?' I asked.

'Get in the car,' Sara said, coldly.

I couldn't quite figure out what was happening.

I obliged. I got into the car without asking any questions.

Maybe she wanted to kill me. Hopefully.

CHAPTER 23

£3013.29

'How's your dad?' I asked.

She hesitated to answer, as if we were no longer used to speaking to each other.

'He is better. He's still recovering, but he got to go home. So we all look after him now.'

'Oh, that's amazing.'

'Yeah.'

The silence that followed felt like it lasted forever. I couldn't recognise where we were going. The driver was quiet as well. It was the middle of the afternoon and raindrops started hitting the windshield. No music was playing; all I could hear was my own heartbeat going crazy and my own breathing, which felt shallow. I hadn't drunk enough that day, and I was wishing I did. I wasn't ready for a round two with Sara. Mostly because that whole time we didn't speak, all I felt was guilt. I wasn't angry at her. I never was.

Maybe we were going to the airport.

I wasn't in the mood for a party or showered enough.

'Where are we going?' I asked, all of a sudden.

'We are nearly there,' she said, with a small, blink-and-you'll-miss-it hint of a smile.

We parked by a building I had never been to before. It sort of looked like a school, but there were no children screaming or having fun.

We got out of the car and the driver went his way.

'I'm confused,' I said. 'Am I seeing people? Because I look disgusting.'

'You'll be fine, come with me.'

I followed her inside the building. It felt like there was no one inside. I felt like a video game character thrown into a haunted place. Sara knew where she was going; her pace was quick, while I could barely keep up. We got into a classroom of sorts. People were sitting in a circle. They were already talking to each other but stopped as soon as they saw us.

'Hi!' Sara said.

'Did you take me to the AA?!' I asked.

'No, you stupid. But along those lines.'

She grabbed a seat and invited me to do the same next to her.

'Welcome!' A big, bald, black guy with a folder in his hand smiled at us.

He looked like he was running the thing.

People around us of all ages were staring at us. My whole body was shaking. I was not one to do well in group situations.

'My name is Robert. Nice for you to join us,' he said while looking at Sara. 'Would you like to introduce yourselves?'

'Sure.' She stood up. 'My name is Sara, and this is Leo.'

'Hello to you. We have already spoken via e-mail but allow me to explain what we do. All the people around you suffer from mental illness or are close to someone that does. It's a safe space. We speak to each other and get to discuss ways of making our lives better, by getting to know everyone's everyday realities.'

I gave Sara a terrorised face.

'You are not under any obligation to share anything. You're more than free to sit and listen or leave whenever you please. But we are here for you.'

'I'd like to share something,' Sara said, while raising her hand.

What was she up to?

'Sure, go ahead,' Robert said, with a big smile on his face.

The room was cold, badly heated. It smelled of school. Really took me back. People around us looked normal. I wondered what their lives were like, if any of them felt like me. I wondered if they'd run away if they knew what I had done.

'I don't struggle with mental health, but I often have difficulty dealing with someone who I love very much. They suffer from bipolar and they often break down because of it.'

She looked at me every once in a while, with glossy eyes.

'I got engaged a few months ago and, while I thought

this was great news for me, I got so wrapped up in my own drama, that I didn't notice my best friend was sinking more and more. I had noticed different behaviours—they were drinking more, and they weren't in contact with me much. I was so busy with finding the right dress, the venue and organising stupidly expensive parties that I didn't notice them being in a crisis. Then my father had health issues, and instead of welcoming their comfort and a shoulder to cry on, I got angry at them. I lashed out and said things I didn't mean. Truth is, I can't live without my best friend, and to see their light dim right before my eyes is extremely painful. Because when they hurt, I hurt too.'

I could barely see her through my tears...I couldn't control them.

'They're my best man, and I wouldn't have it any other way. And I'd like to apologise for what has happened. I will do whatever I can to make sure they're okay and happy again. I was just scared and so worried about myself, I couldn't see them. But I do now. And I'm sorry.'

I smiled at her, while tears were falling down my face.

'Thank you, Sara. I'm sure they'll appreciate that.'

Sara wiped her own tears. She was shaking. She was a good public speaker, but I had never seen her be so fragile.

I took a deep breath. I looked around the room and took courage. I needed to do this.

'I'd like to go next,' I said, timidly. 'If that's okay.'

'Of course,' he said.

'I haven't had the greatest year. My marriage came to an end, and I had to move out of the flat where we had lived together for years. I left a dog I absolutely adored and a job that was comfortable. I started working for a job I despised with all my heart and moved in with a friend. Then my best friend gave me some wonderful news. She was going to get married to the love of her life, and I couldn't be happy for her. All I could think of was how she was about to start this life without me, and something clicked in my head. I had to make sure we would have as much fun as possible at every event leading up to the wedding. Because after that, things would change. I knew I couldn't afford to go around the globe with her, so I realised I needed more money.'

I was looking down, memories rushing through my brain, an anxiety that was pulsing out of my bones. I was the boy wrapped in Blue at that moment.

'I made some questionable choices and started performing certain acts in exchange for money. And with each client, I'd lose a part of me. I'd self-medicate with alcohol instead of my prescription. I'd even do drugs, without caring much about the others around me. I got obsessed with doing this as much as I could, because the more money, the more memorable our last adventures would be. But then I lost track of it all, and at the time of need, I wasn't there with her. She needed me and I was out of the country with a despicable man who may or may not have given me HIV.'

Sara put her hand on her mouth. She was sobbing as much as I was.

'I blame everyone around me, but the truth is, there is a part of me I can't control, and sometimes that takes over and allows me to do stupid things. I pretty much lost my job, my friends want nothing to do with me and I feel so damn alone all the time. I'm nearly thirty and all I've accomplished is the biggest fuck-up of all time.'

That's when I felt Sara's hand touching mine. She was looking at me in tears.

'I thought I had hit rock bottom a while ago, but this is truly it. And I'm so sorry about the things I've done; I don't even know where to start.'

'I'm sure the start is right next to you,' Robert said.

I turned around and smiled at Sara. We were good. We'd been through it all.

'There was a time where I thought I was done with it all. I wanted it to end. But she was there to pick me up. She's here right now.'

'I love you,' she whispered.

'I love you,' I said, looking at her big green eyes.

And then I breathed. I breathed so deeply, like I had been drowning for weeks. I needed help. I needed to do so many things and I didn't know where to start.

'Thank you, Leo.'

I closed my eyes for a second, and for once I didn't see Blue or Red. I saw bright purple.

I held Sara's hand while we listened to the other people's stories.

We both had found peace that afternoon.

———•———————●———————•———

'I couldn't help but notice you're not in Ibiza,' I said in the car.

'I had to cancel. I need to stay close to my dad.'

'Makes sense.'

'I actually got all the money back. It's one more reason I wanted to see you. I'll transfer it back to your account.'

'Oh, okay. Don't you want to have one last big party before you tie the knot?'

'We'll think of something else.'

'Whatever you want.'

The car was going through central London, which I thought was a bit odd.

'Are you taking me to actual AA now?'

'No,' she laughed. 'We are going for a drink, because I'm exhausted from the talking!'

'Good plan,' I said with a smile.

'Here is good,' she said to the driver.

We got out and walked through Soho. She was taking me to *Dean Street Townhouse*. The place where we discussed her engagement. It felt like it happened centuries before. I felt so different back then.

It was a mild evening. The rain had stopped, and the air became clean and crisp. People were having drinks outdoors, under the heaters. They were watching people walk by, while smoking cigarettes and enjoying Happy Hour. We walked towards the restaurant, about to sit and do the same.

'I'll go in and ask if we can just sit outside,' I said.

'Actually, there's something we need to do first.' She turned around and pointed at what was in front of the restaurant.

'I can't do that.'

'It's scary, I know. But I'll be there with you. And we need to find out,' she said while putting her hands on my shoulders.

Dean Street Clinic looked ominous for the first time. No longer was it a place I'd make fun of—it was now the location where I'd find out the truth.

My legs were shaking, I could barely move them. Once again, my heartbeat was ear-splitting. I wasn't sure how I'd react. I wasn't sure what I'd do. I would have been more than happy to never find out. Kind of like when I'd refuse to check my bank balance.

We entered the clinic, and just as I was told, it looked like the entrance to a gay club. The walls were white, with baroque patterns, the chairs were colourful and stylish, and the magazines were brand new and up to date. I kind of wished my psychiatrist's office looked like that.

'One thing at a time, we will fix everything,' she said to me, with the upmost optimism I could only aspire to. 'I feel really good about this.'

'Okay.'

I walked inside the examination room and got my blood taken. I hated needles so much. While I was there, I gave them urine and saliva samples too. I needed to know whether I had anything else.

I was only a few hours away from the text that would reveal my health status. I was shitting myself.

When I left the room, Sara gave me a tight hug. I couldn't even express how grateful I was to her and her friendship.

'Let's get a drink now,' she said.

I smiled at her.

———•———————●———————•———

We were sitting at the same exact table where we sat before. We were sipping on a well-deserved glass of Shiraz and really enjoying each other's stories.

'You need to make a plan,' she said. 'We need to fix you. We need to get you to feel amazing.'

'I feel like that's a revolution, not a plan.'

'Start with the small things. Get your phone. Let's write a list.'

I obliged. I had to entertain her. I took my phone out and pulled up the 'Notes' app.

'Okay, first thing?' I asked.

'You're going to take a shower every day.'

I cackled.

'You've got to start small,' she said. 'You'll look for a new job.'

I had almost forgotten I was still suspended.

'That's easier said than done,' I said.

'I will help you. And it will be something you actually enjoy doing. I feel like one of the reasons you spiral out of control is pure boredom. You're frustrated. I get it.'

'Okay, okay. I'll work on it.'

'You also need to make time for your friends. They're all about to go away or do different things, and you may not see them as much.'

'Are you talking about yourself?'

'I'm not going anywhere,' she said, with a little wink.

'Fine. I should probably look for a place to live as well.'

'Don't stress about that. You can always stay with me while you find the perfect place. Don't rush it.'

I sipped more of my wine and looked at her. I couldn't believe how much I had missed her and her determination.

'You'll go back to your doctor and sort your medication out. Write it down.'

'This is a long list.'

'Yeah, I don't care. You're also going to start writing again. It doesn't matter what. Just write whatever the hell you feel like.'

'I can do that.'

I wrote my notes down, and then a text message came in.

'It's the clinic,' I said. My hands were shaking.

'Okay. Do you want me to read it for you?' she asked.

'Yes, please.'

'Fine.'

I gave her my phone. I was on the verge of crying.

'Just remember we will tackle *whatever* this is,' she said. 'It doesn't matter what this text says.'

'Okay.'

She looked down at the text. I felt like time had stopped. My heart was beating so fast, I thought I'd pass out, right in front of her.

She gave me the phone back.

'Look at it yourself,' she said with the biggest smile.

I sighed in relief. Even without looking at it.

CHAPTER 24

£2977.25

THE BOY CRIED AND CRIED AND CRIED. *He sobbed all night. All he could see was Blue, everything was blue. The trees, the grass, the dirt. He thought he was completely alone. Then he heard a voice. It was a little girl. She shone bright. She didn't look blue. She was golden.*

'Why are you crying?' she asked, with a big bright smile.

'I am lost and sad,' he responded.

She sat next to him, with her bright light keeping him warm.

'Why are you shining so bright?' he asked.

She didn't know what to say. Where she came from, everyone would shine bright. She was born that way.

'Your heart must be safe inside you,' he said. 'I only have a tiny piece left.'

'Let me keep it safe for you,' she offered. 'I will take good care of it.'

The boy trusted her with the remainder of his heart. She held it tight and kept it safe for him.

'Let's find your home!' she said, holding the boy's hand.

Her light lit up a path, and after walking and walking, they finally reached the wizard's house.

'I gathered enough gold now,' the boy said.

The wizard looked at him carefully.

'Where's your heart?' he asked.

'It's here,' the little girl said, while pulling out a big, whole, bright heart.

'That's not my heart,' the boy said.

'I gave you part of mine, so you wouldn't be sad anymore. We can keep it safe together!'

The boy didn't know what to say and hugged the little girl.

Her light made him light up as well. He was now shining bright just like she was, with a whole heart inside him.

'You found the gold, little boy.'

The boy and the girl were shining bright, like pure gold. A light so intense, the boy could no longer hear Blue or Red.

'I don't understand. I thought this was the gold,' he said, showing the gold coins he had earned during his journey.

'That's not gold!' he said. 'Nothing is worth more than a pure friendship. That's the real gold. Now shine bright, my child!'

The boy took the little girl's hand and together they reached the boy's village. Everyone was happy to see the boy. Finally, he was happy like the rest of them!

'Please stay in my village,' said the little boy.

'I have to share my light with other children like you. They also need help,' she said. 'But I will always be part of you, part of your heart.'

The boy smiled and bid farewell to the little girl.

His light shone the brightest in the village, and from that moment on, his heart would be kept safe. The golden girl's heart was the most precious thing the boy could have, and for the first time, he never felt richer.

I threw the words together, like they just flowed out of me onto the keyboard. I had never thought I'd write a children's story, especially considering how disgusting my behaviour had been. But I wanted to do something good. I wanted to shed light on what living with bipolar meant. I'd often be subjected to Blue or Red. Neither one of them did me good. But my friends were the ones who made it all better.

'It's nice you're pouring yourself into some writing,' Doctor Grey said.

'I've messed up so much,' I said, while placing my shaking hands under my legs.

'It happens. We'll start you on the medication again. Just be mindful it will take some time for it to work.'

'It's fine. I just want to get better.'

'You sound better already,' she said. 'People

underestimate what a network of trusted people can do to their health.'

'I also forgot that.'

'Leo, you're always going to live with this condition. There will be times where you feel invincible and times you feel like life is not worth pursuing. Try to chase the real things that make you happy. Your friends, your writing, even the guy you seem to have a crush on. It's all things that help you feel good.'

She was right. Only a few days before I was done. I was standing at a train station, looking at the trains going past. I only needed to take one step, and it would be all over. I only needed an extra glass of wine, and maybe I would have stopped being scared of jumping. Just like when I was inside the bathtub, underwater, playing with the idea to never come up for air.

My chase for easy money was stupid. I was not for rent. I could shine bright. My heart was being kept safe now.

———•———————●———————•———

It was a mild evening. I was wearing a cosy hoodie, and I was walking Squall. He'd pull me forward and make me walk faster. He was probably excited to go home and see his other daddy. The trees around my old road were bare. How I loved them in autumn, with all their colourful leaves all over the lane. I'd sit on the sofa, next to Squall. He'd fall asleep on my lap, and I'd stare at the outside trees, changing with the seasons. That felt like an entirely different life. I knocked on Jake's door.

'I will miss you, my boy,' I said, while looking at a

sitting, panting Squall.

Jake opened the door, slightly flustered. His hair was untidy, greasy.

'Is this a bad time?'

'No, sorry. I lost track of time. Come in,' he said.

The flat looked different once again. Gone were the Indian photographs, the cushions and the dreamcatchers.

'What happened here?' I asked, confused.

'I'm just getting rid of stuff.'

His stubble was longer than usual. The flat was a mess. There was something he was hiding.

'How was your trip?' I asked.

'I actually didn't stay the whole time. I flew earlier.'

'What? Why?'

He poured dog food in Squall's bowl and gave him a cuddle.

'Marc and I broke up,' he said in a cold tone.

I wanted to burst into a laugh, but I decided it wouldn't have been appropriate.

'Oh no, I'm so sorry!' I tried to say it in the sincerest way possible, but probably failed.

'Oh, save it, Leo. It's all good,' he said, heading to sit on the sofa.

'I mean, I am sorry. What happened?'

'It wasn't right. He is a very selfish person and can only think about himself.'

'You just realised that?'

He gave me a death stare.

'Sorry. Go on,' I said.

'There's nothing to say. Maybe the age gap started becoming an issue. He'd want to party every weekend and get fucked on drugs. It became a deal-breaker.'

'I see. Well, for what it's worth, I am sorry. Break-ups suck.'

'I know. But I feel like I should apologise to you. I haven't been myself for quite some time. I didn't treat you fairly.'

'I know a thing or two about not acting like myself. It's been a long time.'

'He was obsessed with you. He hated that you were still part of my life because of Squall, or the fact you are best friends with Sara.'

'Well, that should have been your first indicator he's insane. No one in their right mind would be jealous of my life!' I said while sitting on the sofa arm.

'I think sometimes you forget what you have.'

'I have nothing.'

'You have friends who have your back, you are incredibly intelligent and are very good looking. I think that's a lot.'

'And yet, you dumped me like toxic waste.'

'I know. I mega fucked up.'

'It's fine,' I said while putting my hand on his shoulder. 'I know things weren't going well. I couldn't admit it back then because I had been dealing with depression, and I didn't realise. Not everyone is a psychologist. You did what you had to do.'

'There's also something else I need to apologise to you for,' he said, while looking at the floor.

'The time we had sex, and you told me it meant nothing?'

'Yes, but also...'

'Spill it out!' I blurted, impatiently.

'Marc is the one who spoke to your manager about you shoplifting.'

'You don't say.'

'You knew?'

'Oh yeah, he wasn't exactly hiding it. It's okay. I can't blame him for something I have done. Was it his place to say something? Probably not. But I'm not angry.'

'What are you going to do about your job?'

'I'll think of something. I have some seriously good friends that have my back, no matter what. I'm not worried.'

'Wow. You sound different.'

'Thanks,' I smiled. 'I feel better.'

'We should go for a drink sometimes if you're up for it.'

'Sure, that would be really lovely. There is another reason why I came here today. Other than bringing Squall back.' I grabbed a folder from my backpack and handed it to him. 'It's time.'

'Are these divorce papers?'

'It's been long enough. Have a read.'

'You paid the entire court fee?'

'I did.'

'I'll send you half of the money,' he said, while reading the first page.

'Take your time.'

Perhaps I should have picked a different time. I just had so many things on my list. It needed to be done.

'I'm going to go now. Take care of yourself, Jake.'

'You too, Leo.'

For the first time in over a year, I didn't leave that flat

raging. For the first time I was okay with Jake.

———•———————•———————•———

When I got home, Andrew was in the living room, packing yet another suitcase.

'Hey, doodle!' I said.

'Hey. How did it go?' he said, while giving me a hug.

'It was fine. I'm okay,' I said after taking a big breath and sitting on the sofa with my legs crossed. 'Needed to be done.'

'For sure. Any update from work?' he asked while folding t-shirts in an OCD fashion.

'Tomorrow. Tomorrow I have my meeting and will probably get fired.'

'Look, it's not like I think you did something particularly smart when you stole a pretty expensive suit—'

'Yeah, it was quite dumb.'

'—but. You hate that job. You hate everyone there. Dominic is leaving. You'd be there stuck by yourself, probably forever. Maybe in a way, this is a blessing?'

'Homeless and jobless? Fairy Godmother, sort yourself out!'

'You're not homeless. I'm so far away from selling this place; you'll probably grow old in here. In fact, you can stay for free now. My job is going to pay for my mortgage until it gets sold.'

'I swear you rich people never pay for anything.'

'It's ridiculous, isn't it? But what I'm trying to say is... you have time now. You have time to do what you want. Find a job where you can write or sit down and write a book. Carve your own path.'

'Funny you say that. As a matter of fact, I have been toying with the idea of doing a children's book,' I said with a smile.

'That's an amazing idea!'

'Thanks, Andrew.'

'Look, I wanted to wait until your birthday, but...' He pulled an envelope out of his bag. 'Here.'

'Are you divorcing me too?' I asked.

'Open it.'

I was curious, yet worried. The envelope contained a ticket. A one-way ticket.

I scrunched my face up.

'Come with me. After the wedding.'

'Are you serious?'

'Look, you'll have far more possibilities in New York. We can live together, and you can have meetings with publishers or whatever else you want to do. You have nothing to lose.'

'My whole life is here.'

'Sara is getting married. I'm not saying you're going to be alone, but...everyone is moving on. I don't want you to feel left behind. You could do great things there.'

'I could.'

CHAPTER 25

£2578.06

I was waiting for over five minutes. I was in a tiny little room on the Human Resources floor. They left me there alone, to think about my mistakes, I assumed. I'd have the final answer about my future in the company. I doubted I could come out of it employed. I was somewhat very calm about it. I had been thinking about Andrew's proposal. I had been thinking about it a lot. I was sipping some tea, getting impatient.

Then Katherine came in, along with another HR representative, Cliff.

'Hi, Leo,' he said. 'Thank you for coming.'

'No problem.'

'This will be our last meeting on the matter. After today, we will close the case, no matter the outcome,' said Katherine.

Funny how she got the hang of these meetings. Back in

the day, when I was her manager, I'd take her to HR every other day. She was that shit at her job.

'I am aware of the process, thanks.'

'Fine. We have a customer's witness statement saying they had seen you take a suit to the changing room,' she said.

'Marc Rhodes,' I specified.

'It's anonymous,' said Katherine.

'Of course.'

'We asked around the floor and checked CCTV footage.'

'Okay?'

'We actually didn't find anything.'

'Pardon me?' I said, flabbergasted. Not because I thought I had been caught by CCTV, but all they had to do really, was ask the security guys at the staff entrance. They would have said something. They could have checked stock numbers. So many possibilities. Katherine was such a fucking incompetent moron.

'So, we're happy to put all this behind us. I apologise for the misunderstanding and putting you through this process.'

'I can get back to work?'

'Yes, from tomorrow, or this afternoon, if you wish,' she said. Weirdly smiling.

She couldn't deal with the job without Dominic and me. That was the reason why they didn't go through with dismissal. Cheeky cow. If we both had gone, then she wouldn't have time to put on make-up at work or be on her phone for the majority of the day.

'No.'

'No what, Leo?' she asked.

'No, *thanks*.'

I stood up.

'I have no intention of coming back to this job. So, thanks, but no thanks,' I said, feeling serene.

'Please sit down. Let's discuss this.'

'Katherine. I never liked you when I was your manager years ago, and I most definitely do not like you now that, for god knows what reason, you have managed to bag a promotion. I only tolerated this time because Dominic was there with me.'

Her face went red. I could tell she wanted to slap me or choke me. But she couldn't do anything.

'I am grateful for the opportunity, but I never want to step foot in this building ever again. Have a nice day.'

I left them both in the room and I never felt better. I was unemployed, but I felt so good. I wasn't in a rush to find a new job, as I wouldn't have to pay rent for some time. I walked back onto the shop floor to find Dominic, who was working his last few shifts before he'd also say goodbye to the hell hole.

'Hi, sweetie!' I said.

'Hey, sweetie!' He turned around. 'How did it go?'

'It went great. They had nothing on me.'

'Yay!' He hugged me and picked me up. 'So, when do you start again?'

'I quit.'

'You did?'

'Yeah, I hate this. So much. I don't want to be stuck here without you. It would be fucking awful.'

'What are you going to do with money? Or are you still...?'

'No, I'm done with that. I'll be okay. I just need to reflect on a few things.'

'Fuck yeah, then! Let's go celebrate!' he said, removing his employee pass from his neck.

'Don't you still have a shift to work?'

'Fuck this place. I'm going to Berlin. Who cares about what these bitches say about me?'

I smiled. It was another end of an era.

Another friend who'd go away.

It was bittersweet.

———•———————●———————•———

There was another thing I needed to do that day. I made my way to Balham wearing my stolen suit and my Venetian mask. I looked like an idiot.

I knocked at his door, but no answer.

My fucking luck. I knocked again. Nothing.

I didn't want to text him, as I was counting on the surprise effect, but I guess sometimes things just don't go your way. I turned around to leave and there he was.

'Duncan!' I exclaimed.

His expression was dull.

'You nearly gave me a heart attack with that mask. What are you doing here, Leo?'

'I must apologise.'

'There's no need,' he said while going past me and towards his front door.

'I do. I messed up.'

'Fine, I'll listen.' He put his back onto his front door.

'We are not going inside? I pictured this as more of an

indoor thing.'

'No. Talk,' he said in the coldest of tones.

'Okay, fine. Duncan, we met at a stupid time. I wasn't being myself. I was doing things that I wasn't too proud of and I just acted like an arsehole altogether. Worst of all, I ruined our first date.'

'Go on.'

'I was drinking loads, I wasn't taking my medication, and I even did a few drugs. That's very, *very* unlike me. I freaked out when you were attending to me. I didn't deserve you. Not then.'

'I didn't care, Leo.'

'I did. Because I really like you. I knew I could be better, but I just needed a little more time, and if you forgive me, I can show you that. I won't take that for granted.'

'I am very happy you feel better,' he said while walking towards me. 'But it really shouldn't be this difficult. We had a great kiss, and for a while there, I really thought we could be something, but maybe it's just not meant to be.'

I felt like a sword just disembowelled my insides. It wasn't going the way I had envisioned in my stupid mind.

'I know it's been a while, but I came here because I really think there's something between us. Something special? As cheesy as that sounds.'

'It's pretty cheesy. There's so much stuff you need to sort out. You have the stuff with your ex, your job and your flat. You have your hands full. Don't further complicate things with a romance that has been clearly doomed since the start.'

'Just give me a chance, please.'

'I'll think about it, okay?' he said, putting a hand on

my shoulder.

He looked so different without his signature smile. His eyes were no longer kind nor smitten. He wasn't looking at me the way he did before. I was damaged goods in front of his eyes. I had screwed up big time. I didn't blame him. After all, I wouldn't go for a coked up, drunk, psychotic prostitute-wannabe either.

'Okay,' I said. I was probably crying inside.

'It's not to say we can't be friends, or we won't see each other around. I just don't think we can work.'

'You've made your point.' I was trying hard not to sound devastated. 'I will see you around.'

'Take care, Leo.'

———•————————●————————•———

'That was it?' Sara asked, while smoking a cigarette. 'That doesn't sound like Duncan at all.'

'I broke him,' I said while looking at the floor.

We were sitting on the balcony at Sara's house. She was wearing Alfie's puffer jacket. She looked like a navy Michelin man. Sara could not cope with the cold in the slightest.

'Well, that's shit. Bet you thought you'd get to your thirtieth with a spanking new boyfriend.'

I had completely forgotten. My birthday was that week. I stressed so much about it before.

'Shit, I wasn't even thinking about that.'

'You know, maybe Duncan wasn't right for you. Maybe you just thought he was because he was the only decent male you had around at the time you guys met. Maybe there's someone better out there.'

'Yeah, maybe. I just really liked him, you know?'

'Yeah, I know. But it's only one thing that has gone wrong. You have ended things with Jake officially, you don't have HIV, or any other nasty disease, you are free from your god-awful job and you don't have to pay rent! I think it's an overall great time for you.'

'You look at things in a really weird way. All I see is I'm single and unemployed.'

'You're free,' she said while holding my chin. 'You can relax and look for a place where you can really shine.'

'Ha, shine.'

'What's funny?'

'There's a story I'm working on, and it has something to do with being shiny.'

'Sounds interesting. When am I reading it?'

'We will see. It's just crap on a Word document for now.'

'Stop being so damn negative, man.'

'You're right.'

'Let's go inside, I have something to show you.'

She took me inside, into her guest bedroom.

'Did you invite me for sex? Because you know I'm not cheap.'

'You're the cheapest whore out there,' she said while removing her jacket. 'I wanted to show you this.'

She unzipped a clothing carrier, revealing the most beautiful wedding dress I had ever seen.

It was a laced off-the-shoulder mermaid gown, encrusted with pearls and embroidered with flowers, with a long chiffon veil.

'Wow.'

'Do you like it?'

'It's incredible. No wonder it took you so long to find one.'

'Do you think Alfie is going to like it?'

'If he has eyes. I'm surprised you're keeping it in the house.'

'Well, actually, that's kind of what I wanted to ask you. Can you take it with you and keep it? I am scared I might try it on some day and be busted by him.'

'How many times have you tried it on?'

'Too many. Risked spilling wine on it way too many times.'

'Is that why you're not trying it on now?'

'Yeah, I'm way too clumsy. Please take it away.'

'You sure you trust me with this?'

'Why? Are you so druggy that you may sell it for cocaine?'

'Well *now* I'm thinking about it!'

She punched me on the shoulder.

'Don't even joke with that crap. You'll never touch any of that shit again.'

'Fine, fine. I'll protect this with all I have.'

'Which isn't much,' she said with a big teasing smile. 'Thank you.'

She gave me a kiss on the cheek.

I think I was feeling a hint of happiness again.

Things between us would never change. Wedding or no wedding.

We were soulmates.

CHAPTER 26

£2760.50

HAPPY BIRTHDAY, LEO.

The dreaded day had finally come. I was no longer a twenty-something idiot. I was a full-fledged thirty-year-old idiot. I was born on Valentine's Day, which would make for a very uncomfortable date to do anything with your coupled friends or find a table at any restaurant. It was okay, though. This year it was not only a reminder that I was single but also that I was rejected by the guy I liked. I was alone in the flat, walking around in my underwear. I always thought I was a loner at heart, but living without Andrew felt weird. Even though he would hardly be home most of the time, I liked knowing he would be around, eventually.

Part of me would always wait for my mother's birthday call. If she was still alive, she'd tell me the story of my day of birth, and what a beautiful baby I was. She'd tell me I had grown too fast. She'd tell me she loved me so much.

And my eyes watered, a little.

Then someone buzzed at my door.

I didn't bother putting any clothes on. Hopefully it wouldn't be a complete stranger. I opened the door and Sara was standing in front of me.

'What are you doing here?' I asked.

'Fucking hell, thanks,' she said.

'Sorry. I just woke up. Come in.'

She walked in with a small box and put it on the table in the kitchen.

'Happy birthday, my lovely!' she said while giving me a big hug. 'Please go wear some clothes, as I can feel your penis.'

'You're so demanding today.' I went to grab a robe. 'Happy?'

'Very much so. Cake?' she asked, while opening the box.

'Ah, you star. Bring it.'

'How does it feel to turn thirty?'

'Like I should have died at twenty-six,' I said, while sitting down.

'Fucking Christ. Have some cake and stop being so depressing,' she said while handing me a slice of what looked like carrot cake.

I loved cake.

'What are we doing tonight?' she asked, with a big smile and giant eyes.

'Are you not smooching with Alfie?'

'Nah, it's your day. Valentine's Day is stupid anyway.'

'I don't know. We could go for a drink or something?

I'm not really fussed,' I said while chewing on a massive piece of cake.

'You're being so boring. Would a present make you more excited?'

'We don't do presents.'

'We do this year,' she said while slipping an envelope on the table.

'What the hell is this?' I enquired, while trying to open it.

'It's for the both of us.'

'Got us some strippers?'

'I mean, we can do,' she cackled.

I opened it and there were two tickets. For mother fucking Tokyo.

'Are you out of your damn mind?' I asked.

'Hear me out. You were supposed to go to Tokyo for your thirtieth birthday. Your ex-husband has taken that away from you, so I'm just giving it back.'

'I can't accept this. You're insane.'

'It's non-refundable.'

'I can't believe it. Thank you so much,' I said while giving her a hug and lifting her up. I was stoked to say the least.

We'd go in June, a month after her wedding. We'd roast to death, but I couldn't believe I'd get to have the trip of a lifetime with my best friend.

'Is this our honeymoon?' I asked.

'Fuck yes.'

'You made my day, and it's only 8 a.m. I'm surprised you got up this early.'

'It's fine, I'll head straight to work after this. I just

need to use your printer, if you don't mind. Mine stopped working and I have to get a few bits for a presentation today.'

'Knock yourself out. I'll go take a shower,' I said while getting up.

'Thank god.'

I gave her a kiss on the cheek.

'Thanks for cake and Japan.'

'I will see you this evening,' she said.

It was around lunchtime. Working people were running to get their lunches, while I was walking through Chinatown at a leisurely pace. Jimmy was in town and asked me to see him, I assumed for the biggest apology that has ever existed. I wasn't hungry as I had eaten most of the cake to myself, but I could probably do with a little birthday drink.

He was already sitting at the pub, with a glass of red wine waiting for me. He looked different then. I couldn't quite put my finger on it, but it was probably due to the fact that I despised him now.

'Hey, Leo. Happy birthday!' he said, with enthusiasm. Probably expecting a hug.

I nodded and sat down.

'Is this for me?'

'Yeah, thought I'd order it so you wouldn't have to wait.'

'What are you doing in London?'

'I just wanted to spend a weekend to catch up with

friends.'

'I see.'

'I also wanted to see how you were doing. We left things on a sour note last time.'

I sipped my wine, hardly making any eye contact.

'Yup,' I said.

'How are you?'

'I'm excellent. You?'

'I'm okay. Did you get tested?'

'I did. You'll be delighted to know you didn't pass the virus.'

'That's good! I thought the worst when you stopped replying to my texts,' he said.

'I just didn't want to talk to you.'

'That's fair,' he nodded. 'I really want to apologise. I didn't want to hurt you. It's just...the gay community can be really vicious. Whenever I would tell guys beforehand, they'd want nothing to do with me.'

'So you decided to lie?'

'I guess I was scared. You're a really attractive guy, smart and funny. As soon as I saw you, I was completely in awe. I didn't want you to run away.'

I felt like I could really see Jimmy for what he was. An extremely insecure guy who just so happened to make some serious money. He enjoyed sex, but that same passion is what bit him in the arse. I almost felt pity for him.

'Look, I had to let it go. I learned that dwelling on things that could have happened is stupid. At the end of the day I was really lucky, and that's all there is.'

'You're being very cavalier about it all.'

'It's my birthday, it's lovers' day. I don't really care about it anymore. We're good, Jimmy,' I said while giving him a pat on his shoulder.

'Amazing. Maybe we could still see each other sometimes. We could go on another weekend away,' he said, with his eyes lit up.

'Oh, no. That ship has long sailed. Find someone else. Just be truthful. You don't have to pay for sex. Just be a decent human being.'

'I think part of me likes paying. I find it kind of sexy.'

'Then do whatever you please. I have to go now,' I said while getting up. 'Thanks for the drink.'

'Wait,' he said, all of a sudden. He opened his wallet and started grabbing notes. 'For your time.'

'Keep it, Jimmy. This is on the house,' I put my hand on his hair and messed it up. 'Take care.'

That was the last time I'd see him. Or hear from him.

I felt good.

Sara was being the usual diva. We'd agree on a time to meet, but she'd always be late. Most of the time I'd end up meeting her at her place, and she'd still be drying her hair. To be fair, she did come to my place in the morning, and she'd hardly ever do that.

It was a weird day. I had spent so much time in my twenties dwelling over the day I'd turn the big three-o and now that it had arrived...it wasn't anything special. There were definitely a few things I was happy to leave behind. My marriage to Jake, which took such a big chunk of my twenties, had officially come to an end. Back then we'd make plans for children, more dogs, a farm even. But it all fell apart with a mental condition and one single dog.

'*I'm here.*' I texted Sara.

'*Come up.*'

Of course. She wasn't anywhere near ready.

I wasn't mad. I had brought a bottle of wine exactly for that reason. At least I'd get to have a few drinks while she'd do a full montage of trying every garment in her wardrobe.

I walked up the stairs and her main door was open.

I walked in and everything was dark.

'Dude, you doing a satanic ritual?' I shouted.

Then they all came out.

Surprise!

Fuckers. They gave me a heart attack.

'Oh my god. I'm dying,' I said while holding my poor heart.

'Sorry,' she said. 'We didn't time the lights right.'

All of my friends were there. John, Abigail, Dominic and Andrew.

'Welcome to the dirty thirty club,' said John, giving me a hug while holding a beer bottle.

'Sara, you're the last one,' said Abigail.

'Don't remind me,' she said. 'Let's focus on this little shit.'

'Thanks, guys. I was not expecting this at all.'

I didn't even know Andrew was in town.

'Did she grab you from New York herself?' I asked him.

'I wish,' Sara said. 'He was planning to celebrate you all along.'

'You didn't think I would have left you crying alone

while drinking wine, right?'

I gave him a big kiss on the cheek.

'Thank you.'

'Right, who wants cake and booze? Because that's why I came,' said Abigail.

The room was heavily decorated with balloons and all of the stuff I liked. Pokémon, animals, video games. It looked like a party for a five-year-old—if they were into drinking whiskey, that is.

I grabbed a glass, and I stared at all of them, being there for me. It truly warmed my cold, messed up heart.

'Where's the groom-to-be?' I asked.

'He had something to do with some coworkers. Didn't really ask, didn't really care. It's your night,' she said while pinching my cheek.

She looked amazing. She was wearing a long-sleeved black dress, which really made her physique look incredible. Her hair was down, and she had already done her make-up. That woman was banging.

'Right, so what's the plan, birthday boy?' asked Dominic. 'Are we going out and celebrating?'

'Yeah, I left that for you to decide, Leo,' said Sara. 'Didn't know if you wanted to get your gay on.'

'I'd be more than happy to get our gay on,' said Abigail. 'Name the club and I'll get us a table with champagne and all the rapper crap you can imagine.'

'So much for my quiet ethylic coma I had in mind,' I said, with a giggle. 'If I get to wear some sort of balloon hat the entire evening, I'm down for a club.'

'Well, it's still early and you have all of this booze here to go through. No way we are dancing sober,' said John.

He had also dolled himself up. His hair was newly cut and bleached. He was wearing a sleeveless top and some sort of skirt-trouser concoction. A £2k outfit, for sure.

'Dom, how does it feel to be out of retail?' asked Abigail.

'Really fucking great. I can't believe I don't have to deal with those arseholes,' he responded.

'John and I worked there as well. We know damn well what you're talking about,' said Sara.

'Amen. Fuck that,' said John while sipping his beer.

Then the doorbell rang.

'Did you also order pizza?' I asked Sara.

'Actually, I hope you don't mind, I invited my sister as well?' she said.

'Why would I mind? I love her!'

'Awesome. Can you go open the door? I'm working my way on these bottles of prosecco,' she said while popping one.

'Absolutely,' I said while making my way to the entrance.

I opened the door, but it wasn't Emma.

'Duncan.'

'Hey.'

I had missed his gentle eyes and crazy hair. He was wearing a white shirt. Denim jacket was no more in February. Enter the puffer with the shearling collar. Just as cute.

'Come in,' I said.

'One second.'

I closed the door behind me and went outside the flat.

'Are you okay?' I asked.

325

'I've had a lot to think about.'

'You did?'

'Yes,' he said. 'I don't care how difficult it has been, or how difficult it's going to be. Meeting you was the greatest thing that has happened to me in a long time.'

I couldn't believe what I was hearing. Duncan made my heart race. Every single time.

'What happened on New Year's—'

'Won't ever happen again,' I interrupted. 'The drug part, not the alcohol. The alcohol will most likely always be there. Unless it becomes a huge problem.'

'I'm Scottish.'

'Fair point,' I smiled. 'Honestly, I am in such a better place now. Mentally. Not much else, though. I don't have a job and my flatmate is deserting me.'

'I don't think the people who are celebrating you over there will ever allow you to be homeless.'

'You never know, they are a bunch of rich arseholes,' I giggled.

'So, if you wanted to go on a date...with me—'

'Yes!' I blurted. 'I do.'

'Okay,' he smiled.

He came towards me and grabbed my waist. I put my hand behind his neck and put my fingers through his hair. We had a long, sweet, passionate kiss. My legs were weak, but I couldn't ask for a more perfect one.

I couldn't stop smiling.

Then the door opened suddenly behind me.

'I was wondering what was taking you so long!' said Abigail.

'We were just coming in,' I said.

I reached for Duncan's hand and dragged him inside.
Happy birthday to me.

CHAPTER 27

£4589.05

WEEKS WENT BY and everything was ready for the bride-to-be. I was sitting at the airport on my iPad trying to finish an article on sustainable materials in the fashion industry for a company that hired me to do some freelance content writing. It didn't pay much, but I genuinely enjoyed putting my brain into action. I was also not required to work full-time, so I had extra time to spend with Sara and her wedding shenanigans. I was there for all the phases. The time she got blackout drunk and decided she'd buy drinks for everyone because she had finally found the perfect cake, the time she couldn't stop crying because she was going to be called Mrs a few weeks later, the time she came for a sleepover at mine because she couldn't bear Alfie's snoring, but mostly, I was there to help her with her dad. He was still put under rigorous rest. It wasn't an easy heart attack. I'd sometimes spend some time with her mum just to keep her company, as she was doing everything for him. I'd cook with her quite often. I'd teach her how to veganise things, cooking without oil and many other little adjustments that were necessary to keep Sara's dad as healthy as he could be.

The house was still not sold. Andrew didn't really mind. He liked being at home when he'd come back to London. Which he did, multiple times. I got to spend more time with Squall while I'd send hundreds of query letters to literary agents for my children's book. I hadn't had much luck with that, although those things would usually take forever.

'I got you a croissant!' said Duncan, coming from *Carluccio's* and sitting next to me.

'Thank you,' I said.

'I cannot wait to get to Greece. I've actually never been,' he said. 'Have you?'

'No. I'm really looking forward to it. And we get to be in a hotel room and do all the naughty stuff.'

'Don't be gross,' he said.

Being with Duncan was a surprise every day. I thought his happy, positive energy would dim the more we'd go on, but he was a constant firecracker. I had never had that much fun with a boyfriend before. Well, he wasn't my 'boyfriend' yet. I didn't want to ruin the honeymoon phase with worthless, outdated labels.

'How's the research going?' I asked.

'Well, I can safely say Santorini isn't lacking places where we can get Sara a fun hen do.'

'That's good. Although we'll have to try not to go overboard. She will be getting married the day after.'

'Everyone loves a hungover bride. You should have seen my sister when she got married. I don't think she even recognised the groom. Thought for a second she'd marry his dad.'

'Speaking of Scottish weddings...'

'What?'

'Did you bring your kilt?'

'You need to stop with the sex stuff. Or I'll be horny for the whole flight!'

I gave him a kiss. Slightly teased him with my tongue and then bit his lip.

'Fair enough,' I said.

My article was done and ready to be sent to my editor. It was only going to be fun from then onwards. My little girl would be saying 'I do' in less than seventy-two hours.

The hotel was a massive white structure with everything in it. They gave us access to the whole resort, which meant massages and private beach would be ours to be abused. Duncan and I were upgraded to a suite as I was the best man. The suite was right next door to Sara's. We'd even share a terrace. We had champagne and chocolates on the bed, towels made to look like swans and a whole booze trolley for us to get disgustingly drunk on. We were the last ones to fly, as Duncan was covering for Sara at work and he wasn't given permission by the arsehole-in-chief until that was done.

'We have a Jacuzzi in the bathroom!' he screamed. 'I'm going to jump in it.'

'Save me some room.'

Then we heard a knock on the door.

'Did you order food already?' Duncan asked.

'No, but I could definitely do with a snack,' I said while opening the door.

'You're here!' Sara squealed. 'You brought the dress, right?'

'Of course, I did, silly bitch. I didn't want to die.'

She was tanned already. She had only gotten to the island two days before us and was already on her way to looking like a California raisin.

'Dude. Did you fall asleep for forty-eight hours at the beach?'

'Do you think I've tanned? I don't really see it.'

'You're very close to being mistaken for a different ethnicity.'

'Good. That was exactly my plan,' she said while entering. 'I'm glad they gave you this room. The shower is amazing.'

'Did you have sexy fun with it?'

'Ew, no,' she said. Then sat on the bed. 'So, what's the plan for after our rehearsal dinner?'

'What do you mean?'

'Well, it's my last single night.'

'You're not single.'

'You know what I mean!'

'Yes, I'll find a place for us to go. Then you can be a whore for one last night.'

'Yay! Where's Duncan?'

'In the bath which is where I also want to be in, so get lost. I will see you later,' I said while pushing her out.

'But I need to know if my clients were okay with him taking over!'

'They'll be fine. Bye, woman.'

I closed the door and took my clothes off. I was about to have some hot water sex in my giant Jacuzzi.

———•————————•————————•———

I thought I'd fit in a massage before dinner, as I was feeling mad tired from staying up all night trying to write my article. Duncan was taking a nap, Sara was busy freaking out with Abigail, and I could really use the peace. I walked through a long corridor where everything was white marble. There were beautiful paintings of the buildings in Santorini, all white and blue.

I found the treatment room, and that's when I saw Marc. Also in a robe. Just my fucking luck.

'Hey,' he said.

'Hi.'

'Are you also...?'

'Yes.'

No one else was there. I could hear crickets killing themselves. I wasn't sure what to do. Maybe I needed to come back later. I just really wanted that god damn massage.

'It's been a while,' he said.

I couldn't be stuck in that room for more than five minutes and be forced into small talk with that parasite. There was a voice inside me that was just dying to get out, but I was trying everything in my power to keep it down.

'Is there an apology coming soon or...?' I asked.

'There is, actually.'

Oh, what a shock.

'Marc, why on Earth would you ever think to fuck

me over at work? Like was it not enough to get my ex-husband, live in my flat, play with my dog, hang out with my best friend and ordering my current boyfriend around? Like...do you not think you had enough? Why was my employment such a big issue to you?'

'I'm so sorry. I really am. But you have to understand...'

'What?'

'You have to understand that all I heard for the past year and a half was your name. *Leo is so funny. Leo is so handsome. Leo is so smart. Leo could cook anything. Leo would always play with Squall. Leo is just fucking awesome all around.* I always had to compete with the ghost of Leo Cotton. Even with Jake.'

'Jake and I were married. Of course, we had history. And he still lives in the same flat we both shared. Every little crack on the wall, or anything contained in the flat had something to do with me.'

'Exactly.'

'Look, I don't think you're necessarily a bad guy.'

'It just gets really lonely sometimes. Especially after Jake dumped me,' he said while looking at the floor.

'Oh. I thought you did.'

'No. Our trip to Japan was a disaster. I had no interest in going. I just bought the tickets because I had heard you wanted to go. Jake was furious at that, even though he never admitted it. We left early; we couldn't even be in the same room.'

'So it was you doing all that. Jake wasn't actually the monster I painted him as all this time?'

'I think Jake will always love you. Even if just a little. And I kept getting angry at him. I couldn't imagine *why* he would love *you*.'

'Thanks,' I said, sarcastically. 'You're really working my self-esteem up.'

'But I do now. I saw Duncan falling in love with you... getting excited at every text you sent, or when he'd see you after work. All I hear around me is Leo.'

'If only you knew how I'd felt all that time...'

'What do you mean?'

'I'm the opposite of confident. I think I'm fucking up all the time. I constantly compare myself to everybody and, trust me, I am constantly losing. I am surrounded by all these great talented people that are doing what they're meant to do. I felt left behind. I was in a really dark place only a few months ago.'

'Here I thought being poor was your only issue.'

'Oh, it has definitely been a huge issue.' I smiled.

'I am really sorry, Leo.'

'I'll accept your apology.'

'Maybe we could hang out some time, have a drink after work...'

'Yeah, I may have to think about that. I'm not that big of a person.'

'Fair enough.'

The woman at reception called me over. She said our names in a Greek accent.

'We have made a mistake with the treatments. I am afraid we only have one room available.'

'What does that mean then? Do I come back later?' I asked.

'We have one room available. We could do couples massage if you don't want to wait,' she said, looking at the both of us.

I looked at Marc for a second.

'I don't mind,' he said.

Bleeding Christ.

'Sure, why the heck not,' I said.

Of all the things I imagined myself doing in Greece, being naked in the same room as Marc Rhodes was definitely not one of them.

'Follow me,' she said.

I followed her and Marc.

I rolled my eyes up and thought back to only a few months earlier. If anyone had told me I'd be spending an hour in the same room as Marc Rhodes, both naked, I would have laughed in their face. Punched them too. But here I was.

Dinner was held in the main hall of the resort. The restaurant was beautifully decorated with white linens and delicate flowers. The napkins had blue ribbons tied to them. Everyone looked lovely. Duncan was wearing a tight white short-sleeved shirt. I looked at him and smiled. I touched his hand under the table. I was so glad to have found him.

Sara and Alfie looked like they weren't speaking to each other. The pressure was possibly getting to them. Although, she was probably just fed up with his family. There were so many of them. Alfie had brothers that had already been married and had children. There were so many fucking children, my ears felt like they wanted to

commit suicide. I was glad to see Sven, enjoying him
His happy smile warmed my heart. He had to be r
around in his wheelchair, but he was still there for
We were all pretty tipsy already, but I somehow m
have been shitfaced, because I found myself grabbii
everyone's attention by tapping a spoon to my champagn
flute. Like an American wedding wanker.

Sara looked surprised, but I just went ahead anyway.

'Hi, everyone!' I said, while standing up. The room
went silent. I couldn't go back now.

'For those who haven't had the pleasure to make my
acquaintance, I am Leo Cotton, the bride's best man. I
know what you're thinking. *Why isn't the maid of honour
doing a speech?* She'll have her moment. I just thought
I'd get to it first. I'll be doing the *honours*. Sara Langaard
has been my best friend for a good part of the last decade.
I have shared everything with her. We navigated into the
horrifying dating pools of London and complained to
each other at how shit men were. We would be there for
each other when one of us would catch a cold and bring
food and alcohol when either of us would be upset. Sara
is so incredibly precious that she can't help but being
surrounded by people who love her. Everyone is drawn
to her. She is pure sunshine. Even if she doesn't think so.
But she hasn't always been the gracious, beautiful creature
you see before your eyes. You see, there was this one time
that we both had a stomach bug, and let me tell you...'

Everyone started laughing. Sara turned a weird shade
of purple.

'Actually, for the sake of her career in public relations,
I should probably keep this one to myself. Although

self.
lled
er.

st

g

e

. the sordid details of how the bride
w up and shit herself at the same time,
ess is...'

v a bread roll at me. Hit me in the face. She
5, though. That's what was important.

ine. What I want to say is that Sara is one of
important people in my life. She's been there for
i times and the bad. She is the most loyal person
/ and anyone who swears to spend the rest of their
with her is a wise man. Alfie, I am looking at you. You
t my princess like the queen she actually is. Unless you
int a mob of gay guys whooping your arse.'

I looked at Sara straight into her glossy eyes.

'So, if you all would raise your glasses, I'd like to wish
the best of luck to the bride and groom. Woman...I love
you.'

'I love you,' she said from across the room.

I sat back down and felt free. I knew we'd have more
funny tales to tell in the future.

Plus, she told the story of how I shat myself in Primrose
Hill at my wedding. It was time for payback, bitch.

───•──────●──────•───

We were just about to head out of the hotel, so we
could celebrate Sara's last bachelorette night, when her
sister Emma stopped me.

'Do you have a minute?'

'Yeah, sure,' I told her. 'Hey, we will see you at the
club! I forgot something in my room!'

I waved at them while they all filled a cab. Poor driver.

'Yes, Emma?'

We sat down at a bench.

'I read your manuscript,' she said.

'You did? What? How? When?'

'Sara gave me a printed version a few weeks ago,' she said with a smile on her face.

'I have never given it to Sara.'

'It's called *The Golden Boy*, isn't it?'

'Yeah, I just don't recall...wait.'

That time she came over to my flat because her printer was broken. My story was there. Still by the printer. Nosy bitch.

'I think I know now,' I said. 'You said you read it? That's so embarrassing.'

'It's great. It's such a simple story, but how it tackles mental health, was truly remarkable.'

'Thanks, Emma. It's weird to hear I have done something right.'

'Well, it's not just me. I have sent it around to a few publishing houses, and I have a few who would love to have you on board.'

'You're joking.'

My heart was about to leave my chest.

'We can talk about it when we get back to London. There's even a few in the States, if you were interested.'

'I can't believe this. Thank you so much!'

We hugged. I felt like I was about to cry. My book would see the light of day. I imagined a child who may have struggled with things they couldn't quite understand and then reading my book. They wouldn't feel like there was something wrong with them. They'd say *this is how*

———————————●——————————— •———————

night I was in heaven. Sara and I had the time
lives, and even though we both got incredibly
.mered, she looked like a goddess the day after. Her
.ir was tied up, and the veil was probably eight feet long.
I had never seen anyone look more gorgeous.

I had my hair slicked back, while Duncan's was
uncontrollable. I was looking at him while I pushed Sven's
wheelchair down the aisle, so he could walk his daughter
like she always wanted.

There were tears, there were plenty of laughs.
Especially when Sara paused dramatically before saying
I do. Usual attention seeker. Now we'd all get to make fun
of that moment each time we would be shown the wedding
video.

It was a day of celebration. We all partied for the happy
couple until late night.

It was so exciting I couldn't even go to sleep.

I left a very inebriated Duncan in bed while I decided
to stare at the gorgeous panorama out of our terrace. I
had unbuttoned a few buttons of my shirt, my braces were
just hanging on the sides of my trousers, and my hair
was all messed up. I pulled it back and popped a bottle of
champagne. I wanted to have a drink while I'd watch the
sunrise. I was on such a high. Everything just seemed to
fall into place for once.

Then I heard a noise. Sara opened her door and joined

me on the terrace.

'Shouldn't you be having crazy monkey sex with y
husband?' I asked.

'I heard there was an idiot still awake and havin
champagne without me.' She smiled.

I gave her my glass while I held the bottle.

'Cheers,' I said, and then chugged a big sip from the
bottle.

'It's so beautiful.'

'It really is.'

We watched the sunrise for a short, silent moment. I
put my arm around her. Everything was just so perfect.

'Leo?'

'Yes?' I said, turning my head at her.

'Getting married was a huge mistake.'

our

g

ACKNOWLEDGEMENTS

Wow. I'm just going to board the cheese-train and say that this book took a village!

First and foremost, I would like to thank my mother, for being incredibly supportive and always being genuinely excited about this project. She has never doubted this book would see the light of day and she has cheered me up at every step of the way.

My best friend Sara who, very directly said something along the lines of 'Sit your arse down and write a god damn book.' It's not an understatement to say that if it wasn't for her holding my hand in the darkest moments, neither myself nor this book would be here today.

My critique partners George Raymond Stead and author Pearl Khatri for helping me craft the best story I could possibly tell. And a thank you to all the beta readers who have sent me invaluable feedback.

A special shout out to my editors Paul Ryan, Susan Keillor and Maxwell Anderson for helping me polish and elevate the manuscript to a readable text.

.he artist who has created the cover
.rkhatov (fedos.art on Instagram),
.iunta for creating the alternative cover
and Ami (teawithami) for illustrating the

.ke to thank Abhi for creating the Cloudy Day
.iing logo and Julia Scott (Evenstar Books) for
.gning the interior formatting and helping me juggle
.ie thousand files I needed to upload to all the platforms.

A special thanks goes to Jenna Moreci, Bethany Atazadeh, Lyra Parish and Meg Latorre for posting incredible content on YouTube which has immensely helped me craft this final product.

To all my friends, this book is an ode to friendship, and I am so thankful for each and everyone who has inspired me to create these characters I hold very dear.

Thanks to you, the reader, for taking the time to read a novel published by a new, indie writer. It means the absolute world to me and I couldn't be more grateful.

And finally (this is the last one, I promise) thanks to my partner Jack and my husky Cloud, who have listened to me rambling for the entire publishing process. I love you.

ABOUT THE AUTHOR

Michael Sarais was born in Italy in 1991 and has lived in London for much of his 20s. He was educated at the University of the Arts in London and holds a BA in Fashion Journalism. When he is not crafting tales with incredibly flawed characters, he spends his time playing videogames, watching a myriad of YouTube videos and walking his spectacular husky around the city.

All of My Friends are Rich is his debut novel.